KILL BITE

TOPAZ TRILOGY BOOK ONE

VICTORIA JAYNE SAUNDERS

VJS Books

CONTENTS

Nyla   1
The Basin

1. Aaron   6

2. Aaron   14

3. Interlude   18
   The Basin

4. Aaron   22

5. Nyla   37

6. Aaron   50

7. Interlude   57
   Somerton Outskirts

8. Nyla   60

9. Aaron   71

10. Nyla   80

11. Interlude   86
    The Basin

12. Aaron   87

13. Interlude   91
    Willow Lodge

14. Aaron   94

15. Nyla   98

16. Aaron   104

17. Interlude
    Willow Lodge   112

18. Nyla   116

19. Aaron   128

20. Nyla   132

21. Aaron   140

22. Nyla   154

23. Nyla   164

24. Aaron   181

25. Interlude
    The Chehwinoo   188

26. Nyla   191

27. Aaron   197

28. Nyla   205

29. Nyla   209

30. Aaron   215

31. Nyla   217

Epilogue: Amelia   221
Royersford, Pennsylvania

Nyla

The Basin

Nyla always wondered which was harder to clean: mud or blood.

Every man she'd ever asked confidently said that blood was the more difficult of the two, but that wasn't necessarily a surprise. None of them had spent a humid Tuesday night huddled in their parents' bathroom, frantically scrubbing their favourite pair of underwear under a stream of cold water and hand soap. There was a tried-and-true method to clean blood if it was dealt with quickly.

Mud was different. For one thing, Nyla could never be certain what it was made of. Some muds were thick and dense, more like wet sand, and barely clung to anything other than themselves. Some were closer to water, leaving enormous stains that looked horrifying but washed away with ease. Then, of course, there was the mud she was sluicing through now. It was gooey, almost gelatinous, and threaded with all manner of decaying underbrush and animal feces.

Mud, or blood?

Nyla supposed she'd get her answer tonight; her clothes were bogged down with a healthy dose of both.

Where the hell was Leo?

The formidable exterior lights of Willow Lodge couldn't reach her here, deep in the belly of the Basin. Nyla knew the path even without the bobbing beam of her flashlight; there was a dip in the trail up ahead, a low-hanging branch at the base of the next turn, and then she'd be staring at Basin Lake.

With any luck, she'd *also* be staring at Leo's campsite.

The man was infuriating on a good day. Nyla cursed him and his haughty, rich-boy attitude with every twig that scraped across her skin. He shouldn't be out here. *She* shouldn't be out here, but she couldn't leave him to his fate, even if he was the one who'd decided to tempt it.

All these missing hunters were proving to be terrible for business.

Rain had accosted the Basin for days now, leaving the terrain sticky and treacherous for even the most experienced hikers. Nyla had already stumbled over a hidden stump and struck her knee on a displaced stone. Her legs were battered, bruised, and bleeding, her hair drenched and clinging to her scalp. She was uncomfortable, cold, and hungry. When she found Leo, she was going to demand a day at Clary's Spa as compensation for her trouble. At least she knew he could afford it.

Why did Leo choose *now* to pursue his game anyway? He was hunting deer. Deer! Of all things! Nyla was no expert hunter, but she knew more than most. Between the late hour, the torrential rain, and the fast-approaching end of the season, Nyla would eat her left boot before betting money on Leo bagging a buck on this trip.

A bright orange ribbon caught her attention, tied tightly around the thickest limb of a beech tree. This was where the lodge's property line ended, and the hunting grounds opened. It was a fair hike from the brilliantly golden web of cabins that made up the resort, but that was intentional. The last thing Nyla needed was an accident with a hiker.

Leo wouldn't be too far now.

His tent was easy to spot, even in the dark. Leo wasn't a hunter, not really. He picked up the hobby to impress his business partners, but he had no interest in actually learning the craft. He made rookie mistakes, things veteran hunters clowned him for, like choosing a tent that stood out against the trees like a sore thumb. It was a vibrant and sparkling red, like someone had thrown a full can of paint onto the bushes.

"Leo?" Nyla yelled over the wind, her voice catching on every branch and leaf between her and the gaudy tent. Leo wouldn't have heard her if he was standing three feet away. She trudged closer, making as much noise as she possibly could.

"Leo, come on!" Her boot collided with a sunken log, pain zinging up her shin. Nyla cursed, kicking away the mud covering the obstacle so she wouldn't repeat the mistake. "I'm way too tired for this shit!"

She was practically on top of the tent now, close enough to see the faint glow of Leo's cellphone through the fabric. She rolled her eyes, slapping the drenched rain cover until the screen went black and the tent door zipped open.

"Nyla? What the hell?"

Leo emerged with a stack of blankets wrapped around his narrow shoulders. His rounded face poked out from beneath a heavy layer of plaid, giving the impression of a ridiculously oversized newborn in a swaddle. Nyla was too rankled to laugh, but it was close.

"What are you doing out here?" Leo demanded, lifting his nose. He was immediately defensive, as she expected. Leo wasn't used to being questioned, let alone tracked down in the middle of the night like a petulant child disregarding his curfew.

"I should be asking you the same question," Nyla snapped, crossing her arms over her chest. The flashlight beam bounced wildly, refracting off fat drops of rain. "I told you the Basin is closed. You shouldn't be here."

"You can't *close* the Basin, Nyla," Leo said proudly. "It's not your land."

"It's my lodge," Nyla huffed, tapping her foot impatiently. "And while you're a guest there, you need to follow my rules."

Leo opened his mouth as if to argue, but swiftly changed tactics at the dangerous flash in Nyla's eyes.

"It's my last night here," he tried instead, pleading with her. "Let me stay until morning. It's already after midnight, what harm can it do?"

Plenty, but Nyla wasn't about to reiterate that point.

"Leo, please don't make this any harder than it has to be." Nyla pinched the bridge of her nose between her thumb and forefinger, squeezing her eyes tightly shut. "Come on, I'll help you take down your tent and we can walk back to the lodge together. It's not safe to be out here right now."

"What's not safe about it?" Leo demanded, throwing his arms out wide in exaggerated protest. "I've barely left the trail! The lodge is practically in spitting distance, what could possibly—"

A loud, reverberating crack split the air, silencing everything but the howling wind. Nyla flinched to the ground, expecting a tree branch to tumble from somewhere above them, but the forest was still. Too still, she realized quickly. Her attention snapped to Leo and his tent, hoping for the best and expecting the worst.

Leo was gone.

Nyla stared, unblinking. Was she disoriented from her new vantage point? Summoning her strength, she straightened, scanning the scene in front of her with growing confusion and disbelief.

The tent was there, untouched and almost offensive in its peace. The trees were undisturbed, leaves rustling in a melody of scratches and flutters, like millions of insects writhing over each other. Nyla's gaze skittered over every inch of terrain she could make out in the dark, and Leo was nowhere to be found.

Dozens of scenarios flashed through her mind, each as unlikely as the last. *Had* a tree branch fallen and knocked Leo out of her line of sight? Had he been startled by the sound and bolted? Nyla had been shocked by the crack too, but she wholeheartedly believed she would've noticed if anything happened to Leo. So, what...?

"Leo!" Her call died in her throat as a horrendous screeching echoed through the trees. Nyla jumped, clamping her hands over her ears as the sound reached a painful volume, shaking the very ground she was standing on. A primal, vicious fear swept through her, freezing her blood in her veins. The screeching grew louder, drowning out every other sound. Nyla squeezed her eyes shut, trying to gather her senses.

She didn't want to leave Leo, but—

The screeching crescendoed, knocking her limbs into action before she could think. Nyla didn't know what was happening or what was making that awful noise; she just knew she had to *run*.

Twigs snapped beneath her boots as she fumbled for the path, sprinting blindly towards the lodge. The screeching followed her, snatching at her hair and skin, leaving prickly tendrils of ice embedded in her bones. Nyla swallowed a scream, launching herself over the uneven ground with no regard for grace or caution. She had to escape. She had to—

Silence.

All at once, the woods settled into an eerie quiet, like a switch had been flipped. Nyla was so thrown by the sudden change that she tripped, careening into a jumble of wild raspberry bushes. Fear thrashed in her chest as she scrambled to get up again, clawing at the thick, unyielding mud with trembling fingers. The Basin returned to the unnatural state of calm she'd noticed before, not even the leaves daring to make a sound. Nyla didn't trust it— didn't trust *anything* right now— not until she was safely back in the lodge and could collect herself. She wobbled out of the underbrush on wooden legs, pushing her body to make the final stretch to safety.

The lodge's lights winked into view just as the silence broke, Leo's screams undercutting the sprawling stars above.

Chapter One

AARON

"I'm telling you, that's not me!"

Aaron tried not to roll his eyes, counting to five in his mind before speaking again.

Gary Yearling was making a scene, not unexpectedly. *Lightning Greasers* was a small, mom-and-pop style chop shop, so the oil-stained lobby wasn't exactly teeming with customers. The handful of people that *were* hanging around huddled in plastic waiting chairs, staring unabashedly at the unfolding drama. Aaron didn't care— he was there to do a job, nothing more.

"Mr. Yearling." Aaron sighed, struggling to keep his annoyance in check. "I'm just dropping off the papers."

"You can take your 'papers' and shove them up your ass!" Gary spat, literally. Spittle collected on the dirtied blue linoleum next to Aaron's shoe. "Then take 'em out and shove 'em up Cathy's!"

This was the last time, Aaron decided. He was never taking another infidelity case again.

"You can discuss the details with Mrs. Yearling and her lawyer," Aaron deadpanned, dropping the manilla envelope on *Lightning Greaser*'s reception desk. The clerk blinked up at him from behind thick-rimmed glasses, pretending to busy herself with the shop's paperwork. Aaron let his gaze linger on the stack of crumpled invoices the clerk was (poorly) obscuring with her forearm. The forms had clearly been drafted on a computer and printed, but some of the sections were filled in manually with a pen. A few familiar terms jumped out at him, and Aaron had to bite back a smile.

No wonder Gary Yearling was pitching a fit over the legal system getting involved in his failing marriage.

"I'm not discussing nothing!" Gary snapped, puffing his chest and stepping into Aaron's personal space. Gary wasn't a small man, but his height outweighed his muscle by a worrying margin. Underneath his tattered coveralls, Aaron suspected Gary was nothing more than a wraith. "I don't know where you got those damned pictures, but I'm not having it. Take your *papers* and get out!"

"Right," Aaron huffed, giving up on his attempt to remain civil. Gary Yearling wasn't his client, after all, Cathy was. Or, more specifically, her lawyer. Professionalism wasn't getting him anywhere, so it was time to change gears. "You're not a smart man, are you, Mr. Yearling?"

Gary's mouth fell open, shock silencing him.

"You don't need to answer," Aaron continued, easing back onto his heels. He wanted to speak before Gary regained his senses and started swinging. Aaron wasn't one to engage in unfair fights. "I've got my answer from the agonizing few minutes we've been speaking. If you were a smart man, you'd have taken these papers and let me get on with my day. Instead, you're being stubborn and generally unhelpful, which means that I have long overstayed my welcome."

Aaron leaned an elbow on the reception counter, nodding to the iMac taking up most of the available space.

"Observation is a skill, Mr. Yearling." Aaron allowed himself a bit of theatrics, catching Gary's eye with distaste. "A very useful one. While you've been huffing and howling, I've been paying attention. Let's see."

Aaron made no effort to hide his actions now, making a show of needlessly squinting at the computer screen.

"Is there a... Frida Watson here?"

A small, frail woman raised her hand. Aaron felt a surge of bitter anger coat the back of his tongue. Frida Watson looked to be in her eighties, likely with no knowledge of cars or auto work. She was the ideal customer for scum like Gary Yearling.

"I'm just looking at your invoice, Mrs. Watson," Aaron said conversationally, shooting Gary a cold warning glare when he tried to interrupt. "I notice they've charged you $500 for a GW Transmission Flush. May I ask what brought you to the mechanic in the first place?"

"My check engine light," she squeaked, confusion swiveling her head between Gary and Aaron. Aaron nodded gravely; he'd expected as much.

"It's a good thing I asked." Aaron pressed his lips together, looking concerned. "I think there's been a mistake. A GW transmission flush is rarely necessary." He turned to the clerk. "I believe you've checked the wrong service, ma'am. Simple error. Nothing to worry about."

"Now, wait a minute—" Gary slapped his palm on the reception desk, crowding the clerk. Aaron stopped him with a sharp stare. He retracted his hand, but he didn't quiet. "That invoice is correct! I filled it out myself!"

"I have no doubt," Aaron muttered. He lowered his voice so that the gathered crowd could no longer hear him. "Unlike Mrs. Watson, I know a thing or two about how establishments such as yours make a profit, Mr. Yearling. Unless you want me to announce to the entire lobby that 'GW' is mechanic shorthand for 'Gravy Work' and that Mrs. Watson should've been out the door with a $20 oil change, I'd suggest you shut your damn mouth."

Gary's jaw snapped audibly shut.

Aaron made another nod, this time to the stack of invoices piled next to the keyboard.

"And maybe this is just a hunch." Aaron raised his voice just a touch, enough to make Gary sweat without being overheard. "But in my experience, the only reason a mechanic would hand-write their serial numbers like that is if they were... 'inaccurate.' As a matter of fact, I think the local PD could cross a lot of Ts and dot a lot of Is in a few of their open automotive thefts by perusing your records."

Gary Yearling went pale, sweat beading along the edges of his hairline.

"Luckily for you," Aaron smirked, "I'm not here about that. *I'm* here to serve you these papers on behalf of your jilted wife. Now, if I were to stick around at all, maybe call in a favor or two, I *could* shine some unwanted light on this chop op, but we don't need to go there, do we Gary?"

Aaron reached into his pocket, popped a piece of gum from the packet, and offered a second piece to Gary. He declined.

"Nah, I don't think we do," Aaron mused. "I think you're going to take that envelope into your office, and I'm going to walk out of this shop, patting myself on the back for a job well done. After that, I don't give a rat's ass what you do with your sad little life, alright? What do you say?"

Wisely, Gary Yearling chose to say nothing.

"Have a good day, Mr. Yearling," Aaron said with a grin, pivoting on his heel and heading back into the midday sun.

Man, he really hated his job.

The weather was a poor reflection of his mood, the bright blue sky mocking him with its clarity and promise. Birds sang animatedly from a nearby park bench, and teenagers gathered in the parking lot across the street on their skateboards and bikes. The world was happy. Happy and carefree.

Aaron, on the other hand, was late.

The coffee shop they were going to was on Fifth, about a five-minute walk from the chop shop. Aaron headed there now, keeping his steps quick but refusing to jog. If Pratt caught him literally running late, he'd never hear the end of it. Besides, Aaron wasn't ignorant to the apprehension roiling in his gut.

Tyler Pratt had graduated with Aaron from the FBI Academy, so they'd crossed paths enough times to become good friends. While they'd started their careers in different departments, eventually they'd collided again in homicide and began their six-year-long partnership. Pratt was the closest thing Aaron had to a brother— he felt guilty for avoiding him for so many months.

Aaron spotted Pratt's car, which was impossible to miss. The '89 Ford Taurus with two different coloured doors was parked outside the coffee shop, forcing Aaron to let go of the little bit of hope he had left of hiding his late arrival. If there was one thing he could count on Pratt for, it was tardiness. Not today, of course. Aaron would never be so lucky.

Steeling himself, he pushed through the front door and made directly for the counter.

"I thought you died!"

Annoyance and amusement flooded him in equal measures as he caught Pratt's eye from a table near the window. Aaron flipped him a middle finger before placing his order and joining his old partner with a sideways smirk.

"Get it out of your system now," Aaron insisted, pulling Pratt into a one-armed hug. "Before I get sick of you and go home."

"Private sector's changed you," Pratt needled, already enjoying this far more than Aaron was ready for. He sighed, accepting his drink from the barista. "Who'd have thought the infamously punctual Agent Aaron Tomas Carlo Javier Klein would show up *late*. The Bureau would be disappointed."

"Hey now, no need to whip out my government name," Aaron complained, struggling to hide his smile. "In my defense, it's not my fault. I was on a case."

"Trouble getting a cat out of tree for an old lady?"

Aaron scowled into his drink, taking the jabs in bemused stride.

"Cheating scumbag refusing his court documents." Aaron shrugged, easing into the hard plastic chair opposite Pratt. "That reminds me. *Lightning Greasers*, heard of it?"

"The mechanic on Fleet Street?"

"That's the one. You might want to pass the name along to someone in the fraud department. I doubt their financial records would hold up to scrutiny."

Pratt nodded, making a note on his phone to do just that on Monday morning.

"So, is that your business now?" Pratt grinned, displaying his perfectly white teeth. Aaron had always suspected he got some sort of whitening treatment, but Pratt insisted it was genetics. The same genetics that graced him with shining locks of dirty-blond hair and bright blue eyes. Aaron always told him he should've been an actor, and put his baby face to better use. He didn't want to repeat the choice words Pratt regularly threw back at him over those comments. "Chasing down cheaters and bill dodgers?"

"Among other things," Aaron said, taking an appreciative sip of his latte. "I'm ruling out cheaters, though. Way too messy."

Pratt coughed out a laugh, pausing with his blueberry muffin halfway to his mouth.

"No more infidelity cases?" He shook his head 'no.' "Isn't that your bread and butter?"

Pratt wasn't wrong. As a private investigator, Aaron could pay his mortgage with infidelity cases alone. It was how most in his field made a decent living. Aaron's problem was that he simply didn't want to be in his field.

"I get other cases, Pratt," Aaron said defensively, though it was close to a lie. Infidelity wasn't the first category of assignments he'd stricken from his personal workload. Cheaters joined the growing list of taboos, including missing persons and anything involving tracking down unknown relatives. After that, his job pool was small at best.

"You could always come back," Pratt mused, his nonchalance deliberately and wholly false. "You left a gaping Klein-sized hole in our unit when you left."

Aaron inwardly flinched.

"Kelley has it covered," Aaron huffed, warning Pratt with a piercing gaze to drop it. Pratt listened, but not without an exaggerated eye-roll. "I just wrote off cheating cases for being too messy, and you're trying to convince me to come back to homicide?"

"That's a different kind of messy," Pratt argued. "An interesting one. I got the impression that you wanted to drop this?"

"I do," Aaron lied.

"Then consider it dropped."

Pratt knew Aaron better than anyone. He knew that Aaron didn't idolize the private sector like other investigators he'd met. He knew that if he pushed, Aaron would eventually agree to come back to the FBI's Chicago field office. But he wouldn't. Pratt also knew that if Aaron came back due to his prodding, nothing would change and they'd be right back here again in a few years. No, if Aaron came back, it had to be a decision he made on his own.

"How's Chia?"

Pratt smiled, happy for this change in topic.

"She's great." Pratt pulled out his phone, bringing up the most recent photo he'd taken of his wife and young son. "Recovering like a champ. And Isaiah is sprouting up like a damn weed."

He was right. The picture showed Chia with an impressive cast around her arm, the only evidence that she'd recently undergone surgery for a bone spur in her wrist. Isaiah hung off her free arm, giving his mother a huge, sloppy kiss. Aaron smirked.

"He's what, three now?" Pratt nodded in confirmation. "Jesus. Seems like yesterday you two were fighting about which crib to buy."

"Don't ever bring that up around Chia." Pratt cringed, shuddering. "Three years and another baby on the way and she still hasn't let it go."

Aaron laughed, shaking his head.

"Of course not." He grinned. "You were wrong, after all."

Pratt snorted.

"Is Jabulani flying over for this birth too?"

"If she can," Pratt took a bite of his muffin. "We're still six months away for sure, and Chia's father's health isn't great. I doubt he'd be well enough to make the trip to Johannesburg, let alone the seven-hour flight after that. She wants to come, but we'll have to see. Chia wants her here too, so I'm sure she'll come if she can."

"And your parents?"

"In Rome at the moment." Pratt laughed. The last time they'd met, his parents were in Mumbai. Aaron idly wondered where they'd be the next time he got around to a coffee date. "We haven't even told them yet. You know what my mom's like- she'll cut their trip short and book the next flight home. Dad would never let me hear the end of it."

Aaron eased into the conversation as they spoke, his posture relaxing now that they were clear of dangerous territory. He'd missed Pratt, he realized with a sudden pang of loneliness. Working solo had its benefits, but companionship wasn't one of them. He didn't plan on having any kids, but he loved being an uncle to Pratt's.

A vibration shook his wrist, his smartwatch screen lighting with an incoming email.

"Duty calls already?" Pratt joked, finishing the last sip of his tea. Aaron dismissed Pratt's half-hearted guess, pulling out his phone to peruse the email.

"Probably just my last client following up." He'd meant to send a quick message to Cathy's lawyer when he arrived, but had completely forgotten. "I'll just respond so she knows I didn't forget about her."

Pratt gestured for him to do just that. Aaron tapped the email, freezing with his finger on the 'reply' icon. It wasn't from Cathy's lawyer after all.

Help

The subject line was simple and to the point, almost ominous in its lack of detail. He didn't want to look at a new case while he was still engaged with Pratt, but something stopped him from putting away his phone. Intrigue was slithering up his spine like a snake, constricting around his neck until he felt he couldn't breathe. Aaron wasn't sure where this sense of foreboding came from. He opened the email.

Good afternoon Mr. Klein,

My name is Nyla Jameson. I'm in some trouble, and I need help. Several hunters have gone missing near Willow Lodge, and local law enforcement isn't listening to me. I don't know if you usually deal with this sort of thing, but I didn't know where else to turn.

I can pay you whatever your normal rates are, I just might need some time depending on how much. If you have any questions, my cell number is 555-3290, or you can call the lodge number in my email signature.

Please help me,

Nyla

Aaron frowned, blinking at the screen for a long time. Pratt must've sensed his shift in mood, leaning forward in his chair.

"Klein? Everything okay?"

"Y-yeah," Aaron cleared his throat, shaking himself. He was no stranger to odd requests. Hell, half of the emails he received were barely legible. All the same, this one was off-putting in a way he couldn't quite point out. "Sorry, I thought it was my client but it's a new case."

"Interesting?" Pratt lifted his eyebrows, feigning casual curiosity. Aaron saw through him immediately.

"Not one I'll be taking," Aaron insisted, typing out the same in a reply to Nyla Jameson as politely as he could. Missing persons cases were on his 'no' list.

"Doesn't mean it's not interesting," Pratt pointed out. Aaron had to concede that.

"Interesting enough for someone else perhaps," he grinned, ignoring the pang of uncertainty that sounded in his chest as he hit 'send.' "I'll stick to cats stuck in trees."

Chapter Two

AARON

Insomnia was a problem Aaron rarely found himself plagued with, but tonight was determined to be an exception to just about every rule he'd set for himself.

It was nearly two in the morning, and Aaron was wide awake. After his coffee date with Pratt, he'd come home, sent his closing remarks to Cathy's lawyer, watched a movie, and went to bed. Nothing out of the ordinary had happened, nothing to set his teeth on edge, nothing to make him fidget. So why was he still awake?

His house was silent, almost eerily so. He'd thought about getting a dog, but his working hours were too erratic. A cat would be better, he'd just never gotten around to it. He had one in college, but it was a reformed stray and didn't spend much time indoors. It was barely a pet, really. If he got a cat now, he'd make sure it was an indoor cat. Chicago had far too much traffic to let anything roam. Then again, maybe he wouldn't feel as secure with a cat in the house. Now, if there was a strange noise or some other disturbance, Aaron would immediately investigate. If he had a cat, maybe he would attribute new sounds to the animal and miss a potential break-in. How many times had pet owners ignored possible threats under the guise of annoyance at their furry friends? Was there a statistic on that? Maybe he could—

Aaron bolted upright in bed, rubbing furiously at his eyes. He was thinking circles around *cats* for Christ's sake.

Swinging his legs out from under the covers, Aaron trudged agitatedly into the hall. He was tired. He was grumpy. All he wanted to do was *sleep*. Why did that have to be so difficult?

A glass of water was his first potential solution, so he headed to the kitchen. He didn't bother turning on any lights; his eyes were adjusted to the dark, and he knew the layout of his home well enough to fill in any visual gaps. Nothing was ever truly lightless anyway, not with streetlights, digital displays, clocks, and any number of other inconspicuous sources. He could see just fine without ever turning on a bulb.

The water might help, but it might not. What Aaron really needed was to figure out what was bothering him.

Well, to *acknowledge* what was bothering him.

Cathy and her lawyer had been incredibly grateful for his help. They'd thanked him profusely and promptly settled the balance on the bill without hesitation or complaint. Everything had gone as smoothly as it could've. He and Pratt parted ways with a smile, no hard feelings there. No, it was that damn email.

Aaron groaned in frustration, dropping his elbows onto the counter and cradling his head in his palms. He'd already declined Nyla Jameson's request, so why was he still thinking about it?

Because it was strange, that's why.

Aaron was a sucker for the hard cases, the ones that felt impossible right from day one. His stomach clenched with anticipation when faced with a puzzle that others had written off, his blood sang when he finally solved it, and he was good at picking out the cases that would give him that thrill and satisfy the craving. For a time, anyway. Eventually, the need would creep up on him again, making him restless, and he'd hunt for another case to continue the cycle. Nyla's email tickled the dormant part of his brain that told him this case would be like that— different in that intangible way that made his heart race.

"I told her no," he announced to his quiet house. "I already told her no."

That should've been the end of it, he supposed. Then again, there was no harm in looking into things a little, was there? Nyla had given him a name— Willow Lodge— and a phone number. Surely with that information, he could turn to the internet and find *something* to scratch his investigative itch.

Glass of water in hand, Aaron returned to his room and retrieved his phone. The light from the screen nearly blinded him until his eyes readjusted, leaving the room around him looking like a wall of inky darkness.

Equipped with the phone number in Nyla's email, Willow Lodge wasn't hard to find. Their website was clean and simple, featuring large, high-definition photos of the property and surrounding wilderness. The colour scheme matched the natural atmosphere with different greens and creams. Aaron scanned the website with a practised eye, gathering as much as he could without scrutinizing every word at length.

It looked like a hunting lodge, from the reviews that were posted in their feedback section. That made sense, given the content of Nyla's email. Nothing on the website seemed to indicate that anything sinister could be going on until he reached the 'Bulletin Board' page. The most recent entry was dated one week prior, announcing the closure of an area called 'The Basin.' No explanation was given, just that it wouldn't be available to guests of the lodge for an undetermined amount of time.

Odd. Typically, closure announcements were accompanied by some barebones explanation. Enough to sate idle curiosity, but not quite enough to detail the situation. If hunters were going missing and this closure had something to do with it, Aaron would've expected at least a vague warning.

He changed tactics, returning to his search. He found a Facebook, Instagram, and Twitter account for Willow Lodge, as well as a few unrelated accounts for other establishments with similar names, but that was it. He wasn't sure exactly what he was looking for— articles about missing persons, maybe even a blog post or two. Whatever it was, he couldn't find it. From the perspective of a naïve bystander, Willow Lodge looked like a perfectly safe place to visit.

Very odd.

Aaron leaned back against his pillows, thinking. The lack of evidence supporting Nyla's claim that something was wrong could be indicative of one of two things: one, there was nothing wrong and Nyla was either paranoid or delusional, or two, something was *very* wrong and Nyla was in a precarious position with local law enforcement, the nature of which left them questioning her validity as a witness. Aaron wasn't sure which, if either, he was willing to get involved with.

Neither, he thought adamantly. He already turned her down. The only reason he was looking into this at all was to satisfy his own curiosity. Nothing more.

And yet...

Aaron opened his email almost against his will. No new requests, no follow-ups from old ones. As of right now, his week was glaringly open. He *could* take on Nyla's case, if he wanted to. But he didn't want to. Did he?

Curiosity burned in his throat, that old drive to plunge headfirst into a potential mystery nagging at him with infuriating insistence. After his refusal, Nyla wouldn't be expecting him. If Aaron showed up at the lodge as a potential guest, he could do a quick survey to satisfy his need for answers and she would be none the wiser. If he sniffed a case, he would just reveal himself. No commitment, no risk. There was nothing wrong with that, right?

Chapter Three

INTERLUDE

The Basin

By the fourth time he'd rolled his ankle, Ted Rourke had sworn off favors.

Ted didn't consider himself a 'nice' man. He didn't like people, got bored at social events, and always did the bare minimum at work... all in all, Ted knew exactly why his coworkers thought of him as the office asshole. He embraced it- his piss-poor reputation meant that most of the time, he was left alone. People certainly didn't ask him for *favors*, not unless they felt like being chewed out for half an hour.

But even Ted knew that when James Carver asks you for a favor, you shut your mouth and do the fucking favor.

"No more," Ted spat, stumbling over a tree root. "He could be the goddamn *pope* for all I care. Never again."

It had been weeks since Ted had last heard from James. A measly email, sent from a dummy address, with the instructions on what he was meant to do. Ted almost didn't believe it was from James at all until he ran into him at Tinny's Taco Truck the following day. Faced with a direct question, Ted couldn't turn James down. He was regretting it now, sludging through the dense underbrush circling the Basin.

Why were Jameson and Poulette so hellbent on protecting this shithole? Ted didn't know for sure, but he had a feeling his presence here had something to do with their little petition. James hadn't said as much, but the request had arrived in Ted's inbox just a handful of days after the signed petition was posted on Somerton's bulletin board. It didn't take a genius to fit two and two together.

Now, it was 9 PM on a Thursday, James Carver had been ghosting him for weeks, and Ted was in the middle of the woods, scouting some bullshit permit limits for a doomed construction project. He was crazy. Absolutely crazy.

The Basin was bigger than Ted always thought it was. He'd never been here before, and this trip wasn't encouraging him to come back any time soon. The trees looked like they were *dead* for Christ's sake; tall and spindly, with huge clumps of missing leaves. Why anyone came here for pleasure was beyond him. As soon as he'd finished his task, Ted was hightailing it out of there.

Ted reviewed the contents of the email in his mind's eye: *Wait until the situation calms down. Find the trailer. Get the permit.* It seemed simple enough on paper. Ted had sent multiple return emails asking how long he was supposed to wait, but after a month went by with no answer in sight, he made an executive decision. Six weeks was more than enough for the flames to die down.

James said there'd be a trailer. Well, Ted didn't see any fucking trailer; he couldn't see anything in the darkness. This was supposed to be a quick trip, a side stop on his way home from work, but it had turned into a three-hour trek through the goddamn wilderness. Ted wasn't a hiker, and he wasn't a fucking outdoorsman either. He hated the forest, hated the mountain. All he wanted was to finish this quest and go. Home.

Why was it so cold out here, anyway? August in Somerton was cool at night, sure, but Ted could almost feel himself starting to shake. He remembered one time in college when the power had gone in the middle of a blizzard. He and his roommate had to huddle around a makeshift terracotta heater for warmth, and even then, they'd barely made it through the night. Ted felt a lot like that now, like if he wasn't panting so hard, his teeth would be chattering. The moonlight shimmered through the tree branches, almost like they were coated in a thin sheet of frost.

Frost? No, that was impossible. Not this time of year. Not here. This may have been Ted's first time in the Basin, but he knew the area well enough to know that it was way too early in the year for frost. He was seeing things.

The ground began to even out beneath his feet. Thick vegetation gave way to packed dirt, and Ted almost whooped for joy when he saw a break in the trees. He had to be close. The taste of a freshly cracked can of Coors flashed on his tongue for a second, just long enough to get his heart pumping.

Find the trailer. Get the permit. Ted could do that.

A twig snapped beneath his loafer, and the sound echoed in Ted's ears. He paused, wondering why it caught his attention. He'd been trampling through the forest for hours now, making all sorts of ungodly racket, yet a twig snagged his focus. That was... strange, wasn't it?

He came to a full stop, struggling to get his breathing under control. Ted was a city boy through and through; his boy scout knowledge was practically non-existent, aside from the most basic turn-tail-and-run response if he came across any kind of creature with teeth or claws. Still, some deeply embedded instinct stirred to life in his bones. Something was wrong. He couldn't pinpoint it exactly, but the feeling was unmistakable.

Where was the trailer?

An intense feeling of discomfort started at the base of his spine, creeping into his limbs, and rhythmically tensing his muscles. Inexplicably, Ted felt the sudden urge to run.

"Fuck this," Ted uttered, deliberately stomping toward the break in the trees. Best case, he'd found the build site. Worst case, he'd somehow circled back around to the road and then he'd just leave. Screw James and screw this godforsaken forest. Ted was done.

Another snap of a twig, but this time Ted could've sworn it came from behind him. But... that couldn't be. The woods were silent. Completely and totally silent. Was that normal? Ted didn't think that was normal, but maybe his ignorance was showing. It wasn't like he was expecting a symphony of animal calls, but he thought he'd be hearing *something*, wouldn't he?

Jesus, it was cold. He couldn't think straight.

Ted flexed his hands, his fingers numb with cold and his palms sweaty with nerves. Had he ever felt this unsettled? No, he didn't think he had. He should listen to this feeling, heed the unconscious alarm bells that were sounding in his DNA, but *how*? His car was a three-hour hike away, he didn't know where the trailer was, and his cellphone didn't get service out here. Warning or no warning, Ted was at the mercy of the Basin.

Another snap. Ted jolted, realizing that he was standing stock-still in the middle of the trees. He was a sitting duck for any wayward animal that might find him appetizing. If nothing else, he should move.

Snap.

He should run.

Snap. Snap.

He was running.

Thwack!

Ted ducked under a jutting branch, crashing through the underbrush as quickly as his tired legs would allow. His heart thundered in his chest, choking him, pounding against his ribs, and his ear drums. Sweat needled his skin where it formed and immediately froze, creating a shallow crust of ice along his exposed limbs. *Why the fuck was it so cold?*

The snapping sound consumed him, filling every one of his senses. The world collapsed into darkness and the gut-twisting cracks of shattering bone. Ted tried to yell, opened his mouth to shout his panic into the silent forest. His cries were swallowed by the wet squelch of torn flesh.

The Basin settled into silence, stifling the guttural screams of Ted Rourke's last favor.

Chapter Four

AARON

"Hey, you've reached Nyla! Leave me a message and I'll call you back as soon as I can!"

Aaron dropped his cellphone into the cupholder, annoyed and troubled. That was the third time he'd called Nyla since hitting the highway, and still no answer.

He wasn't sure exactly when his initial plan fell apart. Aaron had a perfect excuse— he was a hiker, looking for new trails to explore— and the equipment to match. At some point early in his journey, he'd lost sight of why he was trying to hide his intentions in the first place. He was barely 20 minutes from his house when he called Nyla the first time to tell her he'd changed his mind and was taking her case.

An hour later, he still couldn't reach her.

Aaron tried to tell himself that wasn't necessarily worrisome. Willow Lodge was located deep in the mountains, and cell service couldn't be stellar. If Nyla was working, she might not be able to answer. He thought about calling the lodge number but quickly dismissed the idea; if she *was* getting his calls and simply couldn't answer for whatever reason, he didn't want to harass her.

His first impression was already unsteady since he'd turned her down and then decided to show up anyway. Aaron didn't want to risk making himself look worse.

The mountains were beautiful this time of year, lush and green, with only the whispers of autumn slinking through the underbrush. Aaron swore he could feel the city smog evaporating from his lungs the further he drove. It was liberating. He may not be much of an outdoorsman, but he could see himself vacationing somewhere like this as long as it had a hot tub and strong Wi-Fi.

From his brief internet sleuthing, Willow Lodge was about a three-hour drive from Chicago, nestled in the heart of Wisconsin. The I-90 took him on a straightforward route across state lines so even without the GPS in his BMW X5, Aaron didn't think it was possible for him to get lost. Once he'd passed Portage, he only needed to pay attention. Signs for Willow Lodge jumped out at him as he rounded every bend, and each time his heart did a little stutter, making him squirm in his seat. Even his palms were prickling with the onset of sweat, just starting to slip over the smooth leather of his steering wheel. Aaron frowned; why was he so anxious?

He knew he was getting close when Route 39 branched into a small, gravel-packed off-ramp. Willow Lodge was located about 15 miles north of a backwoods town called Somerton, which was currently taking up the real estate of every road sign Aaron passed. He hadn't been able to find much more on Willow Lodge when he resumed his snooping over breakfast, but Somerton was a different story. He nearly drowned in the headlines about construction companies and drilling projects competing with conservation groups. It was enough to make his vision swim.

The turn-off for Somerton was a blink-and-you'll-miss-it fork in the road. Aaron made note of the marker for later, continuing down the gravel drive towards Willow Lodge. The road was steeper here as he carefully climbed the mountain; he didn't want to think about what it would be like to traverse in the winter. Even his X5 would struggle if the road was caked in ice. Aaron was beginning to wonder if he somehow *did* get lost when the lodge finally appeared, emerging from the trees like a ship in foggy waters.

The property was familiar to him, meaning the website must've been updated recently with current photos. The main building stood at the forefront, just behind the neatly combed parking lot. It was bright and cheery, comprised of massive, golden oak tree trunks. From his vantage, Aaron could see several rustic-looking cabins spread out behind the central lodge, each one a slightly different shade of gold. He wondered if that was due to the choice of stain, sun exposure, age, or something else entirely. All things considered, aside from the unnatural stillness in the parking lot, Willow Lodge looked to be a completely normal business.

Aaron parked his SUV and stretched. He hadn't bothered to stop on the way, his anxiety wouldn't allow it. Now he was cramped and sore, but he could deal with that later. First, he needed to find Nyla. Her email hadn't specified her position at Willow Lodge, so the front desk seemed as good a place to start as any.

The front door opened with a click and a jingle, echoing through the wooden building. The décor leaned into the wilderness locale, everything looking like it was built from the very trees that no doubt used to stand on this spot. It was older than Aaron expected, at least on the inside. The exterior of the Willow looked like it had been renovated recently, but the interior reminded him a little of an old folks' home, though he couldn't quite put his finger on why. The smell, maybe?

"Hello?" Aaron called, stepping carefully into the lobby. He couldn't see anyone, but a series of clangs and bumps told him that he wasn't alone here. "Anyone around?"

"Hang on!" A yell from down the hallway startled him. He managed to rein in his nerves before he was greeted by a tall, broad woman with sharp, accusing eyes. Aaron smiled politely, ignoring the immediate sense that he wasn't wanted here. "Can I help you?"

"I'm looking for Nyla Jameson," Aaron said, easing back onto his heels. He looked for a nametag on the woman but found none, though his immediate impression was that this woman wasn't his client. "Is she here?"

The woman's eyes narrowed, surveying him with tangible venom.

"Who's asking?" She crossed her arms over her chest, shifting her weight to one hip. Her hostility surprised him.

"My name is Aaron Klein," he told her, preparing to produce his ID and forcing himself to take on a relaxed demeanor. If the locals were already stand-offish, he had a difficult investigation on his hands. Better to try to squash that problem now, before it got out of control. "Miss Jameson contacted me about a case that she—"

"You're the detective!" The woman gasped, her hostility evaporating in an instant. Her face softened, making her look years younger. Aaron guessed early thirties, just a few years younger than him. "Oh, thank goodness you're here. Nyla told me you weren't coming, but I hoped…"

She cut herself off, tying her shoulder-length, silky black hair up in a ribbon she pulled from her wrist. When that was done, she came around the front desk and extended her hand. Aaron took it.

"I'm Clary Poulette," she said urgently. "I run the spa down in Somerton. Nyla asked me to cover for her while she spoke to Bill."

"Bill?"

"The sheriff." Clary waved off his next question before he could ask. She moved with purpose, each gesture quick and confident. "I got a call from her this morning asking me to watch the Willow today, and I haven't heard anything since. I'm not surprised; Bill's probably throwing every book at her he can think of."

Clary was speaking as though Aaron knew exactly what she was talking about. He didn't, but he filed everything carefully in his mind to revisit once he'd figured out what was going on.

"I take it the sheriff and Miss Jameson don't get along?" Aaron hedged, resisting the urge to pull out his notebook.

"That would be an understatement," Clary huffed, grabbing her coat from the back of a grey swivel chair. "Come on, I'll take you to the station."

"That won't be necessary," Aaron interjected quickly, but Clary ignored him, barreling towards the front door with a determined step. "I'm sure I can find it—"

"I'm sure you can too," Clary admitted, holding the door for him. "But Nyla's been radio silent for hours and I'm too worried to sit around here and wait."

Aaron blinked, dumbfounded and frozen in place, as Clary turned from him and headed straight for his SUV. When she reached it, she turned to look back at him as if to ask what the holdup was. Aaron almost laughed. He had no clue what was going on in this town, or what his client needed him to do. He didn't know if he was going to continue to work the case, or turn around and go home, but he wasn't going to decide that standing here in the middle of an empty lobby. Right now, going with the flow was the quickest way he was going to get anywhere at all. Palming his keys, he headed into the parking lot after Clary.

Somerton's sheriff's station was nothing more than a speck of beige amongst a sea of green. The building looked like it'd been plucked from the top of any generic office complex he'd seen in the city and plopped into the middle of nowhere. Aaron tried not to make a face; he'd dealt with small-town offices before, and it wasn't his favourite gamble. He guessed there was a 50/50 chance of Sheriff Bill being helpful or obstructing him at every turn. From what Clary had told him thus far, he was leaning towards the latter.

Since leaving the Willow, Clary hadn't stopped talking. Aaron's ears were aching with the overload of information, but he didn't dare interrupt her. Everything was helpful to him, even if he could barely follow half of it.

Now that they were in the parking lot of the sheriff's station, Clary was mute.

"Are you coming?" he asked her, dangling the keys questioningly. Clary shook her head, sinking further into the passenger seat.

"I'm just after Nyla on Bill's shit-list," she explained. "If you walk in with me, he'll write you off too."

Aaron nodded slowly, handing her the keys.

"Turn it on if you get too warm," he told her, shrugging out of his seatbelt. He wasn't worried about Clary making off with his vehicle. She'd been so worried for Nyla that she'd left her cell phone on the Willow's front desk, only noticing when they'd arrived at the station. Not to mention, he wouldn't have any trouble tracking her down if she did feel like venturing into grand theft auto for the day. Somerton was a far cry from a big city like Chicago. "Be back in a bit."

"Good luck," Clary huffed, muttering something under her breath that he didn't quite catch.

Aaron had about 10 seconds to decide how he was going to approach the situation: from the time he opened the door to the first words he spoke. His gaze darted around the room as covertly as possible, taking in every detail of the station's layout before the receptionist caught sight of him and waved him over to the front desk. It was a fairly open building, with four-foot-tall dividers sectioning off small workspaces for the officers. Aaron observed for a second longer, wondering if this place was always meant to be a station or if it had been converted from something else. Eventually, he couldn't delay the receptionist's impatient gesturing any longer.

"Afternoon," Aaron greeted conversationally. He plastered an easy-going smile on his face, leaning an elbow on the counter as he settled into his role. "Beauty' day out there."

"Stunning," the receptionist agreed, returning his smile. She was a petite woman with kind eyes, likely someone's daughter or niece working for the summer. "How can I help you?"

"I'm looking for someone," he mused, dipping his chin in acknowledgment of another officer as they walked by. "Got a tip that they might be here. A, uh…" Aaron pulled out his phone, pretending to check the screen. "A Miss Nyla Jameson?"

The young woman bit her lip, covering the reaction by turning abruptly to look at her computer screen.

"Miss Jameson is unavailable at the moment," she answered automatically. Aaron donned a confused expression. "She's... in a meeting with Sheriff Hannaford."

"Has she been arrested?" Aaron prompted, noting the uncertainty in the receptionist's voice. The woman shook her head quickly.

"No! No, she hasn't been... no. They're just talking." She paused as if deciding what she was allowed to say. "That's what Bill told me."

"Well." Aaron frowned, pursing his lips. "That leaves me in a bit of a tight spot. Do you know how long they'll be?"

"I don't."

The answer was firm and final, leaving no room for Aaron to press. That wasn't going to work for him.

"If you don't mind," he drawled, peering at one of the pro-police work posters scattered across the walls. They looked like they hadn't been updated since the early 2000s. "I'll just wait around here until they're finished up. Can't be too long if they're just talking, right?"

The receptionist opened her mouth to speak, but nothing came out. Aaron stuffed his hands into his pockets, turning away from her as though he hadn't seen her attempt at dissuading him. Instead, he took notes.

There were three other officers in the station, none of which he'd assume to be Sheriff Bill Hannaford. Two of them were standing, hovering near the third's desk as they discussed something in hushed voices. Office gossip or case details? Aaron meandered to the window, squinting at his BMW, listening.

"Rourke? You sure?"

"Positive. Three of his coworkers saw him leave yesterday and then nothing."

"Ted's a dick." Two of the officers laughed. Aaron scrutinized the window's reflection, but he couldn't make out who was talking. "We sure he didn't just skip his shift?"

"He's a dick, but he's money-hungry." A chair scraped across the linoleum. "He's not giving up a sick day for anything. Man would show up to work missing a limb before he took a day off."

"Excuse me, sir?" The receptionist's voice sounded again, wavering and small. "You can't stay here. It's... it would be considered loitering, and I—"

"BRANDY!"

A thunderous yell shook the coffee mug on Brandy's desk, nearly toppling it. She grasped the handle just in time, turning to face a man that Aaron instantly clocked as Sheriff Bill Hannaford.

He was a boxy man, shorter than Aaron but significantly wider. Thin wisps of once-brown hair clung to the frame of his face, any locks he had on his head had long since migrated to the tangled grey beard covering his chin. He looked tired. And angry.

"You're not supposed to be giving out information to anyone," Hannaford grumbled, eyeing Aaron with disdain. He idly wondered if it was because he was a stranger or because they weren't accustomed to seeing people with skin as dark as his around Somerton. Probably a good mix of both. "Who are you?"

"Aaron Klein." He held out his hand for Hannaford to shake. The gesture wasn't returned. "I was just asking Brandy as to the whereabouts of my client."

"Your client?"

Aaron didn't answer, holding Hannaford's attention until the older man squirmed uncomfortably.

"You some kind of lawyer?" Hannaford eyed him suspiciously, expression guarded. Aaron smiled politely.

"Something like that," Aaron said dismissively. "I've been informed that Miss Jameson has been here for some time. In a meeting with you, I'm told?"

Hannaford pressed his lips together into a thin line.

"I'm afraid I can't give out any information on Miss Jameson without proper identification," he huffed. Aaron's smile widened.

"Of course." He reached into his back pocket, producing his ID and investigative license. "Please, feel free to run my credentials. It shouldn't take long."

Hannaford reluctantly took the ID, scrutinizing it for anything he could point to as possible fraud. Aaron waited patiently.

"The hell is Jameson doing hiring a PI?" Hannaford snarled, shoving the ID back into Aaron's hand. Aaron observed him carefully, piecing together a clear picture of the monumental task ahead of him.

Bill Hannaford was the type of man that Aaron loved to piss off. Blustering, power-hungry bigots with a taste for ignoring the rules as it suited them. After his time in the FBI, Aaron could spot them a mile away. Hannaford was a textbook case of a sheriff who'd gone too long without a good challenge.

How fortunate that Aaron just so happened to be up for one.

"Brandy tells me that Miss Jameson hasn't been arrested," Aaron said easily, taking note of the way the other officers in the building had stopped their gossip to eavesdrop. "If she hasn't been detained, arrested, or charged, there's no reason I can't speak to her, correct?"

Hannaford said nothing, nostrils flaring as he tried to think of an excuse to kick Aaron out of his station. Aaron wouldn't give him one.

"Maybe you can get her to leave," Hannaford said eventually, muttering something under his breath. Aaron didn't quite catch it, but Brandy must have. She immediately started typing something on her computer. "Follow me. She's in the… interview room."

"Lead the way."

Aaron nodded his thanks to Brandy, and then he followed after Hannaford.

"She's been harassing us all day," the sheriff complained, looking anywhere but at Aaron. He didn't pause to ensure Aaron was following. "Came in ranting about some creature in the woods, aliens or some other bullshit. We've been trying to get her to leave, but she's insistent on giving a witness statement."

"Witness to what?" Aaron prodded, studying Hannaford carefully. Everything about him screamed untruth, but Aaron wasn't ready to call him out on anything yet. He was still collecting information, deciding his approach. "I'm afraid Miss Jameson didn't tell me much in her email."

That wasn't entirely true. She'd outlined the very basics of the situation, but Aaron hoped if he played dumb, Hannaford would accidentally give him more details than he needed to.

"Not surprising." Hannaford snorted. "There's nothing to witness. A couple of city boys get lost in the woods and she's convinced the world's gone topsy-turvy. Maybe now that you're here I can get her out of my hair."

Aaron resisted the urge to ask what hair he was talking about when Hannaford held out his hand, stopping him in his tracks.

"Wait here," he commanded, spinning to stalk down a perpendicular hall. Hannaford operated with the certainty of a man that was rarely disobeyed. Aaron picked up his step, falling in line behind Hannaford's bulk.

"I'd like to accompany you," he said pleasantly, but with a firm undertone that left no room for argument. "If Miss Jameson is going to be giving a statement, I should be present."

"I'm not taking a statement," Hannaford growled. Aaron maintained his smile. "You can ask her whatever you want when you get her out of here."

"My understanding is that Miss Jameson is insistent on giving a statement, otherwise I would've met with her at the lodge as planned and not interrupted your busy schedule," Aaron prompted, repeating Hannaford's own words back to him. "It would be much quicker if you simply jot her statement down and sent us on our way, especially if she's been here lobbying you for several hours. Perhaps you'll allow me to negotiate on her behalf?"

Hannaford stared at him, trying and failing to come up with an argument. Eventually, he made a noncommittal noise that Aaron took to mean he was allowed to follow.

Sheriff Hannaford led Aaron down an excessively long hallway. Between the strange layout and ill-equipped storage, he was now certain that this building wasn't initially intended to be a police station.

"She's in there." Hannaford jabbed his thumb over his shoulder, his mood souring considerably. Aaron raised an eyebrow, receiving no explanation before the door opened and he was thrust into the observation room.

'Room' was a generous misnomer. Aaron stood shoulder to shoulder with Hannaford, huddled together uncomfortably in the face of the massive two-way mirror. Aaron wouldn't be surprised to find out that this used to be a broom closet.

"This is your interview room?" Aaron questioned skeptically. Hannaford grunted something unintelligible, staring pointedly forward. On the other side of the glass, arguing animatedly with a deputy, was Nyla Jameson.

Aaron was ashamed to admit that he was surprised. In his FBI years, he'd trained himself not to rule out anything when first approaching a case, but Nyla Jameson managed to subvert expectations he didn't intend to have. She was young, for one thing.

And painfully beautiful, for another.

Nyla was short in stature, no more than 5'4" surely. Aaron would've never guessed she worked at a hunting lodge— her body was all soft curves and plump frame. She looked like she should be running a bakery somewhere, dressed in all pink and frills and lace, not smeared in dirt, sweating through a thin tank top and ripped jeans.

"You're only making this harder on yourself, Jameson." Aaron couldn't see the officer's face, but it was impossible to hide the mocking lilt to his prodding. "Drop the melodrama and this will all go away."

"Eat my ass, George."

Aaron snorted.

"She's been like this all day," Hannaford told him, rolling his eyes. "Combative, difficult, and all-around uncooperative."

"But she won't leave?"

Hannaford shook his head in a vague gesture. Aaron frowned. Something wasn't sitting right with him.

"I'd like to speak with her now," Aaron murmured, not trusting the glass to be properly soundproofed. Hannaford pressed his lips together, his mustache eclipsing his mouth.

"I don't think that's necessary," he insisted, hooking his thumbs through his belt loops. Aaron didn't miss the way his fingers twitched towards his gun, a clear threat if he'd ever seen one. "We'll take her statement, then she can meet you out front."

"With all due respect, Sheriff," Aaron lifted his brows, "I don't require *your* permission to interview *my* client."

Hannaford opened his mouth as if to argue, but quickly thought better of it. Local law enforcement was never pleased to cooperate with private investigations, or federal, for that matter, but Hannaford clearly wasn't the brightest man. With any luck, Aaron hoped he would conclude that the best way to get rid of this new thorn in his side was to simply play along.

It never worked, but it didn't stop people like Hannaford from trying.

"I can give you a few minutes," Hannaford relented, shuffling his feet. He was nervous, unsettled. Aaron wanted to figure out why. "Then you need to leave and let me get on with my day."

"That's all I ask," Aaron promised, taking a deliberate step towards the door that made Hannaford falter back. With a hearty push, the harsh heat of the fluorescents flooded his vision again.

"Thank you for your time, deputy." Aaron poked his head into the interrogation room, noting the bewildered look on the deputy's face. Mason, his nametag read. "If you don't mind, I'd like to speak to Miss Jameson."

"Just who do you think you are?" Deputy Mason stood, thumbs hooking into his beltloops in an exact mimic of the motion Hannaford pulled earlier. Aaron couldn't help but wonder how often these men used physical intimidation to get what they wanted.

"Stand down, George," Hannaford grunted, stepping into the room behind Aaron. "He's private sector."

They shared a look, one that Aaron ignored.

"Private sector?" Nyla echoed, defenses still firmly in place. Aaron caught her eye, hoping she'd pick up on his game and play along.

"Ah yes, I keep forgetting we haven't actually met in person." Aaron smiled easily, taking the seat Mason vacated and settling in comfortably. "Aaron Klein. It's nice to finally put a face to the name, Miss Jameson."

He held her gaze for just a second longer than he needed to, until recognition sparked in Nyla's eyes.

"Oh, Agent Klein!" she greeted in relief, folding her hands in her lap. "I'm so sorry, I thought you couldn't make it out today. I wasn't expecting you until later."

Nyla's brow quirked, barely more than a twitch. Aaron suppressed a smirk.

"Sorry for the short notice." He dipped his chin. "I was finishing up with another client and things went smoother than expected. I decided it was best that I make the trip as soon as possible, given the urgency of your situation."

While they spoke, Sheriff Hannaford leaned against the doorframe, acting nonchalant. Aaron could tell he was listening to every word, trying and failing to decode their cryptic half-truths. He felt a pang of irritation.

"I would've gotten here sooner," Aaron mused, keeping a covert eye on the good sheriff, "but I went to the Willow first. I wasn't anticipating you'd be here. Sheriff Hannaford tells me it's been a full morning for you?"

Nyla snorted, shooting a venomous look at Hannaford.

"I'm sure he did," she muttered. "Not as nicely as you put it. Probably added that I'm batshit insane, too."

"Trust me, Jameson," Hannaford scoffed, "I don't have to tell no one how crazy you are. He's gonna figure that one out for himself real fast."

Aaron shot him an irritated glare, willing him to be quiet. Hannaford ignored him.

"Running in here screaming your yapper off about aliens and monsters and ghosts. Waste of my time."

"*You* were the one who brought up all that cryptid shit," Nyla spat, outraged. "I didn't say a thing about aliens or whatever. If you'd just *listen*—"

"Sheriff, would you mind stepping out?" Aaron clipped, turning to face Hannaford. "I believe it's a reasonable request to consult with my client alone."

Hannaford looked like he wanted to do anything but. Aaron was sure he was running through every possible excuse to decline, but he would come up empty. A benefit of working for the FBI for so long, Aaron knew the law. After a tense silence, Hannaford nodded and disappeared into the hallway.

Aaron wasn't an idiot. He knew Hannaford would be pressing himself up against the two-way glass, straining to hear every word of their conversation. He had no doubt that Nyla knew it too.

"I'm glad to find you here, if we're being honest," Aaron began slowly. "From your email, I wasn't certain you'd be comfortable going to the police. They really are the best people to handle this situation."

They weren't, or at least Hannaford wasn't. But the sheriff didn't need to know that.

"I know." Nyla sighed, deliberately deflating. "Bill told me they need evidence before they can conduct a proper investigation. I get it. That's why I contacted you, I thought you could help me help them. I came down here to give a formal statement, just to have something on the record. I know that red tape can be a killer in most cases."

Aaron almost laughed. Nyla was smart, too smart really. She slipped into her role with ease, making Sheriff Hannaford out to be the sympathetic authority figure with his hands tied. That's exactly what he needed her to do if they were going to walk out the door without further pestering.

"I wish you had called me first." Aaron furrowed his brow, injecting an almost theatrical amount of gravity into his tone. "A statement is useless without an open case. I suspect that's why Sheriff Hannaford has been refusing yours. Understandable, given the volume of his workload."

Alright, maybe Aaron was laying it on a little thick. He couldn't help it.

Nyla frowned, confusion slipping through her mask. Aaron feared for a moment that she would fall out of character, but she didn't. Rather than ask whatever question was burning her tongue, she kept quiet.

"How about this," Aaron pressed on, trying not to sound too eager. "Let's move this conversation back to the Willow so we can get out of the sheriff's hair." Nyla's lips twitched, mirroring Aaron's amusement at the unfortunate turn of phrase. "We can come back when we've got a bit more to work with."

"I can leave?" Nyla's eyebrows shot up, her attention darting inadvertently to the glass behind him. "Right now?"

"Of course, you can leave." Aaron tilted his head questioningly. He got up, stepping towards the door to punctuate his point. "If you'd like to avoid the heat, I can bring my car up to the door while you wait here."

"Thank God." Nyla stretched, a chorus of pops erupting from her spine. "I've been waiting here for like two days now, I'm sure I can manage a few more minutes."

Aaron froze, his hand on the doorknob.

"I'm sorry?" He turned to face her, incredulity and confusion warring for dominance on his expression. Surely, he misheard. "You've been here for how long?"

"About two days," Nyla confirmed, thinking. "The lodge closed yesterday, but I had to get Clary to cover for me today. I couldn't risk shutting down two days in a row. Bill takes every opportunity to make things as difficult for me as possible."

Nyla rolled her eyes, as though this was a minor inconvenience. Aaron was speechless, still processing her words.

"You've been in this room for two days." He meant it as a question, but his tone was flat. Nyla caught his shift in demeanor, frowning and meeting his gaze.

"Well... yeah?" Nyla pulled her lips to the side, recollecting. "Bill told me you can keep suspects in custody for 72 hours without a warrant. I've been here close to 48 now."

"Suspect?" Aaron's voice dropped sharply, a growl slipping into his tone despite his best effort to stop it. "Miss Jameson, you're not—"

"Mr. Klein?" Bill's gruff voice preceded his head, appearing suddenly in a gap in the door. "Can I speak to you for a moment?"

Aaron blinked at Nyla one more time, letting the reality of the situation simmer. Anger formed into a solid mass in his stomach. Silently, he followed Hannaford into the hall.

"You've been treating her as a suspect." Aaron accused as soon as the door clicked behind him. Hannaford immediately lifted his guard, puffing his chest indignantly.

"The disappearances have all been guests of the lodge," Hannaford argued. "We have to consider her a suspect."

"The missing men are hunters," Aaron snapped. "And Miss Jameson is an employee of the only hunting lodge within a 100-mile radius. That's not enough to keep her in holding for *two days*."

Aaron didn't bother mentioning the outright lies Hannaford had told him when he arrived. The cold outrage on his face made it perfectly clear to the sheriff that he knew, and he wasn't about to forget it anytime soon.

"I don't have to justify my actions to you," Hannaford grunted. "This isn't your town, and it isn't your case. Nyla Jameson has been a pain in my ass for far too long—"

"Your official stance is that she's a *witness*, Sheriff." Aaron resisted the urge to call him something far less polite. "And as of what you told me five minutes ago, you didn't believe that there was a crime for her *to* witness. You've kept an innocent woman detained for two days without probable cause. You'll be lucky if she doesn't sue this department!"

"I've got a handful of missing men, one more just this morning! With Rourke gone, I'm looking at seven. Seven!" Hannaford thundered. "I won't let some second-rate, washed-up detective come barging in here, telling me I don't know my nose from my asshole!"

"At least a second-rate, washed-up detective *knows* an asshole when he sees one," Aaron snapped. "You just said that the most recent disappearance was this morning. Miss Jameson has been here with you since *yesterday* morning."

Hannaford bristled.

"That doesn't mean she's innocent!" Hannaford shot back. Aaron had anticipated that argument.

"When was the victim last seen?" Aaron challenged. He knew the answer already from the conversation he'd overheard in the lobby. He almost wanted Hannaford to lie, to give Aaron an excuse to exercise his wit.

"Leaving work," Mason cut in, apparently tired of this charade. "Around 5 pm yesterday evening."

If looks could kill, Deputy Mason would've been dead.

"You have no grounds for keeping her here." Aaron felt his jaw twitch. He wasn't quick to anger, not usually, but this was unacceptable behaviour even for a small-town precinct. "My client is leaving. Now. End of discussion."

Aaron didn't give Hannaford the chance to speak. He stormed back into the interrogation room, rounding the table to a bewildered-looking Nyla.

"Miss Jameson," he clipped, his hand resting politely at the back of her chair. "Follow me if you would. We'll be taking our leave."

Nyla blinked at him, trying to piece together the sudden shift in the atmosphere. Hannaford was still blustering in the hall, throwing an impressive tantrum for a man his age. Aaron stood ramrod straight, hovering next to Nyla like a shield. For all Hannaford's volume and anger, Aaron wasn't going to let him push either of them around.

Nyla stood, letting him lead her through the station and out the front door without a glance back.

Chapter Five

NYLA

"I swear, the next time Bill comes into the spa, I'm waxing that stupid mustache off his face and feeding it to him."

Clary had been spitting similar threats the entire trip to her work, making the backseat of Aaron's SUV sound like a bad indie mafia drama. They were in the parking lot of the spa now, but Clary couldn't resist hurling one last insult for the universe to interpret however it pleased.

Nyla stifled a smile, waving to Clary as she stomped away from them. For all the nonsense Nyla had to put up with from the locals, she knew she could always rely on Clary to have her back, come hell or high water.

"She's not usually so sour," Nyla told Aaron as they pulled away, presumably heading back to the Willow. "Still loud, just not angrily so."

Aaron said nothing, dipping his chin in a terse nod.

He hadn't said much since they left the station. At first, Nyla assumed it was because Clary was happily filling the silence for him but now that they were alone, she wasn't so sure. The X5's radio couldn't pick up any signals and Nyla didn't know anyone that owned CDs anymore, so they sat next to each other in stony silence while the trees filled in around them.

Aaron Klein was nothing like she imagined he'd be. Given the clipped tone he used in his email and the barebones layout of his business's website, Nyla expected a man in his late fifties or even early sixties, gruff and jaded, maybe even sloppily dressed. She supposed she had popular media to thank for those assumptions.

There wasn't a single detail in her mental image that fit Aaron Klein. He was young, mid-thirties at the most, clean-cut and professional. Nyla snuck a glance at his wardrobe again, trying to be discreet and not sure if she was succeeding. Instead of a suit, Aaron wore snugly fitted dark-washed jeans, secured with a leather belt at his hips. His cream-coloured linen shirt hung comfortably around his torso, draping away from his skin just enough to obscure the fine details of his shape, but leaving absolutely no question that he was physically fit. The long sleeves were pushed up to his elbows, revealing honeyed chestnut coloured skin and the outline of unflexed muscles.

But it was his face that struck her as the most surprising. Aaron had thick, wavy, coffee-brown hair that swirled gently towards the front of his head. The sides were cut close to his scalp, leaving the top to grab most of the attention. If it wasn't styled, Nyla guessed the locks would fall to his eyebrows, maybe a bit lower. Aaron's face was kind. Laugh lines crinkled the corners of his eyes, and his mouth turned up naturally when he wasn't talking. Aside from the sharp cut of his jaw and pointed nose, his face was soft and inviting. Nyla suspected he could easily con information out of just about anyone with just a precisely timed smile.

"Thank you, again." Nyla muttered eventually, the silence driving her insane. They were still a few minutes from the lodge. She couldn't sit here fidgeting in his passenger seat the entire time. "I should've realized Bill was jerking me around."

It stung to admit, and it stung even worse to know that it was true. Nyla should've seen through Bill, given their history. She had no excuse for believing his lies, except that she was shaken from the incident in the Basin. Still, she felt stupid. Stupid and helpless.

"Don't thank me for that," Aaron said coolly, a muscle in his cheek twitching. Nyla frowned.

He was angry.

As soon as she realized it, she cursed herself. *Obviously* he was angry— his body language had been screaming it since they left the station. She just hadn't put two and two together until now.

Why was he angry? Was it at her?

Nyla fell silent again, pondering. She didn't think she'd done anything to warrant Aaron's mood, but then again, she had very little understanding of his job. Maybe she'd inadvertently made his investigation harder. Or maybe he was realizing that he really shouldn't have taken her case after all.

Or maybe it was nothing to do with her, and she was overanalyzing this.

"I really didn't think I'd hear from you again," Nyla tried instead. She knew she should let Aaron sort out whatever funk he was in before prodding, but her well of patience was shallow on a good day. "Your email made it pretty clear you weren't interested. What changed?"

Aaron spared her a sideways glance.

"Call it a gut feeling." He shrugged, pulling his vehicle onto the access road that led to the lodge. "Although I didn't expect to find you locked up in the Sheriff's station."

"To be fair, neither did I."

"You want to walk me through how that happened?" Aaron's tone was softening, matching the naturally calm cadence of his voice. Nyla took that as a good sign. "Actually, walk me through everything. From the beginning."

"Sure," Nyla agreed, sitting up a little straighter. She'd been mentally preparing a list of events since she sent the email, going over it several times to make sure she didn't miss anything that could be helpful. "I can give you a full breakdown once we get inside. If it's alright with you, I'd like to grab a shower first. Maybe get a cup of coffee."

"Guess I can't fault you that." He gave her a half-smile. "I suppose I should find an inn somewhere and drop off my things. Where's closest?"

"Here." Nyla jerked her chin towards the main building of Willow Lodge, where Aaron was currently parking. "There's a motel about 3 miles outside town, but you don't want to stay there. Trust me. I can set you up in one of the cabins. No charge, since you're here helping me."

"That might constitute a conflict of interest," Aaron said thoughtfully, scrunching his brows together so that the angles of his face stood out. "The motel can't be that bad, can it?"

Nyla said nothing, just held his gaze meaningfully.

"Alright, cabin it is." Aaron switched off the vehicle, easing open his door. "Lead the way, Miss Jameson."

"Nyla, please." She wrinkled her nose with almost comical distaste. "People only call me Jameson when they want to piss me off."

"Duly noted," Aaron chuckled, shouldering a duffel bag from the backseat. Nyla watched him appreciatively, her attention straying to the sliver of skin that appeared as the hem of his shirt lifted with his reach. If nothing else came from this investigation, at least she'd have a nice view. "After you, Nyla."

With Aaron directed to one of the three single cabins at the Willow, Nyla headed straight for her bathroom.

A shower was the bare minimum of what she needed. Nyla had been stuffed in that cramped room for two days, only allowed out for toilet breaks. She'd slept as best she could, but the little plastic chair she'd called home for almost 48 hours was far from a plush mattress. She was sore, exhausted, hungry, and irritated. If she was alone, she'd set up camp in her cramped bathtub and soak until morning. As it was, her discomfort wasn't Aaron's problem.

When she was clean and relatively comfortable, she pulled up her big-girl pants and met him in the canteen.

"This part is going to be tedious," Aaron warned her, settling into the chair opposite her. Nyla slid him a camping mug filled to the brim with tea, sinking into her own chair with a quiet sigh.

Willow Lodge didn't have an onsite restaurant. Nyla couldn't afford to build one, nor could she afford the salary of a full waitstaff. The best she could do was where she and Aaron were now seated, in a communal kitchen of sorts that functioned more like a snack bar with a dining table.

"I'll take tedious over infuriating," Nyla promised, feeling a twinge of annoyance at Bill. She felt like such an idiot- blindly trusting him after everything he'd put her through. She'd uttered several threats of her own when she'd left Aaron to settle in, embarrassment making her bitter. "Fire away, Detective."

"I thought we were on a first-name basis?" Aaron smirked, taking an appreciative sip of his tea. He was more relaxed now, revealing a certain charm that Nyla liked far too much. She fought back a coy smile of her own, trying to stay focused. Aaron wasn't here to flirt, he was here to work.

"Alright then, *Aaron*," she taunted lightly. "What do you need to know?"

"Everything," he reiterated, pulling a notebook out of his jeans pocket. Nyla swallowed a laugh- the latest smart watch perched on his exposed wrist and here he was writing notes in a dollar store spiral notebook. Maybe her initial assessment of him as a grouchy old man wasn't *entirely* wrong, at least in spirit. "Start with you. How long have you lived in Somerton?"

"Four years now," Nyla answered automatically. She could give him the exact date, down to the day of the week.

"And you've worked at Willow Lodge for the duration of that time?"

"I bought the lodge when I moved here, yes," she clarified, noting the spark of surprise on his face. Nyla wasn't offended. Most people were shocked when they heard that she was the owner. For one reason or another, she didn't strike people as the business-savvy type. "I live onsite, in the cabin just behind us."

"Are you a hunter yourself?"

"No," Nyla dismissed quickly. These answers came to her without thought or hesitation. Out-of-town guests always wanted to chat, so Nyla had performed this song and dance many, many times. "I hate hunting. Well, I hate *going* hunting. Obviously, I don't mind that other people do it, otherwise I'd be in the wrong profession."

"If you're not a hunter," Aaron furrowed his brows, bringing that serious, almost clinical expression back to his face, "then why buy a hunting lodge?"

"It wasn't supposed to be a hunting lodge at first," Nyla said. She'd told this part of the story enough that she could recite it while drunk, high, or half-asleep with equal clarity. Tourists weren't the only ones who asked her about her odd career choices. "I wanted it to be more like a tourist spot for hikers and nature lovers. I didn't realize the area was a favourite for big game hunters until after I signed the deed."

She left out the parts about being misled by her realtor who was just trying to make a sale. It didn't seem important, and Nyla didn't feel like embarrassing herself any more than she already had. Aaron made a note, peering thoughtfully at the page.

"You mentioned disappearances in your email," Aaron began, treading carefully. "I did some research before making the trip up here, but I didn't find any local articles or news reports indicating a problem."

"I'm not surprised," Nyla said, pushing her own mug away. She'd added too much milk to her tea this time and it cooled too quickly. "Bill has everyone on a tight leash right now. Anything that could damage the town's reputation is nixed before it has a chance to gain traction."

"But the Sheriff is obviously aware of the missing persons," Aaron mused, more to himself than to Nyla. "He mentioned them himself when we were at the station."

Yes, Nyla had heard. That was what hurt her the most, knowing that Bill believed her and still made her feel like she was screaming into the void. Nyla bit down on her tongue, forcing back the sting of tears. She couldn't allow herself to cry in front of Aaron. The last thing she needed was for another person added to the list of those that refused to take her seriously.

"He knows," she conceded bitterly. "He just doesn't think there's a problem."

"Seems odd for a sheriff to think there's no problem with people vanishing under his jurisdiction."

"Try telling him that."

Aaron made another note, processing everything she was telling him with clinical focus. Nyla waited patiently.

"I feel like I'm missing a piece of the puzzle here," Aaron said eventually. "Keep going. When did the disappearances start?"

"Six weeks." Nyla chewed her lip absently. "The first hunter disappeared almost two months ago, but I agreed with Bill at that point. It's not abnormal for the odd person to go missing in these mountains. They're vast and confusing, and even experienced hikers can get lost when the weather turns unexpectedly. Add to that a menagerie of big predators and an influx of tourists, and a missing person or two doesn't usually cause alarm. Tragic, but a part of life out here."

Aaron nodded slowly. Nyla might have thought he was just politely listening, but the rapt attention in his eyes told her that he was thoroughly scrutinizing every detail that left her lips.

"Obviously something has happened to change your mind," he pointed out, tapping his pencil against the lined pages of his notebook. "How many people have gone missing in the six weeks since the first incident?"

"Six," Nyla answered hollowly, knowing it was true but not wanting to believe it. "Seven, if I heard you and Bill right."

"Seven," Aaron confirmed gravely. "Another one disappeared today. Someone named Ted Rourke?"

"Ted?" Nyla furrowed her brow. That didn't make sense. Ted Rourke was the only person by that or a similar name in Somerton to the best of her knowledge, and he wouldn't have been anywhere near the Basin. "Ted's not a hunter. He works for town hall."

"Maybe I misheard," Aaron relented, taking a long dreg of his tea. "I only caught the tail end of the conversation."

"Ted would have no reason to be in the woods," she insisted, agitation forcing her foot to tap restlessly on the floor. It couldn't be Ted Rourke. She quickly sorted through her logbook to see if anyone stood out that Aaron could've misheard as Ted. "But I don't know who else it would be. I only have two guests right now, and they're a couple in town for some big tech conference in Hatfield. If someone went missing in the last 24 hours, it wasn't one of mine."

Nyla felt sick. It was foolish of her, but she'd hoped Leo would be the last victim.

"You mentioned an influx of tourists," Aaron prodded gently. Nyla shook herself, refocussing on the task at hand. "Is it possible that increased traffic to the area has inflated the numbers you're used to seeing?"

"I doubt it. Six men have gone missing in as many weeks," Nyla stated, incredulity slipping into her tone. "Seven, I mean. Right. That's more than we lose in a whole year on average. And some of them were experienced guys, ones that know the area almost as well as I do. I just… I find it hard to believe that so many of them would get lost out of the blue like that."

Nyla diverted her gaze, hoping Aaron didn't pick up on the details she was omitting. She didn't want to obstruct his investigation, but… she also wasn't sure how helpful those details would be.

"I'm no expert," Aaron hedged, "but could it be some kind of animal?"

"I *hope* it's an animal." They were treading unstable ground now, and she had to watch her step. "But that doesn't help us much either. Even the most dangerous animals out here wouldn't get through seven people that quickly. If it is an animal, then it's gotta be sick, or hurt, or something."

"So, you think it's something like rabies, then?"

"Not rabies." She'd gone through the same reasons before, over and over again, trying to make sense of it. "Wildlife officers test for rabies every year. We haven't had an outbreak in nearly three decades. It could be an injury of some kind. I read about these tigers in India that killed a bunch of people because they had rotten teeth and couldn't hunt their usual food. I figured it was something like that."

Aaron leaned back in his chair, pressing his lips together until they formed a thin line. Nyla shifted in her seat, forgetting her tea altogether, and watching Aaron's face as he sorted through his thoughts. It was fascinating to see; he was almost completely still, and yet the tension in his jaw and the occasional twitch of his cheek muscle betrayed how hard his mind was working.

It was midday, usually a busy time at the Willow. Even without guests, locals liked to park in the Willow's lot to take advantage of the mountain trails nearby. Nyla had been dissuading people from coming by for weeks now, and had had some success. Right now, with her guests attending their conference, she and Aaron were the only two people on the property.

"Humor me for a minute," he mused, drumming his fingers on the table. "If it's not an animal, and it's not happenstance, what else do you think it could be?"

"A human?" Nyla guessed quickly. Too quickly, she realized. Aaron's lips quirked; he knew she'd thought about this before. "That's the only other explanation I can come up with. Either way, *something* needs to be done. Men are vanishing out here, and Bill couldn't care less than if he stepped on an ant."

Aaron's face tensed again, donning the same stony expression he'd had in the car. Nyla paused, falling silent to properly observe his reaction.

"About the sheriff," Aaron began haltingly, clearing his throat. "What he did... there's no excuse for it. If you need help filing a report against him, I'd be glad to lend a hand. People like him have no business in law enforcement."

His words gained speed and conviction as he spoke, and Nyla realized that he was angry again— but not at her. He'd never *been* angry at her. He was angry at *Bill*. Nyla smiled, touched by the small gesture of solidarity.

"I don't think anything would come of it," she said honestly, shrugging despite the severity of the situation. "Bill's been trying to run me out of town for years. This place was built by old blood; families that have been here for generations. They don't like newbies, especially not young girl-folk newbies with left-leaning ideologies."

Aaron lost his attempt to bite back a chuckle.

"Throw in the fact that I'm a woman running a business in a male-dominated industry, and I'm a walking target for town politics. Though I kinda feel like I'm preaching to the choir."

Nyla nodded at Aaron, with his dark skin and nearly-untraceable accent. He granted her a lopsided grin.

"My mother immigrated from Bolivia," he acknowledged, an almost mischievous sparkle in his eyes. "I understand your position better than most."

More than that, Aaron understood in a way that Nyla never would. As alone and shut out as she felt in Somerton, she didn't have the added complication of a different skin tone. Clary had enough trouble getting people to take her seriously here, and she was more on the European side of her blended Italian-Maliseet heritage, at least visually. To be frank, Nyla was surprised Bill listened to Aaron at all.

"Apart from the obvious," Aaron continued, glancing at his notes. "Is there another reason Sheriff Hannaford isn't acting? Seven missing men isn't generally something you can sweep under the rug."

"That's—" Nyla paused, biting her lip uncertainly. This was the part of the story she wasn't eager to tell, the kind that made Mason laugh in her face and convinced Bill to lock her up, albeit illegally, for two days.

Aaron stared at her expectantly, his expression encouraging and patient. She took a measured breath, telling herself that this was the right thing to do. Aaron was here to help. She needed to give him that chance.

"The last man to go missing before today," Nyla blurted, forcing the story out before she could change her mind. "Leopold Thompson."

Aaron nodded, following along.

"I've known Leo for two years," she explained, rolling the apprehension out of her shoulders. "He's a regular, comes by every season and stays for nearly a month. He's a trust-fund baby; his dad owns some big real estate company on the west coast. He knows nothing about hunting, but you can't tell him that.

"Every year," Nyla pushed on, her words starting to string together, "Leo traipses all over the mountain, looking for the biggest game he can find. He hunts for bragging rights, but he almost never catches anything. If he's still empty-handed by the last weekend of his trip, he'll head down to the Basin."

"The Basin?"

"It's a place where all the inexperienced hunters go," Nyla said. "The terrain is easier, and there's a freshwater lake nearby. If you're just learning how to hunt, it's a great place to fill your quota. A lot of the old guard don't like going there. It's a pride thing."

"I recognize the name from your website," Aaron hummed. Nyla knew he'd researched her and the property before arriving, but she still had to stifle a smile at the blatant acknowledgement that he'd been snooping. Then again, she *was* paying him to snoop. "You announced that it was closed. I take it you own the property?"

"God no." Nyla felt a blush blooming on her cheeks. "The Basin is public land. I put the notice up to try and discourage people from going, but I can't officially stop them."

The words struck a hollow chord, reminding her of the last conversation she'd had with Leo before he vanished. As if sensing her melancholy, Aaron pushed the conversation forward.

"So, Leo went to the Basin?"

"Exactly," she said urgently. "They *all* did. I make my guests leave a detailed itinerary in the Willow's logbook; that way, I have something to hand over to the authorities if anything ever happens to them. It's standard wilderness safety protocol, but you'd be shocked how many hunters grumble about it. I was looking over the itineraries of the missing men, and I saw a pattern. Every one of them was planning to go to the Basin as their last stop."

Nyla pulled out her phone. She'd taken pictures of the logbook to show Bill, but she'd never gotten the chance. Now, she handed the phone to Aaron. He perused the screen, eyebrows furrowing as he took in more information. The itineraries all spanned different dates, but Nyla knew she was onto something. Every itinerary ended with the Basin, all except—

"Leo wasn't going to the Basin." Aaron frowned, sliding her phone back across the table. "It says here that his last stop was Rocky Brook."

"I know," Nyla admitted, fidgeting. "He falsified his itinerary."

"And you know that because...?"

"Because I caught him," Nyla huffed. "Most people listened when I started warning them off the Basin, aside from some hotheaded city dudes that would rather die than listen to a woman. And Leo.

"He doesn't listen to anyone." Nyla looked away, sadness surging in her gut. Leo was stubborn and arrogant, but he was always kind to her. "I tried to tell him it was dangerous and that he should stay away. He agreed, but I knew it was a lie. He was way too calm about it. On the Saturday before he was due to check out, I saw that he'd listed Rocky

Brook as his destination. I knew *that* was a lie too. Rocky Brook is a six-hour hike one way. Leo wouldn't do that if his life depended on it."

"Did you confront him?"

"I followed him," Nyla confirmed. She remembered the burst of anger and frustration that exploded in her chest when she realized what Leo had done. Even now, Nyla could feel her fingers shaking. "I tried to catch him before he left, but he high-tailed it out of there as soon as he could. Probably so he could avoid me. Unfortunately for him, the Basin isn't far from the lodge, so I just picked up and went after him."

"You weren't worried about the danger?" Aaron questioned, his pencil pausing on the paper. Nyla shook her head.

"I know these woods," she assured him. "And I wasn't planning on looking for long. Leo doesn't like to 'rough it,' so his setup sticks out like a sore thumb. It's half the reason he's a shitty hunter. A deer could spot his gaudy-looking tent from ten miles away."

"So, you followed Leo to the Basin. Did you find him?"

"Yes," Nyla rankled, wanting to shut down the memory before it fully surfaced. She didn't, and a cold sweat began to form along the slope of her back. "He was barely off the trail, set up in one of the more trafficked spaces. I told him he was being an idiot and he needed to leave, but he blew me off. Said I was overreacting."

"And then you left?"

"I wish," Nyla paused, deciding whether to continue. She'd come this far already— what did she have to lose? "I yelled at him some more first, hoping if I made enough noise then whatever animal was skulking around might get spooked and leave him alone. If it was a human out there, then I thought Leo would have a better chance at making it out if they thought he wasn't by himself. Obviously, it didn't work. Hell, maybe I made it worse. I don't know."

Nyla bit her lip, the silence heavy. Aaron waited.

"Nyla?" He prompted, his fingers twitching, almost like he wanted to reach for her hand. To her own annoyance, she almost wished he would. "What is it? What happened after you confronted Leo?"

"I..." she paused again and took a breath. "I don't know what happened, okay? One minute we were standing there arguing, and the next Leo was just... gone."

Aaron's brows knit together.

"I know it sounds insane," Nyla rushed to admit, her gaze darting back to the floor. Bill's face flooded her memory, sneering in cocky disbelief. She didn't know what she'd do if she looked up to see the same expression on Aaron. "I'm not saying it was anything supernatural or alien or whatever, I'm not. I don't know *what* it was."

She shifted again, the words leaving her in a flood.

"Leo turned to walk back to his tent, and then this huge explosion shook the forest. I thought it was lightning hitting a tree, but I didn't see anything. Then... I don't know how to explain it. I felt like something was... watching me. Or chasing me. I don't know. It felt like something was *there*.

"I ran," Nyla rasped, exhaustion creeping over her. "I didn't even stop to think about Leo, I just made a break for the lodge. I was so scared that I didn't stop until I was almost back."

Nyla fell quiet, contemplating her confession. She could've told him the full story, that she stopped because she'd heard Leo screaming. She probably should, but fear held her tongue. Nyla summoned enough bravery to look up at Aaron only to find him staring at her, his expression carefully shuttered. He probably thought she was insane. Did she really want to cement his opinion of her before his investigation had even begun? To risk him calling it quits now and heading back to Chicago? Leo and the others deserved better than that.

"I know I sound crazy," she murmured, softening the blow her story had dealt. "That's what Bill said. And Mason. And everyone else at the station. I'm just telling you what happened."

Aaron was quiet for a long time. Nyla wished more than anything that she could read his mind, see if he thought she was as mad as she felt.

"I can see why you asked for help," Aaron said eventually, sinking back into his seat. Nyla started— he sounded puzzled, but not defeated. "I don't think I've ever dealt with something like this before."

"So... you don't think I'm making it up?" Nyla blinked.

"Of course not." Aaron shook his head sternly. "You have nothing to gain from lying to me. I can see that you're shaken up. Something happened, I'm just not sure what."

"That makes two of us," Nyla prompted, daring to hope. Aaron pursed his lips in thought. "But you'll help me figure it out? Really?"

"Yes," Aaron promised, dropping his pencil onto the table with a definitive clatter. "I think I will."

Chapter Six

AARON

Aaron fell backward onto the bed, pushing his hands through his hair. Anger singed his blood, clouding his judgement. He shouldn't have agreed to take Nyla's case so quickly, but the thought of declining made him feel ill. He couldn't turn his back on her— not after what he'd seen at Somerton's sheriff station.

His jaw twitched just thinking about it.

When Aaron was with the FBI, he'd developed a reputation as a hard-ass. He wasn't, not really. He just had a strong respect for the rules. When rules were broken, people got hurt. People who didn't know better. People who didn't quite fit in. People who looked like Aaron. People like Nyla.

Sheriff Bill Hannaford was the kind of man that contributed to the tumultuous culture of law enforcement in the States. Men like Hannaford were a part of the many reasons Aaron ultimately decided to leave the Bureau. Men like Hannaford could pull a gun on a child and get off with two months of paid leave.

Nyla was right. Filing anything against Bill wouldn't bring about the kind of consequences they wanted, but Aaron was going to go through the motions anyway. Nothing would change if nobody at least *tried*.

In the meantime, he had an investigation to conduct.

A small thrill leapt through his chest at that. Most of the cases he worked on in the private sector were formulaic, with not much detective work involved at all. This was different. This felt like getting back in the saddle, despite the fact that he hadn't quite wanted to do that in the first place.

The problem he faced now was where to start.

It was well into the night when he retired to his room. Nyla had given him a tour of the grounds, pointing out each building and indicating whether they were occupied. By the time he'd taken his notes and finished his initial scope of the property, Aaron's day was over. The sun set quickly in the mountains, and it wouldn't be helpful for him to stumble around in the dark. Tomorrow, he could begin investigating in earnest.

Not that that was particularly helpful to him right now.

Aaron heaved a sigh, his attention darting aimlessly around the room. How was he supposed to help Nyla anyway? He was no woodsman— sure, he was in shape, but Aaron didn't even like *hiking*, let alone trudging through the forest looking for missing men or rabid animals. He didn't flounder often, but Aaron felt like he was on the brink of spiralling if he didn't pull himself together.

"Right," he muttered, shaking himself. "First thing's first."

Aaron had left the Bureau on good terms. More than once, he'd gotten offers of assistance should the need ever arise, and now seemed like as good a time as any to cash in. Scrolling through his phone contacts, Aaron found the name of someone in the Wildlife division that he'd done work for a few years ago, Frederique Carter. Fred was a good man, if a little eccentric. He'd have some advice for Aaron, even if he couldn't help outright.

He drafted an email, explaining the situation and requesting an onsite investigation if possible. With that sent, he returned to his contact list.

Pratt wasn't the best at networking, but Aaron kept in touch with other members of his old team. Kelley, for one. She was a born negotiator, and while her no-nonsense attitude didn't lend well to charisma, she knew how to navigate red tape. If anyone could get him the information he needed, it would be her.

Rather than an email, Aaron sent Kelley a text inquiring after missing persons reports from nearby State lines. Hannaford wouldn't be privy to the details of missing men from out of town, not unless he opened an official investigation. That would mean handing his case over to the FBI, and Hannaford wasn't likely to do that unless he had no other choice.

With those nets cast, Aaron pulled out his notebook. As much as he hated to admit it, he could understand why Nyla wasn't believed. Her story was reminiscent of alien abduction fanatics, except for the absence of hysteria that usually came with those tin foil hat types. Aaron could tell that Nyla understood the fantastical nature of her tale, lending to a reluctance to share it in the first place. Ironically, it made her all the more trustworthy in Aaron's mind. He believed that she was genuine, that what happened to her had really happened, however insane it sounded. His job, now that he'd accepted her case, was to find a reasonable explanation amidst all the strange evidence.

In the morning, Aaron would have another look around the Willow's property. Ideally, he'd do a third scan in another day or so when the layout was still fresh in his mind but with enough time passed to notice new details. Tomorrow afternoon, he would get Nyla to show him to the Basin, where she'd found and confronted Leo. That would be his starting point. With any luck, things would fall into place after that.

That still left him with the question of what to do right now...

Aaron sat up on the bed, stretching. He needed a shower, but that would only take about 10 minutes. He wasn't tired, at least not mentally. Physically, he was drained. And hungry.

Nyla had told him the canteen was open 24 hours. Perhaps a late-night snack was what he needed to settle his mind.

It took quite a bit to unsettle Aaron, even when he was with the Bureau. Some of the things he'd seen would be traumatizing to most, but after so long, he'd become desensitized. So why, then, was the thought of wandering around Willow Lodge's property alone, at night, giving him the jitters?

"Too many cheaters and missing pets," Aaron scoffed, shrugging on his denim jacket and forcing himself into the chilled air. As much as he loathed to acknowledge it, his step was quick, and he didn't linger in one place longer than necessary.

Pratt would be cackling if he were here.

The canteen was illuminated before he got there. Aaron assumed that was normal until a squeak of surprise met his slamming of the door.

"Oh!" Nyla whirled, dropping the butterknife she'd been using. Aaron started too, his spine snapping to attention as her hand reflexively went to her hip. Upon inspection, Nyla had a container of bear spray strapped to her belt.

"Sorry!" Aaron held his hands up defensively. It pleased him to see that Nyla was able and willing to defend herself if needed, but that didn't mean he wanted pepper spray to the face. Seeing him, Nyla immediately dropped her hand and bent to pick up the butterknife. "I didn't mean to scare you. Didn't think anyone else would be up."

"It's fine." Nyla smiled, shaking the surprise off her. "I didn't expect anyone else up either."

Aaron wandered into the room properly, glancing around. He'd had a decent look when he was here the first time, but he'd been too focused on gathering as much intel as possible to appreciate the space for what it was. The lodge's entire interior atmosphere screamed cozy and comfortable, which was a stark contrast to the anxiety he'd felt outside.

"Can't sleep?" Nyla guessed, a knowing smirk on her face. Aaron chuckled, nodding.

"How'd you know?"

"Most people find it hard." She shrugged. "At least when they're used to the city. It's not often that you find yourself somewhere that's actually quiet. There's always some sort of noise going on in town."

She was right. Aaron had noticed the almost oppressive silence the moment he'd shut his door.

"Hungry?" Nyla pressed, holding up a jar of peanut butter. Aaron grinned.

"I thought a snack might help." He peered around her, spotting a loaf of bread. "What's on the menu?"

"Peanut butter and cheese," Nyla answered proudly. Aaron blinked.

"Cheese?"

Nyla turned, looking puzzled for a moment until she spotted the blank expression on his face.

"Right," she stammered, twirling a lock of her hair uncomfortably. It was golden brown, almost blonde, and tinged with pink on the ends. Aaron idly wondered if it felt as soft as it looked. "That's a weird one to most people."

He swallowed a smile.

"It's pretty good," she insisted, nodding towards the block of marble cheese she'd been slicing. "If you want to try it."

"Why not?" Aaron laughed, easing back into his chair. He was always up for trying new things, especially food. "So... how did you come up with this, exactly?"

"When I was a kid," Nyla began, pulling out two more slices of bread, "my cousin thought that 'jelly' was spelled with a G. Like 'gel-y.' Whenever he wanted a PB&J, he'd ask for a 'PB&G.' But I always thought he was saying 'PB & cheese,' not 'G.' Eventually I got curious and made one for myself."

Two plates landed in front of Aaron, each with an innocuous-looking sandwich. Nyla took her seat next to him.

"By the time I figured out what he was actually saying, I was too embarrassed to admit I'd misheard," she said, laughing at herself. "So, I just ate the sandwich. And it was surprisingly delicious. Been my go-to midnight snack for years."

Aaron nodded along, pulling his plate towards him.

"You're gonna want something to drink though," Nyla mentioned quickly, before he lifted the sandwich from the plate. "Cheese and peanut butter aren't exactly the easiest things to swallow. Milk okay?"

"I can get it," Aaron offered, making his way to the small fridge. He took a guess at which cupboard the glasses would be in and succeeded on his second try. "I can't say I've ever thought about adding cheese to peanut butter before."

"I promise it's not gross." Nyla smiled sheepishly. "Could've been a lot worse. That same cousin also used to put ranch on his ice cream."

Aaron must've made a face, because Nyla laughed.

"Don't worry, you couldn't pay me enough to try that one."

"Thank God." Aaron chuckled, placing a glass in front of Nyla before taking his seat. She was already a few bites in, so Aaron felt no qualms about hastily sampling his own sandwich. He wasn't sure what he was expecting, but Nyla was right. The combination was weirdly good, if a little bland. Maybe with some chili powder or—

He stopped himself. No way was he considering a spicy cheese and peanut butter sandwich. Not a chance.

"Verdict?" Nyla prompted, taking a long sip of her milk. Aaron gave her a thumbs up, already taking a second bite. "See? I'm not totally crazy."

"Maybe just a little," Aaron teased, sipping his own milk. "But I'll give you a pass on this. I'm not sure what I was expecting, but it wasn't good."

"I make a living on surpassing expectations." Nyla winked, happily returning her attention to her snack. Aaron had no trouble believing her.

There was something so inherently likeable about Nyla. Even sitting quietly next to her, snacking on one of the strangest sandwiches he'd ever eaten, Aaron couldn't deny an intangible spark in the air. Nyla reminded him of bottled sunshine if something like that were possible. It made it all the more infuriating that Hannaford had taken advantage of her in a vulnerable state. Aaron pushed that thought away, not wanting to ruin his mood.

They ate in comfortable silence, listening to the sounds of the forest around them. Aaron noted a number of bird calls, something that sounded like a fox, and a couple of other noises he couldn't place. None of them fazed Nyla, so he didn't worry himself over them.

"So, what about you?" Nyla began, draining the rest of her glass. "We did a lot of talking about me this afternoon, is it your turn now?"

"We talked about you because I'm investigating *your* case," Aaron reminded her, finishing off the last bite of his sandwich. He knew before he'd swallowed that he'd be making this again, and he'd be adding chili powder. "My background isn't relevant, unless you're asking for credentials."

"Doesn't mean I'm not curious," Nyla told him shamelessly. "How does one end up a PI anyway?"

"Depends on who you ask." Aaron grinned. "Me? I wasn't exactly retirement age when I left the Chicago field office."

"Field..." Nyla scrunched her brow, making her light dusting of freckles stand out in stark contrast. Aaron didn't like that he noticed that. "You were with the FBI?"

"For ten years," Aaron confirmed. "I joined when I was twenty-four. Been working private sector for two years now."

"Why'd you leave?" Nyla pressed. Aaron realized with a jolt that he was about to tell her, without even stopping to think about it. What was it about Nyla Jameson that made him feel so at ease? He'd worked with his fair share of attractive women, and none of them had ever affected him like this.

"I think that conversation requires a bit more than milk," he joked, feeling unsettled.

If Pratt were here, Aaron knew what he'd say. He'd tease Aaron about his 'Mama Bear Override,' as he'd termed it several years ago. Aaron strived to be professional, efficient, level-headed, and cool under pressure. That all tended to fly out the window when someone was being taken advantage of.

Nyla's situation with Sheriff Hannaford had Aaron's protective personality traits thrumming in his veins. Between her bright smile and her willingness to trust, it was like she specifically crafted to be his kryptonite. Aaron would have to be careful here. Very careful.

"I wanted to thank you," Nyla said eventually, glancing at him from the corner of her eye. Aaron jumped, forgetting that they'd been talking just moments before.

"What for?"

"Treating me like I'm a human being." She shrugged again, downplaying the nervous waver in her throat. "And not like a crazy person."

She wasn't crazy. Aaron could tell that much, even accounting for his inherent biases. Nyla was scared, stressed, and confused, but she wasn't crazy.

"That's the least I can do," Aaron promised, feeling an intense urge to ease her discomfort with his hand on hers. An urge that he pointedly ignored. "I'm going to help you, Nyla. We'll figure this out."

She graced him with a grateful smile.

"I hope you're right."

Chapter Seven

INTERLUDE

Somerton Outskirts

Donnie really hated his best friend.

That sounded bad, but it was true. Liam and Donnie had been basically brothers since they were in diapers. Growing up in Somerton forced most kids of similar ages together a lot, but none more so than Donnie and Liam. They were neighbors, shared a birthday, and had the same hobbies. They even liked the same girls; it was as if life had predetermined their friendship before they were old enough to sit up on their own.

So then why was Liam such a colossal dickhead?

Donnie trudged through the tall grass, kicking viciously at anything that would break under his boot. This section of Climber Street was poorly traveled and overgrown, so of course this was where Liam had to lose his wallet. Not Liam's wallet, *Donnie's* wallet. That he shouldn't have let his friend borrow in the first place.

The sun was peeking up over the trees now, but that didn't mean Donnie could see any better. The grass was wet and muddy, the ground sludgy and soaked. Unless his wallet was sitting on the very top of the terrain like some sort of beacon, he'd never find it. Liam was going to have to replace every single thing he'd lost— cards, ID, cash, condom— everything. And Donnie was going to make sure he did it, too. Before his mom found out.

He was coming up on the turn that led to their street, so Donnie knew his luck was running out. Liam would've taken this turn on his board, and he'd definitely lost the wallet before then. Their street was well-manicured and open, so Donnie would've seen if his wallet had ended up there. Of course, Liam had to lose it on a back road nobody used anymore since they expanded the interstate.

His optimism was hanging by a thread when something caught his eye on the other side of the road.

Donnie launched himself out of the muck, sprinting across the decaying pavement without looking. No cars came this way, he wasn't worried about getting hit. He just didn't want to lose sight of whatever he'd spotted. It was dark, possibly brown. Just like his wallet.

He was sure Liam told him he'd rode the right side of the street. This- whatever it was- was on the left, in the ditch that occasionally filled with the mud cascading off the mountain when it rained. They weren't supposed to get too close to that ditch- it was a huge part of the reason this road wasn't used anymore. Too many accidents.

As Donnie got close, he knew he wasn't looking at his wallet. Disappointment filled his chest, but curiosity blossomed in equal measures. Whatever he'd seen, it wasn't a natural fixture. Maybe someone had lost something else? He continued his approach, slowing when the stench hit him like a wall. Donnie retched, shocked at how viscerally his body reacted to the scent. What *was* that?

A dead animal, it had to be. Maybe a skunk? Whatever it was, the late summer humidity had done a number on it, that's for sure. The air was heavy with rot, creeping into his nostrils and clinging to his skin. Donnie would need a shower when he got home just from standing near the thing.

Damn morbid curiosity. He was already this close, might as well have a look at the body. It might be cool- or terrifying. One way to find out.

Donnie took another step towards the ditch, stopping suddenly as his limbs locked into place. It was like his brain and his body were disconnected; he wanted to approach, to sate his curiosity, to see what was stinking so bad, but his muscles refused. There was a pull in his gut, yanking him to safety, to home, screaming at him to turn around and leave this thing where it was. Let it decompose in peace.

Now he *had* to know.

Ignoring the pulsing in his ears, Donnie stomped over to the ditch. He could handle roadkill, he told himself. He could even handle someone's unfortunate pet, struck by a vehicle or snatched by a predator. He'd seen worse.

Within three feet of the ditch, the smell merged with the sight of something foul, freezing Donnie in place. It was far too big to be an animal that would roam into town. It couldn't be a... a person, could it? Donnie squinted at the shape in the grass, obscured by foliage and rot. No, no it couldn't be a person. It couldn't.

Donnie forced himself to keep looking until his attention caught on its skull.

Bile filled his mouth, nausea striking him hard in the stomach. He turned to spit, but instead was slammed with a fit of vomiting he couldn't control. His phone. He needed his phone. He had to call someone, anyone. His mom, or Liam, or—

Another bout of vomit. Donnie couldn't stand here anymore, not with that— that *thing* staring up at him. Not with those dead, bloodshot eyes searching him. Gathering his strength, Donnie threw himself away from the ditch, towards his house. He couldn't move fast enough. He could almost feel the thing watching him, maybe even following him. Cold, sharp fear stabbed the back of his neck, making him stumble over himself as he sprinted away— away from the road, from the ditch.

Away from the unrecognizably eviscerated body of what was once Leopold Thompson.

NYLA

"Thanks for coming!"

Nyla waved politely, watching the retreating couple just long enough to notice the longing glance that her guest, Mrs. Hilary Green, gave to the display of Clary's spa products in front of the check-in desk.

"You know those are 25% off if you buy them here," Nyla mentioned casually, ignoring the annoyed look coming from Mr. Kyle Green.

The couple was Nyla's last reservation for the week, and then the Willow would be empty save for her and Aaron. Normally, she'd be discouraged by that. Summer and autumn were the two seasons she could count on to have a full house throughout the month; it was only in winter and spring that she relied solely on weekend bookings. Right now, though, she couldn't get them out of here fast enough.

"Are they made with organic ingredients?" Mrs. Green asked, floating over to inspect the display more closely. Nyla smothered a smile.

"All local," she confirmed, sizing up the sour look on Mr. Green's face. She didn't want to push her luck too far, but Nyla was confident she could sell them at least a couple of soap bars or face masks. "Clary Poulette owns the spa here in town; she handmakes all of their products."

Nyla could almost see the interest spark in Mrs. Green's eyes. She was on the right track, now she just had to seal the deal.

"The 'Witch, Please' soap bar is my favourite. It has witch hazel and aloe to reduce skin irritation and redness. Clary comes from a Maliseet family, so a lot of her recipes are adapted from traditional medicines."

"Maliseet?"

"They're an indigenous tribe," Nyla explained. "Mostly from Canada."

That did it. Mrs. Green lifted a sample of the soap bar reverently, ignoring her husband's warning huffs.

"I'll take one," she announced. "Is it cash only?"

"I still have your reservation open here," Nyla said, nodding to the computer screen in front of her. "I can charge the credit card you have on file before I close the account. Does that sound okay?"

"Perfect." Mrs. Green smiled. "Thank you, dear."

"No problem! Have a fantastic day!"

Nyla felt bad for some of the couples she saw coming through these parts. It was quite clear on most occasions that only one of the two were actually excited to be here. The other was just being dragged along for the ride. Mrs. Green fell into the latter category, and she'd made her displeasure known from the moment they'd checked in. Hopefully her purchase put a slightly more positive spin on her experience. Clary would certainly be grateful for it.

After the couple left, Nyla released a bone-weary sigh. She'd been up since the crack of dawn, as per usual, but her morning had been far less productive than she would've liked. Aaron told her that he'd be looking into some things today, but hadn't specified what. Nyla wanted to be available to answer any questions, but that meant she couldn't busy herself with one of her many time-consuming projects. The problem with being the Willow's only employee was that everything fell squarely on her, even when she had more pressing matters to attend to. Like a group of missing men.

Was Aaron even awake yet?

He must be. Nyla hadn't seen him, though she thought she'd heard someone bustling about before the Greens showed up to checkout. She didn't know what to expect from a private investigation; Nyla wasn't deluded into thinking it would be as exciting and action-packed as the media liked to portray, but that didn't leave her with much to work with. Her curiosity was burning, and the urge to track down Aaron and interrogate him hit her like a punch to the gut. Would she be bothering him if she sought him out? Would he tell her if she was?

Frustrated and undecided, Nyla sank into her desk chair. Aaron knew where she was. If he wanted to ask her something, he would. Otherwise, she should just stay put.

Anxious energy tingled along the surface of her skin, loudly disagreeing with her choice for more than one reason. With no other guests and nothing to occupy her mind, Nyla found herself looking to the door at every little sound, hoping to see Aaron's face on the other side of the glass. She probably shouldn't be enjoying his company as much as she was, but she didn't feel like worrying about that right now.

She was just toying with the idea of going for an innocent-and-totally-not-nosy walk when the front doors to the lodge burst open and Clary stormed in.

"Thank the Creator you're okay!" She exclaimed, jogging to the front desk and reaching over it to wrap Nyla in a hug. "Why aren't you answering your phone?"

"It's on airplane mode," Nyla answered, baffled. "I can't find my charger. I was keeping it alive for an emergency."

"This *is* an emergency," Clary snapped, crossing her arms over her chest. Her hair was parted into two long, slick braids that were fraying at the edges like they'd been unraveled and re-braided multiple times. Clary had a nervous habit of fiddling with her hair. Nyla circled the desk, planting herself in front of Clary and trying to read her expression. She was frazzled and fidgety, with no sign of her usual confidence.

"Why didn't you call the lodge?" Nyla shook her head, dismissing her own question before Clary had the chance to answer it. "What emergency? What's happening?"

"They found—"

"What?"

Nyla blinked, wondering why her voice sounded so masculine, until she spotted Aaron striding into the foyer behind Clary.

"Whoa." Nyla chuckled before she could stop herself. She'd turned to smile at Aaron in greeting, but her attention caught on his appearance before she could formulate a proper hello. "Good morning, Suits."

Aaron paused mid-step, glancing down at himself in confusion. Nyla shared a look with Clary while he was distracted, raising her eyebrows in silent appreciation. Clary pressed her lips together, smothering a grin.

"What's wrong with the suit?" Aaron frowned, shrugging his shoulders so that his jacket fell more naturally over his torso. "It's Armani."

"Nothing," Nyla promised, refraining from pointing out that the cut of this particular suit accented his frame in a way that made it difficult for her to look anywhere else. "Just don't see a lot of them around here, that's all."

"I wasn't planning to trek through the woods until after lunch," Aaron argued, adjusting his button-down shirt's collar. The soft salmon colour peeked from beneath the light grey suit jacket, warming his already glowing skin. "I'll change before that."

"*Suit* yourself." Nyla smirked, making Clary snort in amusement. "See what I did there?"

"Alright, I'm changing now," Aaron announced pointedly.

"I could call you *Mad Men* if you prefer," Nyla offered. "*Law and Order*? *NCIS*? I've got a million of these."

"One more word and I'm going back to Chicago."

"Suits it is."

"Emergency!" Clary cut in suddenly, as though she'd just remembered why she'd come in the first place. "Mom said they found something on the edge of town. One of her regulars was telling her about it. There are rumors going around that it's a body!"

"What body?" Aaron demanded, his eyebrows pinching together in concern, the suit debacle forgotten. Clary flicked her attention between him and Nyla, unsure who to be directing her fragmented information towards.

"I don't know who it is," she said, visibly calmer now that she'd expelled her news and verified Nyla and Aaron's safety. Clary was almost as disliked as Nyla— being both indigenous and Canadian— so the two only really had each other to rely on in Somerton. Clary knew as well as Nyla did that if anything happened to her, no one would be bothered to let Clary know. "The police won't say. All I know is there's a swarm of cop cars surrounding Climber Street."

"Will that be on the GPS?" Aaron asked, pulling out his phone. Nyla shook her head.

"Doubt it," she mused. "It's an old road, not used much anymore. I can show you where it is."

"Great." Aaron opened the Maps app on his phone and handed it to her. "I'll go and see what I can find out. I'll call you if I learn anything."

"You won't need to call me," Nyla scoffed, pushing his phone away. She retreated behind the front desk again, taking the lodge's landline off the cradle and laying it down on the closed logbook. "I'm going with you."

"Nyla, this is a crime scene." Aaron sounded both disbelieving and annoyed. "It's doubtful they'll even let *me* get a decent look, let alone a civilian."

"So I'll hang out in the car." Nyla shrugged, rounding the desk one last time and flipping over a laminated sign that read 'Be Back Later.' "Climber is hidden behind a bunch of back roads. It'll be way easier if I just take you there myself."

That was a lie. There was a decently simple way to get to Climber Street, but she wasn't about to tell Aaron that. Aaron glanced at Clary, but she made no move to correct Nyla either.

"Do you need someone to watch the front desk?" Clary asked, following Nyla as she made her way to the parking lot. She could only assume Aaron was following as well. "I have to get back to the spa, but..."

"Absolutely not." Nyla shook her head hard. "You've done more than enough for me. Go home; the lodge will survive without me for a few hours."

Clary smiled, returning to her massive navy-blue pickup. Nyla was still convinced she'd bought the thing just to spite the salesman that tried to get her into a tiny little smart car, but Clary had never admitted that.

"So." Nyla turned to Aaron with a grin. He was looking more than a little miffed at being ignored. He'd get over it. "Shall we?"

The drive to Climber Street was silent. Nyla was sure Aaron noticed how straightforward the directions really were, but to his credit, he didn't say anything. She didn't know how much more truth-bending he'd let her get away with; at some point, she'd have to start picking her battles carefully. For now, though, Nyla was happy to sit in satisfied silence in the front seat of Aaron's X5.

They spotted their first cop car a fair distance from the turnoff. Aaron pulled over to the side of the road, straightening his jacket.

"I was kidding about the suit," Nyla promised, giving him a sheepish smile. "It looks great."

Aaron gave her a withering look, opening the SUV door without a word. Nyla bounded after him.

"I thought you were staying in the car," he said, though he didn't sound hopeful. Nyla chose to say nothing, scurrying to keep up with him. She thought she saw him roll his eyes, but that might've been a trick of the light.

Climber Street was unusually busy, the typically barren road now dotted with both people and vehicles, all trying to get a look at whatever scandal was unfolding. Somerton was a small town, and word spread quickly whenever something happened. Nyla wasn't surprised to see the locals snooping about, but it still left a bitter taste in her mouth. There was no way she wouldn't be recognized by several people and her involvement in the situation would inevitably spark more rumors about her. She told herself firmly that it didn't matter, but it still stung.

"This is a closed crime scene." The voice of an officer met them before they'd reached the patrol car, coming from the open window. He hadn't bothered to look at who was approaching, still staring firmly at a mindless game on his phone screen. "I'm going to have to ask you to return to your vehicle."

"Aaron Klein, PI," Aaron stated, removing his ID from his pocket. Nyla noted the abrupt shift in his tone from relaxed and casual to authoritative and confident. She wasn't sure which version she preferred, both were appealing in their own ways. "I'm investigating a case in the area, and I believe this may be related."

The officer leaned out the window, elbow resting on the doorframe. Nyla recognized him as Jeff Vasey. He was a newer member of the precinct. He didn't completely hate her yet.

"Can't let you through," he insisted, scanning Aaron's ID with disinterest. "Deputy Mason's orders."

"Not Sheriff Hannaford?"

Vasey gave Aaron a look. Not a kind one.

"Sheriff Hannaford is on a temporary sabbatical," he said, clipping his words in a tone that almost dared Aaron to ask more questions.

"That's new," Nyla interjected instead, trying to keep her distaste out of her voice. She was sure Aaron wouldn't appreciate it if her poor relationship with the Somerton Sheriff Station caused them any further problems. "He was working yesterday, wasn't he?"

Vasey nodded jerkily like he wasn't sure if he was supposed to answer her. Nyla had gotten that uncertain reaction before, mostly from new residents who knew they were supposed to dislike her and hadn't yet figured out why.

"Effective as of this morning," Vasey grunted, choosing to direct his response toward Aaron, circumventing Nyla altogether. She rolled her eyes, unsurprised. "Mason's in charge in the interim."

"Great." Aaron grinned, smacking the top of the car good-naturedly. He glanced at Nyla, making pointed eye contact with Vasey as he straightened. "*We'll* speak directly to him then. Let's go, Nyla."

She didn't miss the deliberate word choice, making her inclusion obvious to Vasey even though he hadn't wanted her to accompany him in the first place. Aaron's hand clasped her shoulder firmly, ushering her along at a brusque pace. Vasey yelled after them to stop, but by the time he'd removed himself from the vehicle, Aaron had guided her well out of speaking range. Nyla ignored the temptation to peek over her shoulder to see if Vasey would bother giving chase. When only the sound of their footsteps met her ears, it was clear that he hadn't.

"That shouldn't have worked," she told Aaron with a smirk. He granted her that, dropping his grip on her shoulder as they approached the center of the commotion. Nyla couldn't help the spark of disappointment that flickered in her chest.

"Small-town law enforcement generally isn't as organized," he told her, his voice returning to its more relaxed cadence. This was the version of Aaron she preferred, she decided. "You can get away with a lot, as long as you know what you're doing."

"And lucky for us, you know what you're doing?"

Aaron only winked.

They found Mason next, speaking to a cluster of officers gathered in the middle of the road. There was a teenage boy standing off to the side with another officer. Nyla thought she recognized him, but she couldn't quite pick out his name. Dylan? Danny? Something like that.

"Jameson." Mason's growl grabbed Nyla's attention before she could finish shuffling through her memories, followed by the sound of approaching boots. Aaron pulled her to a stop with his hand returning briefly to her shoulder, angling himself gently in front of her as a physical buffer. "What the hell are you two doing here? Klein, this isn't your territory."

"I was hired to investigate Miss Jameson's claims of foul play," Aaron said coolly, all business again. "I believe I'm entitled to some transparency, given the situation."

"You're entitled to nothing," Mason snapped, but his voice lacked its usual fire. Nyla watched from her safe space behind Aaron, noting with concern the thin sheen of sweat on Mason's face. It wasn't that warm out today, and Mason was a fit man. Why, then, did he look like he was about to pass out from exhaustion?

"Miss Jameson made her concerns clear to you days ago," Aaron continued, offering Mason a deceptively polite smile. Despite the instinctive discomfort she felt whenever she was addressed by her last name, Nyla found she didn't mind as much when Aaron did it. "Had you taken her seriously at the time, I wouldn't be here. Now, don't think I'm unsympathetic to your situation, but seeing as this body was found on the edge of the very woods that border Miss Jameson's property, that makes it pertinent to my investigation."

"You're not the law, Klein," Mason argued, rapidly losing gusto. Hannaford was stubborn and bullheaded; negotiating with him was both impossible and infuriating. Mason was a bit more lenient in Nyla's experience, mostly wanting to get back home to his son at the end of the day. "I don't have to let you pass."

"It would be much easier for you if you did."

"You're a real pain in the ass."

"I could be worse."

With a frustrated huff, Mason waved him through.

"Look," he spat in warning. "Look, but do not touch. No pictures, no questions, no souvenirs, no poking, no prodding. In, look, and out. Understood?"

"Understood," Aaron repeated, placing his arm around Nyla again and leading her to the source of the chaos.

At first, Nyla didn't know what she was looking at. She expected to see police tape, a body bag, a tarp, something, but from what she could tell, everything was exactly as it should be. If there wasn't an overwhelming police presence and a notable sour scent in the air, she wouldn't know anything was amiss. Somehow, that made her feel worse.

"Stand back," Aaron murmured to her, his hand squeezing her waist for a moment. "If it's not too grotesque, I'll wave you over."

"I'm not squeamish," she argued, but her gaze flickered uncertainly to the tall grass, where a swarm of flies was hovering. She often saw thick clouds of them clinging to road kill or the discarded innards from her guests' prizes, but never at this magnitude. Nyla didn't want to imagine the potent scent of death that was necessary to attract so many.

"It's not about being squeamish," he said. "If this is one of your missing hunters, then there's a good chance you'll recognize them. Depending on the state the body's in, you might not want to see it like this."

"How bad could it be?" Nyla asked before she could stop herself. It was meant as a rhetorical question but once it left her mouth, Nyla wasn't so sure. Aaron pressed his lips together.

"Wait here."

Nyla hadn't made up her mind about arguing with him when Aaron turned and headed straight for the center of the action. Her muscles flinched as if to follow him, but she stopped herself, instead watching anxiously as he made his way to the ditch. In Aaron's absence, she homed in on the sounds around her— whispers, murmurs, gasps, sobs. Small-town gossip was a beast in and of itself, twisting natural curiosity into a callous, entitled demand for details. The mood here was different, somber, like a funeral.

Something was wrong. Nyla could feel it in the air. She shivered, rubbing absently at the goosebumps rising on her forearms. She should've brought a sweater.

Aaron reached the side of the road. Crouched. Paused.

Nyla held her breath.

A few seconds passed before he stood, slipping his hand into his pants pocket. Nyla couldn't see his face very well as he walked back to her, but from what she could make out he looked... troubled.

"Well?" She asked when he reached her, still staring firmly at the ground, lost in thought. At the sound of her voice, he glanced up. His expression was guarded, completely shuttered. Nyla couldn't venture a guess as to what he was thinking.

"We should go," he told her quietly, just as their presence caught the attention of one of the other officers. Aaron nodded for Nyla to head back towards the SUV. "We'll talk at the lodge, alright?"

Nyla agreed, deciding that now wasn't the best time to question him. The officer who'd spotted them was heading their way, quickly. Nyla didn't recognize him at all, meaning he was probably from the next town over and far less likely to be as easily manipulated as Mason and Vasey. They were almost clear of the scene when he caught up to them, tapping Aaron lightly on the shoulder.

"You with the feds?" he asked, raising his eyebrow skeptically. "I didn't think you were supposed to get here until tomorrow."

"I'm sorry?" Aaron turned to face him, arms folded. Despite the clearly unexpected question, Aaron remained composed. Nyla envied that about him. "The FBI is being brought in?"

"Well, yeah." The officer snorted, though the gesture was shaky. "Whatever did— *that*— is way above our paygrade."

"Is this the first time you've had a case that warrants FBI intervention?" Aaron asked, his shoulders suddenly rigid. Nyla squinted worriedly at him, keeping quiet. The change was subtle so that the officer didn't notice, continuing the conversation without pause.

"First time in Somerton, yes," the officer confirmed. "I'm from the Hatfield precinct, so I was a little hesitant to bring in the feds so quickly. Not after I saw the—"

"The Milwaukee field office is a good group of agents," Aaron promised the officer, cutting him off mid-thought. Nyla felt her stomach twist uncomfortably. That was the second time he'd avoided mention of the body's condition in front of her. "You did the right thing by calling them."

"Oh, it's not the Milwaukee office," the officer corrected. "They're caught up in some sort of drug trafficking operation at the Canadian border. Homeland Security has them running at capacity. We're working with Chicago."

Nyla heard Aaron suck in a breath. She placed her hand discreetly on his elbow, whether in comfort or warning she wasn't quite sure.

"Chicago?" Aaron repeated woodenly.

"Yeah." The officer huffed. He'd have to know by now that they weren't with the FBI, yet he was still answering their questions. Nyla guessed he was trying to avoid going back to whatever horrendous scene had everyone on edge. "The lady I spoke to said her name was Kaley. Or was it Kennedy? Kelsey?"

"Kelley?"

"Yeah, that's it. Rebecca Kelley."

Aaron had gone as stiff as a board. The officer glanced down at his phone, oblivious to Aaron's sudden tension. Nyla gently tugged his sleeve, gesturing towards their vehicle. She wasn't sure what had come over him, but here was not the place to talk about it. Aaron nodded curtly, saying goodbye to the officer, and walking stiffly in the direction of the X5.

"What was that about?" Nyla asked as soon as they were out of earshot. "Aaron? Who's Rebecca Kelley? Do you know her?"

Aaron swallowed. Hard.

"Yes, I know her," he said forcefully, pressing his lips together until they formed a thin line. "Her, and her team. Agent Kelley was my successor when I left the Bureau."

"You worked with her?"

"I worked with all of them," Aaron said, running a hand through his hair in frustration. Nyla's fingers twitched as if to smooth away the tangle of curls he'd created, concern lancing through her chest. "As of tomorrow morning, my old team is going to have their hands on this entire case."

"Is that... bad?"

Aaron finally met her gaze, looking uncertain.

"To be honest, Nyla," he said on an exhale, deflating into the driver's seat of his BMW. "I have no idea."

Chapter Nine

AARON

Shit.

Aaron took the turn into Willow Lodge a bit too hard, jostling Nyla in the passenger seat.

Shit, shit, shit.

When Aaron woke up that morning, he'd had a clear plan of attack for handling this case. He'd ordered steps 1-7, starting with a thorough sweep of the grounds and a detailed documentation of everything that looked like it could be useful to him, from strange tracks to broken locks. Now, he couldn't even *remember* his steps, let alone execute them.

He'd been expecting a body, he just hadn't expected it to look like... that. With so many missing men, one was bound to turn up eventually and, given the timeframes they'd been missing, the likelihood of them being alive was slim at best. No, the body hadn't derailed him completely, even in its grotesque state. Everything that came after that is what did him in.

His team was coming. *Aaron's* team. Shit.

Kelley, Pratt, Andrews, German, maybe some new faces though he didn't suspect as much. Pratt would've mentioned if they'd hired anyone new since they last spoke. Aaron knew all of them better than some of his own family and, aside from Pratt and occasional conversations with Kelley, he hadn't spoken to any of them since he left the Bureau.

Aaron needed an aspirin. Or an antacid.

"Do you think Hannaford is on sabbatical because of what happened with me?"

Nyla's voice startled him— he'd almost forgotten she was in the car. Aaron shook himself, gathering his scattered thoughts.

"I think that's very likely," he said honestly, giving Nyla a tight smile. She watched him carefully, searching his face for something. Likely, she already knew what he would say and was trying to distract him. Aaron was grateful. "That tends to be the most we'll get in terms of punishment. I still plan to submit a report, but I wouldn't get your hopes up."

"Thought so." Nyla sighed, sinking into her seat. They were at the lodge now, neither of them moving to get out of the SUV. Nyla glanced at him, curiosity plain on her face. "So... what did you see?"

Aaron didn't need to ask what she meant. They hadn't spoken about the body, not since the bombshell of his team arriving had been dropped on him.

"Nothing good," he admitted. The confession made him shift uncomfortably. He mirrored Nyla's sunken posture, letting his head fall back against the seat. "It was the right decision, staying back. I wouldn't have wanted you to see the state he was in."

"So, it was a man," Nyla confirmed. Aaron pressed his lips together.

"I think so, yes."

"You think?"

Aaron angled his head until he was looking at her, concern pinching his brows together.

"Nyla," he began haltingly. "I'm going to be honest. If I didn't know what I was looking at, I'm not certain I'd have identified it as a person at all, let alone tamp down a gender."

Her eyes rounded warily, her skin paling.

"What do you mean?"

What to tell her?

Aaron had seen his fair share of mangled corpses over the years. It didn't get easier, necessarily, but he did become numb to it after a time. Compartmentalizing was at the forefront of the FBI's mental health evaluations. Even still, this crime scene left an icy trickle of dread inching down his spine.

The body wasn't in one piece, it wasn't even in several. The person had been *shredded,* and that was putting it mildly. Blood soaked the ground into a muddy pit of rancid death, sucking the flesh and bones into the earth. Aaron had, discreetly, taken some pictures on his phone for later analysis, but he wasn't about to show Nyla. Even thinking about the scene left him feeling a little ill.

"Calling it a vicious attack seems... inaccurate." Aaron said, noting the distress in Nyla's eyes. "If it was one of your hunters, I'm starting to lean into the rogue animal theory, if only for the sake of my own sanity."

"It was that bad?"

Aaron laid his hand gently on Nyla's knee, squeezing encouragingly.

"It wasn't pleasant," he murmured honestly. "But it's something for us to go on. Without a body, we weren't working with much. Now, we have a case."

"Well, the FBI has a case."

Right. That.

Aaron swallowed the urge to groan. He liked his team, missed them even, but he didn't want to see them again like this. Not when he was limping along in his new career, knee-deep in the exciting world of tax evasion and counterclaims.

"Let's go inside," he told her. Aaron stretched, trying to ring the stress from his bunched muscles. "We can gather what we know and go over a few safety precautions. I have some leads to follow up on, then maybe we'll have a better idea of what we're going to do."

"Sounds like as good a plan as any," Nyla agreed, launching herself from the SUV with more gusto than was necessary. Aaron suppressed a grin. "Would you frown at me if I poured a drink?"

"Only if you didn't pour one for me, too."

While Nyla sipped her whiskey, Aaron followed up on his leads.

Kelley hadn't responded to his message from the night before; unsurprising, given that they'd been called to work on this very case. Frederique had promised to look into the matter between his other Wildlife duties but hadn't made any promises.

Aaron frowned at his phone, thinking hard. The events of the afternoon had derailed his plans to investigate the abduction site, so he wasn't as prepared as he'd wanted to be. Wildlife was his best bet right now, so he drafted another email to Fred. In it, he enclosed the pictures he'd taken of the body with a warning about their graphic nature. Aaron knew Fred was trustworthy. He wasn't worried about sharing the evidence he'd acquired under less than legal circumstances.

The lodge's phone rang, and Nyla jumped up to get it.

They were lounging in the front office of Willow Lodge, Aaron taking over Nyla's desk and Nyla draped over one of the guest chairs. They were working in easy silence, something Aaron appreciated after dealing primarily with clients that couldn't stop pestering him. Nyla at least seemed to understand that he needed to concentrate.

"Willow Lodge," Nyla chirped, reaching over him to pluck the phone from its cradle. The move had her nearly in his lap, with nowhere safe for his eyes to land. Aaron glanced away, at the innocuous diamond-patterned linoleum. "No, I'm sorry. We're not accepting reservations right now—"

A pause. Aaron tried to ignore the way Nyla's breast pressed against his shoulder as she inhaled. God damnit she was soft. Why hadn't he noticed before?

Because she was his client, and he wasn't *supposed* to notice how soft her body felt, how warm he was wherever she pressed against him, how her hair smelled fruity, with just a hint of—

Aaron slammed hard on his mental brakes, bringing those thoughts to a screaming halt.

"Oh, um, yes," Nyla bit her lip, glancing down at Aaron. They were barely a hand's width from each other, and Aaron suddenly found himself inadvertently appreciating the smattering of freckles on Nyla's nose. "I understand your position, it's just—"

More arguing from the other person on the line. Aaron raised his eyebrows at Nyla, silently asking if everything was okay. She nodded, though her expression was uncertain.

"Of course." She sighed, twisting the phone cord around her finger. Aaron couldn't remember the last time he'd seen a working corded landline. He supposed they were more reliable than cell coverage in this area. "Yes, yes, I understand. Alright. I'll see you in the morning."

The phone clunked down on the receiver, but Nyla didn't sit back down.

"You okay?" Aaron prompted, leaning back to get a better look at her face. Nyla didn't say anything at first, avoiding his gaze. "Nyla?"

"Yeah," she muttered, finally easing back into her own chair. Aaron tried to ignore the disappointment that tickled his chest. "Everything's fine. It's just that... well, I have a reservation for tomorrow now. A big one."

"Okay," Aaron began slowly, trying to read her. "I thought you weren't taking reservations until this was sorted?"

"That was the plan," she acknowledged. "Unfortunately, I didn't really have the chance to say no to this one."

"Why not?"

She finally looked at him, and Aaron knew before she opened her mouth that he wasn't going to like what she had to say.

"That was Agent Kelley," she said. "Your team is going to be joining us at home base as of tomorrow night."

The reality of Nyla's words didn't sink in right away. Aaron stared at her, hard, letting his brain catch up.

"My team… is staying here," he repeated slowly, feeling like every gear in his brain had come to an abrupt stop. Nyla watched him warily, as if he was a frightened animal that would bolt as soon as the opportunity arose. "My team is staying here."

"Are you okay, Suits?" Nyla asked, poising to get up. "Do you need some water or something? I can get you a bottle if you want."

"No, no." Aaron shook his head, his senses crashing back into place with conviction. He blinked his vision into focus, meeting Nyla's uncertain stare. "I'm sorry, I'm fine, really. I think that was just one surprise too many for today."

"You sure?" Nyla pressed, hesitant to untense her muscles and relax into her chair. "You looked like you were going to pass out."

"Nothing so dramatic." Aaron laughed, although he couldn't blame her for thinking as much. His skin felt clammy, his cheeks pale. He was certain he looked about as sick as he felt. "That's not ideal for us, but we'll make it work."

Nyla raised her eyebrow at him, surveying his easy posture with warranted skepticism.

"Are you going to tell me what happened?" She prompted, finally easing back into her seat. Aaron tried not to let his attention linger on her legs as she crossed them beneath her, the hems of her denim shorts slipping further up her thighs until her tan lines showed. He cleared his throat, covering his perusal with a cough.

"I'm not sure what you mean." Aaron shrugged. Damn, that sounded weak. He could do better than that. "I wasn't expecting the FBI to get involved with this case, and having them around means we won't be able to get away with as much. We'll just have to find our way around it."

"That's not what I'm talking about and you know it," Nyla accused, nudging him with her knee. Aaron feigned ignorance, but he had a feeling he wasn't getting out of this one. "You said this was a conversation that required something stronger than milk."

Nyla held up her whiskey, gesturing toward him in mock cheers.

"I've kept my end of the bargain," she taunted. "Your turn."

He thought about dismissing her again, abandoning the idea immediately. He hadn't known Nyla for very long, but it was long enough to know that she wouldn't drop this issue until he gave her *something* to go on. With a sigh, Aaron put his phone down.

"It's really nothing to write home about," he insisted. "I haven't spoken to most of my team since I left the Bureau. I'm not exactly looking forward to all the questions I'm about to be subjected to."

"Questions about coming back?"

"Bingo."

"And... you don't want that." Nyla surmised, looking to him for confirmation. Aaron dipped his chin. "Okay. So, you can't just tell them that?"

"I can, and have," Aaron said, rubbing the back of his neck absently. "It's a bit complicated."

"Sounds like you're the one complicating it," Nyla teased. Aaron gave her a lighthearted scowl. "They don't agree with your reasons for leaving?"

"Well," Aaron hesitated, unsure how much to reveal. He stalled by taking a sip of his drink. "It's... it's not that, exactly. It's more that—"

I didn't give a reason? The excuse I came up with was pathetic and it would've been better if I'd said nothing at all?

"It's more that they don't understand," Aaron said, getting as close to the truth as he could without immediately invoking more questions. "Things have been a little tense ever since I went to the private sector. I don't want any unresolved issues getting in the way of solving this case."

Nyla frowned, the skin between her eyebrows creasing as she tried to work out what he wasn't telling her.

"What's there to understand?" She prodded. "It's not like—"

Nyla's words died on her lips, swallowed by the sudden darkness that blanketed them. Aaron's hand immediately went to his holster, but Nyla's exasperated huff stilled his movement.

"Generator," she grumbled. "There've been rolling blackouts all summer. The lodge is *supposed* to be on backup power. The thing hasn't worked right since July."

Aaron heard Nyla get up, saw the brief flash of her phone screen as she checked the time.

"The hook-up is out back," she told him. "I'll just be a minute."

It was pitch black, so Aaron couldn't see Nyla move toward the back door, but he could hear her. He stood, reaching out as she passed him and grabbed her arm.

"Jesus Christ!" Nyla cursed, slapping his hand away before she could contain her reaction. "What's the matter with you? You don't just grab people in the dark!"

"Sorry." Aaron stifled a chuckle, hearing the panic in Nyla's protest. "You're not going outside alone. I'll come with you."

"The generator is right next to the door," Nyla complained. She turned on her phone screen again so that Aaron could see her, still pointedly glaring at him for the fright he'd given her. "I'll be able to hear you the whole time. You don't need to follow me."

"But I'm going to," he stated, leaving no room for argument. Nyla rolled her eyes, though she didn't try to stop him again. Instead, she took his hand, flipping on the phone's flashlight so she could see where she was going. Aaron's thoughts stumbled, startled by the warmth that accompanied her grip on his palm. Nyla's hand was delicate and small in his, and Aaron had to force himself to refocus on her words.

"This thing is about to die," she informed him. "We'd better be quick. And don't let go of me, I don't trust you in the dark anymore."

Aaron couldn't hide his laugh this time, schooling his decidedly unprofessional thoughts and following dutifully behind Nyla as she made her way to the Willow's generator. Outside, he could see more of his surroundings even without Nyla's flashlight. Although the floodlights were out and there were no streetlights to be seen, the moon was shining just above the tree line. Aaron took a long, hard look around the Willow's property, scouting for any signs of foul play.

"Stupid thing," Nyla muttered, pulling a keyring out of her shorts' pocket and opening the steel casing on the generator's connection. "I've been meaning to replace it, but it's just not in the budget right now."

For late August, the air was surprisingly cool. Aaron shuddered, stepping closer to the building and glancing at what Nyla was doing. He couldn't follow her actions with any clarity, but it looked like she was trying to reset the generator.

"Come on." Nyla gave the generator a gentle kick. "Betty, I really need you to work with me here."

"Betty?" Aaron grinned. Nyla held up her hand.

"Don't," she warned. "She's a cranky old thing. If you insult her, we're going to have to light the coffee table on fire for warmth."

Aaron didn't need to be told twice. He was already shivering, he wouldn't hesitate to light the furniture on fire if it meant getting some relief.

"Is it always this cold at night?" Aaron asked conversationally, trying to hide how much of a wuss he was being. He blamed it on his *madre's* side of the family— she always said Bolivians weren't built for the cold, at least not in the savanna region where she was born. "I thought we'd get a few more weeks of summer weather before I break out the winter suits."

"The weather has been weird lately," Nyla replied, trying Betty again. A sputtering sound erupted from the motor, which Aaron took to be a good sign. "I don't remember it ever being this cold in August. This is October weather."

Aaron made a mental note to avoid travelling to Wisconsin in October.

The night air was crisp and clear, carrying sounds from impossibly far away. Aaron thought he should feel relaxed and calm, but he couldn't shake a budding seed of anxiety in his chest. He found himself repeatedly checking Nyla's progress with the generator, shuffling his feet, and glancing toward the back door. He almost felt like they were being watched, like the gentle tingle of someone's eyes on them bounced off his skin every few seconds. Aaron scanned their surroundings again, finding nothing.

A deep, echoing bellow sounded from far off into the distance, startling Aaron out of his skin.

"What the fuck was that?" He jumped closer to Nyla, preparing to draw his weapon if it became necessary. Nyla glanced up at his distressed tone, smothering a grin.

"It's a deer." She snickered, patting his arm in mocking comfort. "A buck, it sounds like."

"It *sounds like* a damn dragon," Aaron said pointedly. Nyla shook her head at him, making it clear that he was being dramatic.

"There we go," Nyla huffed, stepping back as Betty roared to life. Aaron felt a surge of relief, though he couldn't explain why. Surely he wasn't nervous about a deer, no matter how monstrous its call sounded. "Let me just close this up and we can go back in."

Aaron bit back the inexplicable urge to rush her, gritting his teeth to stop them from chattering. The sounds of the forest faded into quiet, unsettling him more than the amplified sounds he'd heard earlier.

"I think it was frozen," Nyla announced, sounding troubled. "I've got to look up the forecast when we get inside. I shouldn't have to worry about warming up the generator for at least a few months— hey!"

Aaron didn't wait for Nyla to stop speaking before taking her hand again, pulling her along behind him as he made directly for the lodge's back door. The tingling feeling had settled on the back of his neck, like thousands of tiny spider legs scuttling over his skin. The cold was making him jittery, anxious, encouraging him to move. Nyla stumbled after him as he hauled her inside as quickly as he could, slamming the door shut in the same motion. Nyla lost her balance, tripping into him with the speed of his movements.

"What's the rush, Suits?" Nyla panted, blowing her hair out of her face. Aaron still had a hold of her hand, staring over her head at the closed door. "Aaron? Are you okay?"

Was he? Aaron paused to catch his breath, thinking back to what happened. He couldn't explain the overwhelming sense of urgency that crashed over him, driving him to get them both to safety. She pressed her hand against his chest, righting herself and staring up at him worriedly.

"Sorry," he murmured eventually, offering her a shaky smile. "I guess I'm not as comfortable in the woods as you."

Nyla's expression didn't indicate that she believed him, but Aaron couldn't blame her for that. He didn't believe him either.

"Come on," she nudged, nodding her chin in the direction of the lobby. "It's freezing and I have a whiskey to finish."

It was an offer of distraction, one Aaron was glad to accept. He gestured for Nyla to go ahead, quietly following after her as he tried to suppress the lingering chills clattering his bones.

Chapter Ten

NYLA

"Does everyone have their walkies?"

Nyla perched on her tiptoes, scanning the gathered group for anyone looking unsure of themselves. Everyone met her gaze confidently, so she took that as a good sign. The more inexperienced guests she guided on hikes tended to be anything but confident, second-guessing themselves and scrambling to relocate equipment they were sure they'd seen just a moment ago. This group may be new to hiking, but at least they were comfortable following directions. Unsurprising, given their profession.

Aaron was beside her, diligently scouring the map. It was old, and not particularly useful anymore, but Nyla felt like he was just desperate for something to do so he didn't have to talk to the handful of FBI agents milling about the lodge.

The morning sun hadn't yet broached the horizon, leaving the windows practically useless for illuminating the lodge's main building. Nyla and Aaron had met in the lobby an hour earlier, having discussed their plan for the day beforehand. Not long after, Agent Kelley arrived with her team in tow. Nyla wasn't sure what she was expecting upon meeting the group. She was introduced to everyone as they checked in, none of whom were obviously surprised that Aaron was here. Maybe they were briefed by the deputies at the sheriff's station, or maybe Aaron himself had warned them, but either way, they weren't visibly phased by the situation.

Well, except Aaron. He'd been fidgeting all morning.

Rebecca Kelley was the first person that Nyla met. She was in her late-thirties, slightly taller than Nyla- although that wasn't hard. She had a friendly face, with short, curly

80

blond hair. Nyla greeted her warmly, and the gesture was returned. Next was a man named Christoph Andrews. He was quick, efficient, and quiet, so Nyla didn't gather much information about his personality. After him was Tiago German, a shorter, balding man with a pointed face and sharp eyes, and, finally, Tyler Pratt. Pratt was the youngest of the group, looking about Aaron's age with thick black hair and almost lazy confidence about him. Aaron was silent all the while, until Pratt caught his eye and he offered a genuinely happy greeting. They were friends, then.

As the team sorted through their assigned lodgings, Agent Kelley spoke to Nyla and Aaron about their experience thus far. After making the trip to Somerton, Kelley's team had met Deputy Mason at the station. They went over the details of the case, and of course, Nyla's name was mentioned. She wasn't surprised, and she'd spent most of the interaction answering questions about what she'd seen and heard. Aaron hovered beside her all the while, jumping in when he felt she shouldn't be answering something. She was more at ease with him there; at least she knew that, despite his clear discomfort, he was going to bat for her.

"We'll need to see the crime scene," Agent Kelley mused, her lips pursed. "The one you found, Miss Jameson. Leopold Thompson's campsite?"

"Nyla, please," she interjected, fighting off the initial spark of irritation the use of her last name often triggered. "Sure, I can take you. I lead hikes to the Basin all the time."

"Great," Agent Kelley smiled gratefully, taking her room key in the same breath. "We'll meet back here in twenty minutes, if that's enough time for you?"

"I was taking Aaron there today anyway," Nyla confirmed. "I'm ready to go when you are."

"Aaron?" Agent Kelley's attention flickered to Aaron, tensed at Nyla's shoulder. Something like mischief passed over her expression before she schooled herself, nodding to Agent Pratt that they were heading to the cabins now. "Right. See you soon then, Nyla. ...Aaron."

"Did I say something wrong?" Nyla whispered to Aaron when Agent Kelley was out of earshot. He deflated like he was already looking forward to retiring for the evening.

"No, you didn't," he promised, shaking his head. "FBI Agents aren't usually on a first name basis. Kelley was probably just surprised I haven't been asking you to call me Agent Klein."

"Would you *like* me to call you Agent Klein?"

Aaron gave her a sour look that made her laugh.

"Alright, no 'Agent,' then. I like Suits better anyway."

"Is it too late to change my mind?"

It was, and Aaron's resigned frown indicated he knew that already.

Once everyone had returned to the lobby and all gear was accounted for, they prepared to set out for the trails and Nyla felt like she was finally back in her element. The Basin was an easy hike, not something she would normally stress about with any group, let alone one of this size. She expected to feel a jolt of fear at the thought of returning to the spot where she'd seen Leo disappear, but perhaps the reality hadn't struck her just yet. She was excited and anxious to be doing something, anything at all that could help.

"The trail should be pretty dry by now," Nyla announced, shouldering her small backpack. Quick hike or not, whenever she went with other people, she liked to be prepared for the worst. Especially when she had no idea how these agents would react in the woods. She'd seen everything from natural confidence to full-blown panic attacks. Nyla herself had had a rocky introduction to the forest, having grown up in suburban Philadelphia. Her first real exposure to nature was a school-sponsored field trip to a popular camping ground, and Nyla had accidentally stumbled into a patch of poison oak. She got itchy just thinking about the outdoors until she was seventeen when her dad got fed up with her fear and forced her into a week-long camping trip in Vermont with him and his girlfriend. Ever since that trip, Nyla just couldn't feel at home in the city anymore.

"How far from the lodge was the abduction site?" Kelley asked, looking a little out of place now that she'd changed into more casual clothes. Nyla pointed in the direction they were headed, mentally calculating the distance.

"It's about 2 miles south-east of here," she concluded. "The hunting grounds open up just before that. The perimeter is perpendicular to the lodge's property, so all the hiking trails head north. There are tons of signs around, and the hunting range is marked by bright orange ribbons."

"Do you have many accidents?" Pratt piped up, shouldering his own bag. Nyla did a head count before answering, double-checking her pockets for her lighter, pocket knife, and walkie. "With the hunting ground being so close to the trails, isn't that dangerous?"

"Most hunters don't stick around the property line," Nyla answered, making her way through their small group until she was at the front door. "Between the activity at the lodge and the guests that like to explore a little ways into the woods, there isn't much to hunt. Every guest is fully briefed on which areas are safe and which ones to avoid. I haven't had an accident between a hunter and a hiker since I took over ownership, and I'm pretty sure Oscar's record was clean too."

"Impressive," Pratt commented, shrugging his lips. "In my experience, people aren't the best listeners when it comes to rules."

"True," Nyla admitted, nodding for them to head outside. The sun was peeking over the mountains now, so it was time to get moving. "I'd be worried if more big game was spotted around the trails. Even if someone wanted to hunt close to the lodge, they wouldn't bag anything bigger than a rabbit. Maybe a raccoon, if they're feeling feisty."

"So, experienced hunters don't go into the Basin, then?"

Nyla didn't hear who asked that one, but she answered anyway.

"Not usually no," she told them, stepping quickly on the even terrain. "The Basin is kind of like the bunny hill at a ski resort. There's a lake, so you'll always get some kind of animal there, but it's not going to be anything to brag about. I see a lot of fathers bringing their kids on their first trip, casual hunters, people just picking up the hobby, that kind of thing. The Basin is hunting on easy mode."

"The men who've gone missing," Kelley pressed, "you would consider them inexperienced?"

"Actually, no." Nyla bit her lip, glancing up at the trail markers she'd placed years ago. There was a sign pointing to Basin Lake., but seasons of rain had washed away the lettering. "Most of them were seasoned guys. Leo was a bit green, but the rest of them typically hunted deeper in the mountains."

"Why the change in scenery?"

"The weather, mostly." Nyla caught Aaron's eye as he walked alongside her. He nodded for her to keep going. "It's been raining off and on since last month, so the trails have been garbage. It's been too dangerous to go much further than a few miles out."

"Why not just reschedule?" German spoke for the first time since they'd arrived, sounding gruff and tired. Nyla almost laughed.

"Clearly you've never met a devoted hunter."

They trudged on in relative silence, the dense foliage forcing everyone into pairs of two. Nyla and Aaron remained at the front, leading the way. She was starting to get anxious with his continued slump; it had only been a few days, but Nyla found herself looking forward to needling him. This version of Aaron was putting her on edge.

"Can I be honest?" Nyla whispered to him, unable to keep her thoughts to herself any longer. "I kinda figured you'd leave once your team got here."

"Why?" Aaron furrowed his brow at her, looking more like her hiking buddy than a PI in that moment. He wore a thin, grey linen shirt with the sleeves rolled to his elbows, and navy-blue cargo shorts. He looked at home in the woods, despite his insistence that he was a city-dweller by nature.

"Well," she chewed the inside of her cheek, feeling silly all of a sudden, "I asked you to come because no one was taking me seriously. There's a full investigation now, so I'd understand if you wanted to bail."

Aaron looked like he didn't even want to entertain that thought with an answer, but he spoke anyway.

"You hired me, Nyla," he said with a gentle smile. "If you'd like to dismiss me, you can. Otherwise, I'm here to help."

"Well, I'm not about to fire you," she assured him, laughing nervously. "If it wasn't for you, I'd probably still be locked up under Bill's watch."

"Don't remind me," Aaron muttered. "I meant what I said. I'll file that report as soon as I'm back in Chicago."

"My hero," she teased, and some of the stress seeped out of Aaron's stance. Satisfied with her work, Nyla led them deeper into the mountain woods, pointing out any interesting features they saw along the way. She tried to keep everything as informative as possible, unsure what would help in their investigation. By the time she's gotten to the various types of evergreen trees they could find in the area, she felt it was safe to assume she'd exhausted her potentially useful facts.

"Did you get the ME's report back yet?" Aaron called to Pratt, almost like he sensed Nyla was running out of steam. She smiled at him gratefully.

"Not yet," Pratt said. "I talked to him this morning and he told me it would be at least another day. From his initial observations, he thinks it could be an animal."

"What kind of animals are out here, Nyla?" Andrews cut in, sounding a little nervous. "Anything big enough to pose a risk to public safety?"

"We get all kinds out here," she told them honestly. There was no point in sugar-coating anything, not when lives were at risk. They were coming up on Leo's tent now, and the feeling of dread she'd been anticipating struck her hard in the chest. Nyla sucked in a breath, trying to hide her nerves. "Bears, wolves, coyotes, mountain lions. Brown bears would be the most dangerous, if I had to pick."

"Dangerous enough to potentially kill seven people?"

"Not likely." Nyla came to a stop just beyond the turn that opened into the Basin. She could see the red of Leo's tent through the trees here. "Nothing in these woods would do that, not normally anyway. Animals don't kill for fun, and nothing would eat that much that quickly."

The forest twitched around her, twigs and leaves rustling softly to undercut the levity of her voice. Nyla chewed absently on the inside of her cheek, listening for... something. She wasn't sure what. The wind was generally gentler in the Basin due to the sunken landscape and ring of lush trees that surrounded it, but today it was chilled. Gusts of air swept over her skin, leaving a trail of goosebumps.

Aaron looked at her questioningly. Nyla realized she hadn't told them why she stopped.

"Leo's tent is just over there." She pointed, trying to sound calm. "That's where I spoke to him the other night."

Kelley and her team moved to approach, but Aaron held back.

"You don't have to do this, you know," he coaxed, glancing behind them to where the others were already approaching Leo's tent. "You can wait here. I'll come get you when we're done."

"No, no," Nyla insisted, shaking her head. "I need to be there. You guys have questions, right?" Aaron hesitated, which was as much confirmation as she needed. "It'll be easier to answer them if I'm with you."

"Alright," Aaron relented, turning his head to watch the team work for a moment. He placed his hand gently on Nyla's shoulder, giving her a reassuring squeeze. Instantly, Nyla felt her heartbeat calm. "If you change your mind, I'll get you out of there immediately, understood?"

Nyla's lips twitched into a smile, nodding. With a deep breath, they returned to the scene of the crime.

Chapter Eleven

INTERLUDE

The Basin

The group moved through the trees. Noisily. They wouldn't know he was following them even if he wasn't relegated to the shadows. Inexperienced, unobservant. It was laughable.

Nyla Jameson led the way, Aaron Klein at her side. They were talking, low and comfortably. He couldn't hear what they were saying, but he could see the unease on Nyla's face. Whatever it was, she didn't like it. He wasn't sure what that meant, but it didn't matter. She was distracted, that's all he cared about.

He slunk along behind them, keeping to the shaded spaces beneath the trees. If they bothered to look, they might see him. They didn't. As far as they knew, they were alone. They *should* be alone. They weren't.

He could strike now, if he wanted. No one would see it coming, least of all Nyla. He could creep closer until he was within range to successfully rush them. He wouldn't get them all, but he didn't need to. There was only one he truly cared about anyway, and he was sure she was the easiest target.

Still, he didn't want to risk more than he had already. Rushing in now was a stupid idea, even in the face of his rage. He couldn't justify it. Not yet.

He settled back on his haunches, prepared to wait.

Chapter Twelve

AARON

"If this is an animal, what are we even doing here?"

German's voice drifted in a stage-whisper above the crunch of foliage beneath Aaron's boots. He resisted the urge to reprimand him, seeing as he was no longer German's Unit Chief.

"Kelley obviously thinks there might be something here," Andrews answered back, sounding as annoyed as Aaron felt. "Otherwise, we wouldn't have flown in."

Andrews was right, but that didn't mean any one of them had to like it.

It was strange, being around his old team and not barking orders. Aaron sensed it was strange for them too, as more than once he'd caught them looking to him for guidance before they remembered themselves. He wondered how Kelley felt about that. He would never step on her toes, of course. He respected her far too much to even think about it. Maybe that knowledge was enough to keep any feelings of resentment at bay.

"If the ME determines it was an animal, then our services are no longer needed and we can go home," Kelley clipped, kneeling in the thick of Leopold Thompson's ruined campsite. Aaron cast a concerned look over his shoulder at Nyla, who'd hung back at the edge of the trail. That was for the better, given the state of things. For all her strength, Nyla knew her limits. Aaron appreciated that about her.

Leopold's tent was nothing short of ravaged. The fabric had been torn to shreds, leaving nothing for the poles to cling to. They stuck out at odd angles, looking like a decaying skeleton with the barest hint of flesh hanging off the bones. Aaron scanned the scene with a practised eye, keeping Nyla's story in the forefront of his mind. She hadn't mentioned any damage to the tent, but then she hadn't stuck around for long. This could've happened during the incident, or it could be the work of curious animals. Either way, from what he could tell, everything lined up with what she said. There was no unnatural damage to the surrounding area, no trees or branches that looked recently broken. Aaron wasn't an expert on wildlife by any means, but there *was* something 'off' about the way things were laid out.

"I don't see any blood," Pratt commented, squatting next to Aaron where he'd perched to inspect a shred of tent. "Weird for an animal attack. Not to mention all the untouched rations."

"Nyla," Aaron called out, startling her. She made to take a step forward, but he held up a hand. "If Leo left food out here, what would happen to it?"

"It'd be long gone by now," she answered honestly. "We're a bit too close to the trail for big game animals, but scavengers will go just about anywhere. If he had anything unsecured in his tent, it would've been like a bat signal to hungry raccoons."

"And yet nothing here looks like it's even been picked over," Aaron muttered, eyeing a crushed bag of potato chips. He picked them up and turned them over in his hands, surprised to find that the contents of the bag were almost mushy in texture. He tested the bag, but he couldn't find any holes where water may have seeped in. Would they be this soft if they'd only been trampled? "Which means that no other animals have been by since Leo vanished."

"What would cause something like that?" Pratt asked, more to himself than to Aaron. That was good— Aaron didn't have an answer.

"Do we know if anyone's been here since the incident?" Kelley asked Nyla abruptly. Aaron answered instead, standing to catch Kelley's attention.

"Not to our knowledge," he said clinically. "Until yesterday, the sheriff's department didn't think there was anything worth investigating. As far as we know, Nyla was the last person to see this place, not accounting for unregistered hikers or hunters."

"And tell me again what happened when you were here?" Kelley continued speaking to Nyla, ignoring Aaron's interjection. He stepped around Pratt, planting himself directly in Kelley's line of sight.

"I'm not sure," Nyla answered honestly, hugging herself. It wasn't overly cold, but Aaron could swear he saw her shivering. There was a bit of a breeze, and after standing still a moment, he found himself rolling down his sleeves. "I was arguing with Leo and then there was a loud bang, and I couldn't see him anymore."

"You didn't stay to investigate?"

"I thought a tree fell," Nyla rebutted. "Or maybe there was a rockslide. Or something. I don't know, but it was dark and stormy. I don't think I would've been able to see anything even if I did stay."

"But you didn't," Kelley confirmed. Nyla bristled.

"Forgive me if I didn't wait to see if whatever happened to Leo was contagious."

Aaron smothered a smirk. Kelley caught his eye, quirking a brow.

"Nyla isn't a suspect, Kelley," he stated firmly.

"I'm not treating her like one," she argued. It was Aaron's turn to raise a brow. Kelley glanced at Nyla, lowering her voice so she couldn't hear. "I just want to cover all my bases. You should know that."

"This one is covered," Aaron insisted, holding her gaze. "Nyla had nothing to do with this. I'd bet my reputation on it."

"You sure you aren't betting your reputation on a pretty face?"

Aaron's stare hardened.

"I'm just saying," Kelley shrugged, diffusing the bluntness of her statement, "you're not usually so quick to dismiss people as suspects."

"I've been here longer than you have," he reminded her. "Trust me on this one, Kelley. Nyla is nothing more than a witness. The last victim was seen while she was in custody, and he was reported missing before she was released. She's clear."

"She was in custody?"

Aaron cursed. Apparently, Somerton's sheriff station was trying to handle the Hannaford situation quietly. He wasn't having that.

"I'll explain when we get back to the lodge," he promised. Kelley shook her head, glancing at her watch.

"We have an interview scheduled with the kid who found the body," she told him. "You can come with us and fill in the gaps on the way. In return, I'll let you speak to the kid."

That was more than fair. Aaron nodded his agreement, casting one last curious glance at Leo's ruined tent. Something was bothering him, but he had no idea what.

"I think we've gleaned all we can from this place without a proper expert," Kelley announced, turning to address the others. "Let's head back. Nyla?"

"Yes?"

"Can you dissuade people from coming this way, if at all possible?"

Nyla bobbed her head quickly, shrugging in the direction they'd come.

"I don't have any other guests booked," she explained, "but sometimes hikers stop in looking for directions and maps. I'll tell anyone that comes in."

Aaron was sure she'd already been doing that, but he knew Kelley would feel better hearing her agreement out loud, a conclusion that Nyla had clearly reached on her own. She was good at reading people, that much Aaron could plainly see.

"Good." Kelley wiped her palms on her linen pants, brushing away any lingering flecks of dirt. "Let's move out."

She brushed past Aaron, accidentally bumping his elbow and making him drop the bag of potato chips he was still holding. He frowned at it but made no move to pick it up again. Whatever was standing out to him did so at the edge of his mind, hovering just out of reach. There was no obvious way for water to get into the bag and soak the chips, and yet they were the texture of mashed potatoes. What would cause that?

Aaron pushed the thought aside for now, catching up to Nyla as she led the way back to the lodge. He'd ask her later, when they were alone. He trusted each and every member of his old team, but he just couldn't shake the feeling that there was something more going on here. Better he figure it out before making a complete idiot of himself.

He absently laid his hand on Nyla's shoulder again, pretending he didn't notice he was doing it. Touching her was soothing to him in a way he wasn't yet ready to acknowledge and, luckily for him, Nyla didn't seem to mind indulging him. With a shared look of reassurance, they set off for the Willow.

Chapter Thirteen

INTERLUDE

Willow Lodge

They left.

The FBI agents, along with Aaron Klein, left an hour ago. He wasn't sure where they were or how long they were going to be gone, but now that he knew it wasn't a short coffee break, he didn't care. Nyla Jameson was alone for a while, and that's the only thing that mattered.

She busied herself around the lodge, taking care of whatever housekeeping she'd been neglecting since the FBI took over her business that morning. She looked troubled, worried, on edge. That was good. As long as she was in the lobby of the lodge, he could see her. If she retired to her cabin, he wasn't familiar enough with the layout to know for certain if he'd be able to continue tracking her. Best to keep that from happening.

Luckily for him, Nyla didn't seem to be in much of a hurry. It was like she was working in slow motion, deliberately performing each task with the focus of someone wanting a distraction. He waited, getting more and more anxious by the moment. If the FBI returned, he might not get another chance at this. He needed her to come outside. Now.

Nyla didn't see him as he swept through the grounds, searching for something to draw her out. She didn't see him as he circled the main building, his eyes locking on a set of trash bins nestled behind the back exit, next to the dormant generator. She didn't notice the disturbance as he shattered the padlock with a set of bolt cutters he'd brought along, lifting the lid to peek inside. It was full. Perfect.

Nyla *did* notice when he kicked the bin onto its side, spilling its contents, crashing onto the gravel with a cacophony of bumps and bangs. He retreated to the corner of the building, watching.

The back door swung open, and Nyla groaned in frustration when she saw the destroyed garbage.

"Damnit," she cursed, stomping over to the bin. "I swore I locked that. Stupid raccoons."

She bent, gripping the edge of the bin and pulling it upright. It was large and unruly. She struggled. He waited.

"I know for a fact that you guys have plenty of trash to sift through down at Tinny's," Nyla muttered, huffing as she started to reach for the bags he'd torn. "Leave my bins alone."

She hoisted the bag into her arms. She turned. He moved.

Nyla cried out as his foot collided with the back of her knee, knocking her flat on her back with the trash bag on top of her. She rolled it off in disgust, whirling her head around to see what hit her. He stood there proudly, sneering at her prone form on the ground.

"*Bill?*" She hissed. "What the hell?"

Hannaford didn't bother to answer her. He curled his lip, winding his foot back for another kick. Nyla saw, lurching backward on the gravel to dodge. He clipped her ankle and she yelped, scrambling to stand.

"What do you think you're doing?" she snapped, disbelief and anger warring in equal measures in her tone. Hannaford jabbed his finger at her, rage colouring his face a deep red.

"You," he spat. "You just couldn't leave well enough alone, could you?"

Nyla backed up a step, slipping on the gravel with her bruised ankle, but she didn't fall.

"I've got the fucking FBI swarming all over my county," he growled, shaking. "And here I am, off work because some little cockroach ratted me out to her bodyguard!"

"I didn't do anything, Bill!" Nyla countered. "It's not my fault that you don't know how to do your damn jo—!"

He lunged at her, cutting her off. Nyla turned and bolted, skidding around the corner of the building. Hannaford was between her and the back door— she'd have to go around the front. He couldn't have that.

Thundering after her, Bill let his instincts take over. Nyla had a head start on him, but his legs were longer. He caught up to her quickly, grabbing her by the hair and yanking her to the ground. She screamed, kicking and fighting him. He hit her, his knuckles connecting with her cheek.

Nyla spat blood, twisting in his grip as Bill mounted her, winding up for another punch. Nyla's adrenaline took over, clawing and scratching at him. He barely felt it. Bill hadn't meant to kill her, at least, he didn't think he had, but now he wasn't sure he'd be able to stop himself. Nyla sensed this too, and her body turned into a flailing weapon. She elbowed him in the thigh, drove her knee into his gut, dug her nails into his wrist. Bill hollered as a blow landed on his ribs.

He had his gun. He could shoot her.

No sooner had the thought crossed his mind when Nyla freed her pocket knife from her shorts. She flipped the blade in her grip, plunging it into Bill's calf. He screamed, collapsing onto his side. Nyla scrambled to free herself from underneath him, launching towards the front door of the lodge. He couldn't follow her, not fast enough, but he had to try. Biting down against the pain, Bill limped after Nyla.

He got there too late. The door shut in his face, and he heard the lock twist. She'd be at the counter now, calling the station. Or Aaron Klein. Someone. Bill Hannaford was going to prison, and there wasn't a damn thing he could do about it.

He remembered the back door, unlocked. Swinging.

He was going to prison anyway. Might as well finish the job.

Chapter Fourteen

AARON

Donnie Kasack wasn't much help.

In truth, Aaron hadn't expected him to be. The kid was what, 15? He'd seen some messed-up stuff for his age. Hell, even the grown adults Aaron spoke to were at least a little traumatized by the body. He still hadn't shown the images to Nyla. He didn't plan to, not if he could help it.

Kelley and Pratt were speaking with the boy's mother. It likely wasn't going to turn into anything useful, but they were grasping at straws here. Aaron was still waiting on Fred to answer him, but he had probably been contacted by Kelley, too. That was the problem with working with the Chicago field office: all of their resources overlapped. With the two of them looking for the same answers, it was doubly concerning that neither of them had heard back from Fred yet.

The ME report was also late. Later than it should be, considering the low workload a small-town medical examiner would have on their plate. Aaron tried to ignore the sinking feeling in his stomach. This case was rattling him, and he couldn't even explain why.

"I think that's all we'll get here," Pratt said, pinching the bridge of his nose until his skin paled. "A whole lot of nothing."

"Maybe the station had more luck," Kelley mused, but she didn't sound hopeful. "Klein? Want to join us, or head back to the lodge?"

"I'll join you," he answered automatically, glancing at his phone. He'd told Nyla to call him if anything came up while he was gone. The fact that she hadn't meant he wasn't in a rush. "Thank you, by the way. For letting me in on your investigation."

"You're more helpful to us if you're informed," Kelley said, shrugging. "It's not the first time we've bent a rule or two to accommodate."

"Rules that you probably wrote," Pratt joked, elbowing Aaron in the ribs. "Come on, Klein. You may be retired, but you're still you. Why wouldn't we work with you?"

"It'd be easier to work with you if it was official," German prodded, and Aaron inwardly groaned. He knew this was coming, which was exactly why he'd been dreading this meeting. "You could always come back. Kelley might even let you have your old position, if you ask nicely."

"*Kelley* has said no such thing," Kelley responded pointedly. German held his hands aloft in surrender.

"Thanks, but no thanks," Aaron insisted, and he meant it. "I prefer the freedom of private industry."

As he said it, he realized that it was true, actually. Yes, most of his cases were mind-numbingly boring, but there was an odd feeling of comfort knowing he didn't answer to anyone. Pratt seemed like the only one to accept that, as he gracefully changed the topic of conversation. Aaron guessed it was just because they'd had this conversation already.

"Do things seem a bit lively to you?" Pratt leaned out the window, squinting at the station's parking lot as they pulled in. He was right— Aaron could see more people huddled in the front lobby than there'd been when he was here with Nyla. A person or two would make sense, but he counted at least... ten?

"What fresh hell are we walking into now?" Pratt cursed, vaulting from the SUV with purpose.

'Fresh hell' was a good way to put it. Aaron could feel the frantic energy in the room as soon as they walked in, emanating from a group of officers arguing at the back of the room. He didn't recognize all of them, and some were clearly from a different station. Aaron strained to hear what they were saying, but they kept their voices low. Kelley followed his attention, subtly shifting closer to catch what she could. Aaron had done the same his first time in the station, but he didn't think he could get away with it unnoticed again. Not now that everyone knew who he was and who he worked for.

They were standing at the desk for a solid 5 minutes before Brandy noticed them, rushing to greet them with murmured apologies.

"Bit busy this afternoon?" Aaron glanced at the group of officers again, huddled together and whispering urgently. Brandy looked down at her computer screen, pushing her bangs away from her face.

"Sorry about that," she apologized again, sounding less than sincere. "We had an incident up at the lodge. We're all in a bit of a tizzy."

"The lodge?"

Aaron felt his stomach sink, the beginnings of concern and bewilderment surging in his chest. Brandy blinked slowly, trying to work out if she'd just confessed some sort of secret.

"Well, yes," she muttered, eyes darting to where the officers were conversing. She tried to catch their attention, floundering under Aaron's piercing stare. "It's under control now."

"We were there two hours ago," Kelley argued, donning a piercing stare of her own. Brandy paled, panic flickering in her wide eyes. Aaron almost felt sorry for her. "Everything was fine when we left. What happened?"

"And why weren't we notified?" Aaron didn't bother keeping the anger from his tone. He wasn't surprised that Mason hadn't contacted *him*, but Kelley's team should've been called right away. That they hadn't left him feeling vaguely nauseated. "Has there been another disappearance?"

"No!" Brandy dismissed quickly, beads of sweat prickling her forehead. "No, nothing like that. This was different. I was told that you didn't need to be contacted for—"

"Agent Klein?"

Deputy Mason pulled away from the main group, much to Brandy's relief. Aaron turned his attention away from the receptionist, his expression icy.

"There was an incident at the lodge?" He lifted a brow, daring Mason to lie.

"It's been handled," Mason grunted, shuffling. "Your investigation won't be impacted."

His remark was directed at Kelley, but Aaron wasn't letting himself be dismissed. He glanced at Kelley to confirm, and she gave him the barest nod in understanding.

"*Our* investigation hasn't been narrowed down to a single incident, Deputy," Aaron clipped, emphasizing his involvement. "Therefore, it would be impossible for you to guess what will and will not affect our case. What was this incident, and *why weren't we notified?*"

His tone left no room for arguing, but Mason looked like he wanted to try. Aaron held his ground, every muscle tensed and rigid. He wasn't even breathing. Eventually, Mason all but rolled his eyes.

"You weren't notified," he drawled, like the words tasted sour, "because it's not your business. The incident was with Sheriff Hannaford, so that's our department, not yours."

"Sheriff Hannaford?"

A cold dread crept down Aaron's spine, chilling him through the early afternoon heat. There was an air of defensiveness about the entire precinct, which would make sense if one of their own was involved in—

"Agent Klein?" Mason barked after Aaron as he turned on his heel, heading directly for the parking lot. "*Agent Klein!* The situation is—"

The door slammed before Aaron heard the rest.

Chapter Fifteen

NYLA

"Son of a bitch." Nyla winced, hissing through her teeth at the sting of antiseptic. She didn't recognize the paramedic, which meant he was probably from the next town over. Hatfield, maybe. She wasn't used to seeing so many new faces around that weren't guests at the lodge— it was almost unsettling. Adding to her discomfort was the paramedic's stubborn quest to speak to her as little as possible. He worked quickly and efficiently, determining that stitches weren't required on her cheek, but recommended x-rays to look for broken bones. Nyla wanted to decline, but her ribs *did* hurt.

The lodge was absolutely swarming with people, none of whom were in any rush to speak to her aside from taking her statement. After Mason nearly kicked her door down and restrained Hannaford, he'd called in a favor from the Hatfield station and promptly vanished without so much as a nod in Nyla's general direction. Something about a conflict of interest. Nyla guessed he just didn't want to deal with the situation.

She didn't blame him. It was messy, and not just because of the blood.

Nyla eased back into her chair once the paramedic was finished, taking as deep a breath as she could manage. He handed her a blanket, though it was still midday and sunny. Nyla took it automatically, smoothing it over her lap, and thanked him for his help just as an officer waved him over for a statement. Nyla had given hers twice now, and she suspected she'd need to do so a third time before she was allowed to make any calls.

Trying to settle her nerves, Nyla took stock of the damage she and Bill had caused. It wasn't much in terms of structural problems, but the lobby was torn completely to shreds. She sighed, knowing already that she didn't have enough in the budget to fix it.

Tears threatened, and she vehemently choked them back. Nyla refused to cry when Bill was still around here somewhere, when he could catch a glimpse of her. He'd tried to take her life and only managed to take parts of her property. Nyla wouldn't let him take her dignity, too.

The screeching of tires grabbed her attention, reminding Nyla that she was expecting the return of an entire team of FBI agents. She sat up straight, anxiety surging in her chest as Aaron's X5 swerved into the parking lot, kicking up a cascade of dirt. Relief swept over her and Nyla tried to push herself up to wave him over, but her ribs screamed at her to sit still.

The SUV had barely stopped moving when Aaron launched himself from it, finding her immediately amongst the crowd. He ignored the officers that tried to stop him, flashing his ID without a word and jogging straight for Nyla.

"Are you okay?" He demanded, skidding to a stop in front of her. He crouched until they were at eye level, his hands grasping her arms gently. "Did he hurt you?"

"I'm okay," she promised, placing her right hand atop his, offering a small smile. The warmth of his touch grounded her, and Nyla had to work twice as hard not to cry. "I've had worse injuries from hikes."

It was true. Nyla had once taken a serious tumble over a small cliff near King's Point, losing her footing as she tried to catch one of her hiking group who'd tripped while taking a photo. She'd broken three ribs, one ankle, and her collarbone. It hadn't bothered her at the time, she was just glad the other hiker was safe. Now, though, she couldn't help a small twinge of resentment as Bill's attack reawakened those old aches. She was in pain, and no matter how skilled she was at hiding it, Aaron clearly noticed.

Anger darkened his expression as he surveyed her, concern wrinkling his forehead and tensing his jaw.

"What the hell happened?" Aaron snapped, and Nyla had a moment of confusion before realizing his hostility was directed at the officer that appeared beside him. "Where's Sheriff Hannaford?"

"With all due respect, Agent Klein," the officer rumbled. "We have a few more questions for Miss Jameson, and then you're free to ask whatever you'd like."

"Have you already given a statement?" Aaron asked Nyla, softening his tone for her. She nodded.

"Two, actually," she clarified, ignoring the stink eye the officer was shooting her. Aaron pressed his lips together like he was expecting that, and stood to face the officer, effectively blocking him from Nyla's line of sight.

"If you have further questions for Miss Jameson, you can direct them through me," he declared, his firm words teetering on the edge of threatening. "She's given her statement, and now she needs time to recover."

"I wasn't aware you were a lawyer in your spare time, Agent," the officer taunted. Aaron shifted his weight forward, challenging.

"I wasn't aware your jurisdiction was full of loose cannons, Officer."

Silence hung between them, thick with distaste.

"What questions do you have for Miss Jameson?"

"I need to clarify what transpired after Miss Jameson contacted 911," he deadpanned, sounding less than amused. "I'm sure you can appreciate the predicament we're in, Agent Klein. Accuracy is paramount."

"I believe 'predicament' is a kind word for what happened here," Aaron said, crossing his arms over his chest. A spark of gratitude filled Nyla's throat as she watched; Aaron was tall and well-muscled, but his frame wasn't particularly wide. He positioned himself strategically, forming a firm wall between her and the officer. "From where I stand, local law enforcement has been allowed to abuse their power for so long that once it was challenged, they felt it appropriate to attack a civilian with such severity that it required an ambulance."

"Actually, the ambulance was called primarily for Sheriff Hannaford." The officer leaned with false ease to glance at Nyla. "He sustained a severe concussion and multiple stab wounds, one close enough to his femoral artery that, had it been nicked, would have resulted in his death."

Aaron turned his head, meeting Nyla's gaze over his shoulder. She shrugged, wincing at the way it tugged her sore muscles.

"He was trying to kill me," she defended calmly. "I wasn't about to let him."

Aaron faced the officer again, but not before she caught the ghost of a smile twitching his lips.

"I just want to go over this one more time," the officer insisted, sounding tired. Nyla squinted against her building headache to see his nametag: Benn. "Then I'll leave Miss Jameson to her recovery."

"It's fine, Aaron," Nyla assured him, laying her palm against his back in much the same way he'd done to her several times before. "We can go over it as many times as you need to, but the facts won't change. I didn't do anything wrong."

Officer Benn said nothing while Aaron allowed him to properly face Nyla. She started from the beginning for Aaron's sake, from the time she'd heard the bins falling to when Deputy Mason arrived.

When she'd escaped Hannaford after he'd pinned her, Nyla thought she'd saved herself by locking the lobby door. The first thing she did was call the police, screaming over Bill pounding on the walls. He wasn't moving quickly, not with the injury to his leg. Nyla had brought the knife with her, clutching it to her chest. There was blood on her shirt, and her pants were caked in dirt after their struggle. She only let herself breathe once dispatch confirmed a car was on the way, but that had been a mistake. Seconds later, Bill burst in through the back door, charging her again. In her panic, Nyla hadn't thought to lock it.

She'd held the knife out in front of her as he barreled through the lobby, swinging it to some degree of success. She slashed Bill's arm, sending his gun careening across the room. She stabbed into his shoulder when he grabbed for her a second time, and finally lost her grip on her knife when the blade sank into his hip. Blind to his pain, Bill used the adrenaline pumping through him to wrestle Nyla to the floor, his hands around her neck and his knee driving into her ribs. She remembered not being able to breathe, struggling under his weight. She kicked and flailed until she knocked over the window display of Clary's spa products, which included a large, heavy-bottomed jar of bath salts. Nyla grabbed it and swung, colliding hard with Bill's skull. He teetered, knocked senseless, and Nyla was able to scramble to the door just as Mason arrived.

Nyla told her story to Officer Benn, but her attention was on Aaron and the way his cheek twitched in agitation the more violence she described. Once she was done, Officer Benn left them, just as he'd promised.

"Are you sure you're okay?" Aaron asked her when they were alone, crouching in front of her again. His hand reached up to cup her cheek, his thumb tracing gingerly over her newly bandaged scrape. Nyla relaxed under the touch, soothed by the care with which he assessed her. Had anyone ever been so gentle with her before? She couldn't remember.

"I'll live," Nyla promised, her hand automatically moving to her ribs as she inhaled. They hurt, yes, but upon further reflection she was confident they weren't broken. When she was hospitalized before, the pain had been sharp and stole her breath with each inhale. This time, it was more of a dull throb. "Some rest and I'll be right as rain."

Aaron nodded, pressing his lips together into a tight line.

"I'm sorry I wasn't here to stop this," he told her, searching her face for something. Nyla didn't know what, or if he found it, because suddenly he was standing. "Which is your largest cabin?"

"Oh, um," Nyla thought back to her logbook. "The biggest one is 7, with three rooms, two bathrooms, and a kitchenette. German, Pratt, and Andrews are in that one. Kelley is in 5, which is the same size, but it's right next to 7 so I thought it was the best place to put her."

"Any unoccupied?"

"That would be 4," she said. "It's the next size down. Two rooms, one bath, and one half-bath, but no kitchenette."

"Great," Aaron announced, reaching into his pocket and producing his cabin key. "Agent Pratt should be along shortly, and he'll wait with you while I gather my things."

"You're leaving?" Nyla blinked, panic gripping her chest.

"Not leaving," he promised, giving her a reassuring smile. "Just moving."

"You want a bigger cabin?" Nyla frowned, thinking. "I mean, that's fine, I only gave you a single because that's all I had open at the time. Are you... is someone going to stay with you? One of the other agents?"

"No," Aaron clarified, searching the parking lot. Another car had just pulled up, and Nyla could see Pratt in the driver's seat. He looked equal parts annoyed and worried, almost perfectly mirroring Aaron's expression when he spoke to Officer Benn. "Someone else is going to stay with me yes, but it's not one of the team."

"Then...?"

"You," Aaron concluded, shooting her a knowing smirk. "Clearly, I can't leave you alone without you getting yourself into some sort of compromising situation with the sheriff's station. So, I'm not leaving you alone anymore."

"Aaron," Nyla blinked, her mouth working in shock, "you don't need to babysit me."

"I know you don't need a babysitter," he said, turning to face her again. His expression softened, with just a hint of regret. "More like a bodyguard. Look, as much as I'd like to promise that Hannaford is going to prison and will never get the chance to come after you again, he's a sheriff. Law enforcement has a nasty habit of protecting their own, even when they don't deserve it. I can't guarantee that Hannaford leaves here and finds the back end of a cell."

Nyla took a steadying breath, knowing he was right.

"I'd rather have you close until we figure this thing out," he said, waving Pratt over as he emerged from his vehicle. "That way, if he does come after you again, I'll be there."

"And we won't need an ambulance?" Nyla taunted. Aaron donned a bitter smirk.

"If Bill Hannaford tries to lay another hand on you, an ambulance won't be necessary." he promised, "I'll make sure the only way he leaves this property is in the back of a hearse."

Chapter Sixteen

AARON

Aaron's temper hadn't been tested to such a degree in a long time. He prided himself on his ability to keep his composure under pressure; it was an important factor in his relatively quick rise through the ranks at the Bureau. And yet, Sheriff Bill Hannaford was doing everything in his power to undermine Aaron's stubborn patience in the short time he'd been in Somerton.

Nyla was in her cabin now, packing a bag for Aaron to carry over to their new accommodations for the foreseeable future. It had been a spur of the moment decision, one that Pratt was no doubt going to tease him for, but it was necessary. He didn't trust the justice system to keep Nyla safe from Hannaford, so Aaron would simply have to do it himself.

He liked her. More than he cared to admit aloud.

There was no point in denying it to himself, at least. He liked Nyla— liked her spunk, her charm, her wit— he couldn't help it. There was nothing wrong with that; Aaron was a single man, and only a few years older than Nyla. His attraction to her wasn't the problem. His job was.

Nyla was, first and foremost, his client. It would go against every code of ethics he could name to strike up a relationship with her. Not to mention, if any of this ended up in a courtroom, their involvement could jeopardize the case. That's if Nyla even reciprocated his feelings, which he wasn't sure about. She seemed to like him well enough, but perhaps she was just grateful for his help. Aaron was too close to the situation to tell.

Better to acknowledge his attraction and move on. Not that Pratt would let things go that easily if he found out, but Aaron could certainly try.

When Aaron returned from escorting Nyla to her cabin, Kelley and the rest of her team had arrived. He wasn't surprised to see them— it was enough that Nyla was attacked by the local sheriff after he'd been put on probation for misconduct. Throw in the fact that Nyla was the person most affected financially by the string of disappearances, and the whole situation became undeniably relevant to their investigation. What did surprise him, though, was that they seemed to be waiting for him.

Pratt waved Aaron over as soon as they locked eyes, and nodded to the officer they'd been speaking to before. Officer Benn, if Aaron remembered correctly.

"We were just getting the rundown on what happened," Pratt said, conferring with Kelley. "Before we spoke to Hannaford."

"I don't think that's necessary," Benn protested, but it was weak. Aaron suspected he'd made his displeasure with the idea known before Aaron arrived.

"German is already over there." Pratt continued as if he hadn't heard Benn, confirming Aaron's assumption. "Kelley was going to send me as a second, but I think you should go."

"Me?"

Aaron blinked, looking to Kelley for confirmation.

"It's a good suggestion." Kelley nodded, shocking him more. "German is new to Hannaford, but you're not. He'll be less likely to spin some complicated lie if you're in the room to negate his claims."

"He'll also be less likely to answer our questions at all," Aaron argued. "He's not exactly my biggest fan."

"Perfect." Pratt grinned wickedly, wiggling his eyebrows in exaggerated menace. "If you unsettle him enough, he'll start making mistakes."

Aaron didn't miss the hint of glee in Pratt's voice. He knew there were ulterior motives here— Aaron may be retired, but he was still a Fed at heart. He was deeply familiar with manipulation tactics, and Pratt and Kelley were being more than a little obvious with theirs.

It was no secret that they wanted him back. If they treated him like he was a part of the team, they hoped Aaron would start feeling nostalgic and want to come out of retirement. It wouldn't work, but he could let them try.

"Alright," Aaron shrugged, sinking his hands into his pants pockets. "Lead the way."

Bill Hannaford was at the hospital in the neighboring town of Hatfield. Aaron took note of the directions from Pratt, asked him to keep an eye on Nyla, and promptly headed out to meet German onsite.

When Aaron arrived, he knew immediately where Hannaford was located. The hospital wasn't large, and a quick scan of the recovery ward revealed two officers stationed outside a closed door, with German leaning casually against the opposite wall.

"There you are," he greeted as Aaron got close, clapping him on the shoulder. "Come on, let's get this over with before these guys burn a hole through my head."

They *were* glaring hard. Aaron was surprised they hadn't given themselves a headache with all the squinting. He'd meant what he said to Nyla— law enforcement protected their own, even when they didn't deserve it. If Kelley's team, and, by extension, Aaron, weren't the enemies before, they certainly were now.

Inside the room was dull and lifeless. Aaron would never get over the stark contrast between hospitals in metropolitan centers and hospitals in rural communities. The walls in Hannaford's room may have been white once upon a time, but they were now mottled and yellow, almost brown in places. The linoleum had seen better days too, with some spots worn through to the dark grey subfloor beneath. It was clean, Aaron had no doubt, but it didn't *look* clean.

Hannaford didn't look much better. Healthwise, he seemed fine. Some bandages on his leg and arm, a stitch or two on his head. Of the skin Aaron could see, he'd definitely have some bruising, but he was in one piece, and he was alert. He was also pissed as shit.

A sour, dark look passed over Hannaford's face when he laid eyes on Aaron, and he had no doubt that, if given the chance, the good sheriff would've pointed a knife at his chest, too.

"Afternoon, Sheriff," German greeted politely, pulling up a bright blue metal chair. Aaron thought he recognized it as being part of an old school desk, or maybe it was just the style. "How are you feeling?"

Hannaford gave German a sneering grunt, questioning whether the pleasantries were genuine or taunting. Aaron knew better. If Pratt were here, everything out of his mouth would be sarcastic or disingenuous. German wasn't like that. No matter the situation, German was one of the most honest men Aaron had ever met. He wouldn't say something if he didn't mean it. When they met, Aaron was ashamed to admit that he thought German's terminal honesty would make him a terrible FBI agent. Thankfully, he'd been wrong.

"We just have a few questions for you," German continued, consulting his file. Aaron hadn't bothered to look at it. It was likely empty, given the little evidence they had so far. The act of perusing it was just for show. "I know you're probably looking forward to a nap, so we'll try to be quick."

"Hard to sleep when you're chained up like a goddamn animal," Hannaford spat, shaking his cuffed wrist for good measure. That did surprise Aaron. Most cops got the benefit of the doubt when in hospital under watch; Hannaford must've given them hell to be handcuffed even with two guards outside.

"I'll bet," German smiled sympathetically. Aaron knew that German wasn't feeling sorry for Hannaford, not necessarily. After working together for a few months, Aaron's curiosity had gotten the better of him and he asked German how he always managed to be open and kind to the sick people they often dealt with. His answer had been surprising, but also so very like German.

"Everyone has something you can relate to," German had told him. "You just need to find it."

That's what German was doing now, finding things about Hannaford that he could relate to and empathize with, so he could maintain his kind composure. Even something as simple as needing to rest was common ground that German could work with. Aaron was glad that German could do that because he certainly couldn't.

"What do you want?" Hannaford snapped, nearly snarling. "You want me to admit I attacked the bitch? Yeah, sure. I attacked her. Now get out."

Aaron felt his hackles rise, tamping the reaction down.

"Oh, we know," German continued calmly. "Even without the physical evidence, Miss Jameson has cameras on the property. We're not here for a confession, Sheriff Hannaford."

"Then piss off."

"When did Nyla Jameson move to Somerton?"

Aaron's voice shocked Hannaford into dropping his temper, just for a second. It was obvious that Hannaford hadn't expected Aaron to speak at all, let alone ask such a seemingly innocuous question.

"Four years ago," he answered cautiously. Aaron could almost see the gears whirring in his mind, trying to figure out if he was walking into a trap.

"And she bought Willow Lodge right away?"

"That's right," Hannaford agreed slowly. German was making notes, deferring to Aaron now that they were getting somewhere. "Lived there from day one. It was called Oscar's back then. Oscar Gilbert. Kicked the bucket and left the property to his old lady, but she didn't want no part of it."

"So, Nyla moved in, changed the name, and took over the clientele?"

Hannaford snorted.

"No," he shook his head. "She wanted to turn it into some granola hippie resort or some shit. Hikers, tree huggers, that ilk. I told James he never should've let them sell the place to her, but you can't tell James nothing he don't want to hear."

"James?"

"The mayor," Hannaford grumbled, casting his gaze away from them. "James Carver. Don't bother trying to call him. You'd have better luck sending smoke signals."

"Clearly Nyla's plan for the lodge didn't work out," German cut in, directing Hannaford's attention back to him. "Any reason for that?"

"Hunting's too good in this area." Hannaford scoffed, condescension oozing from every pore. "She was never gonna kick out the old blood. Been coming here for generations."

"So, she adapted," Aaron continued. He'd learned all this from Nyla already, so his focus was largely on finding inconsistencies in Bill's story. "Started appealing to hunters *and* hikers."

Hannaford grunted confirmation.

"What started the feud between you and Miss Jameson?" German added, settling into a rhythm. When Aaron was Unit Chief, he typically conducted interviews with Pratt or Kelley, but he had a good rapport with the entire team. Finding his routine with German again felt familiar, like putting on an old coat. "Were townsfolk opposed to the changes she was making?"

"Jameson has an attitude," Bill grumbled. "No one liked her when she moved in. Except Poulette, but she's not exactly a town favourite herself."

"That's Clarissa Poulette?" German clarified. Hannaford nodded.

"What do you mean by 'attitude,' Sheriff?" Aaron pressed. He knew Nyla was no stranger to sass, but he had a feeling that's not what Bill meant.

"Fucking kids these days," he rolled his eyes. "All about change. Progress. Whatever bullshit buzzwords they happened to hear on their phone. Jameson came in, guns blazing, trying to make all kinds of 'improvements,' What's worse is all her bitching and moaning actually started to work. The young people in town jumped on the bandwagon the second they knew it pissed off the old folks."

"So, Nyla gained a bit of momentum behind her movement, then?"

"Yes," Hannaford growled. "Made my life a living nightmare."

"And what did the mayor think of this movement?"

"James?" Hannaford wheezed a laugh. "He's about as useful as a sack of cow shit. Can't make a decision to save his life, and that's if you can find him long enough to ask the damn question. Everyone comes to me when they need something done, because I'm the only one who can tell my ass from my nose around here."

Aaron very much doubted that, but he bit his tongue.

"Jameson and Poulette wanted to turn this place into a tourist trap," he continued, unprompted. Aaron suppressed a smile. They'd touched on a sensitive issue, and the information was flowing freely now. "Bring in new businesses, form partnerships with big names. They wanted a *ski resort* of all things. You think we have that kind of money? Not a chance."

"How did the town react?"

"How do you think?" Hannaford dismissed, which made Aaron think the reaction wasn't as negative as Hannaford wanted them to believe. "Jameson is a pain in the ass, and she's loud. She'd do well with a husband to beat some sense into her."

Aaron's temper flared again.

"She made herself hard to ignore," German cut in, his tone sounding a little clipped. Aaron suspected his 'relatability' was waning. It wouldn't fade entirely, but it would wear thin if Hannaford continued to aggravate them. "So, you had to do something."

"I came up with a compromise," Hannaford said. "Ungrateful bitch. I drew up a contract with Adrian Stamkos, had the whole thing ready for James's signature. What shows up on my desk the morning after I announced it? A fucking petition to abolish the contract!"

"Adrian Stamkos?" German frowned, staring at his blank file while he searched his memory. "Of Stamkos and Stein?"

"The very one."

Aaron sifted through his own memory until he came up with the information. Stamkos and Stein was a pharmaceutical research company on the west coast. They had factories all over the country, but if Aaron knew anything about rich people, it was that they were always looking for more money.

"Stamkos and Stein were going to build a facility here," Aaron guessed. "Which would open a lot of job opportunities for the nearby communities."

"Real estate would boom, hospitality, retail, everything." Hannaford nodded. "It was perfect. But not good enough for Jameson and her sheep. Obviously, they didn't want to make any actual changes, they just wanted something to complain about."

"I'd imagine a project like that would be quite destructive to the surrounding environment," Aaron prodded. "Seems to be a bit counterproductive to Miss Jameson's vision."

"You sound like her," Hannaford snarled, eyeing Aaron with contempt. "You think a ski resort wouldn't knock down a few fucking trees?"

Aaron started to point out the environmental impact of a factory versus a tourist lodge but thought better of it. It wouldn't be helpful.

"When was this deal made with Stamkos and Stein?"

"Five months ago," Hannaford said. "The contractors started leveling the grounds about 2 weeks later, but that fucking petition has slowed things down."

"Sounds like a lot of your problems would be solved if Miss Jameson were out of the picture," German pointed out, his words heavy with implication. "Awfully convenient then that Willow Lodge has been caught up in this missing hiker scandal. Shockingly convenient, you might say."

"Don't try it," Hannaford snapped. "I know what you're fishing for, and I'm not biting. I ain't got nothing to do with those idiot city boys getting lost in the woods. Hell, you can blame that on Jameson too. If she didn't try so damn hard to bring in newbies, we wouldn't be having this problem. The old guard wouldn't get themselves turned around like that. And they wouldn't be bested by a goddamn animal, that's for sure."

It wasn't lost on Aaron that Bill was clearly unaware of the full scope of the problem. He didn't correct him. With a mixture of seasoned and amateur hunters on the missing list, word would get back to Bill eventually.

"Thank you for your time," German announced, standing. Aaron nodded curtly, acknowledging the Sheriff and communicating to German that he'd asked all his questions. "If we have any further questions for you, Sheriff, we'll be back."

"Whatever," Bill huffed, sinking back into his pillows. Aaron watched him for a moment before following German into the hall.

"So, you think he had anything to do with the hikers?" German asked as soon as they were out of earshot of the officers. "Some sort of half-baked revenge plot against Miss Jameson?"

"No, I don't think so," Aaron mused, slowly shaking his head. "Nyla's business is already hanging by a thread. If he did orchestrate the abductions, why then try to kill her when his plan is working?"

"Maybe he snapped after he was put on probation?"

"Maybe," Aaron relented. "But I don't think so. He kept saying the 'new hunters' were the ones going missing, but according to my records, that's not true. Either he's playing dumb, or he really doesn't know."

"We'll keep him on the radar," German concluded, pulling out his phone. "But I'm inclined to agree with you. He's a colossal jackass, but I don't think our Sheriff is a serial killer."

Chapter Seventeen

INTERLUDE

Willow Lodge

Rebecca Kelley was tired. More than tired, really. She was exhausted. Exhausted, and frustrated.

She'd known from the beginning that this case would be annoying. Small-town investigations were notoriously riddled with mistakes and prideful roadblocks— Kelley had guessed exactly the kind of reception they'd get as soon as she saw the name of the Sheriff's station. And, of course, she'd been right. Perhaps a bit too right, considering that the sheriff himself was chained to a hospital bed for attacking their only witness.

She hadn't expected just how weird this case would be. She also hadn't expected Klein. Yes, he'd messaged her about a case he was working the day before they'd been summoned, but wishful thinking had Kelley assuming it was a different case. She was going to respond to him when they were settled in their investigation, and then his name had come up at the station.

Working with your old boss in reversed roles was never something Kelley wanted to do, not that Klein would ever dream of undermining her. He was nothing if not respectful, but it didn't lessen the pressure behind her eyes.

"Kelley?"

Pratt's voice preceded a knock on her cabin door. Kelley sat up straighter.

"It's open."

It was a bit of a shock to her that Pratt stayed with the Bureau after Klein left. The two moved up through the academy together, and they pulled the best scores in the district when they reunited at the Chicago office. Kelley suspected that if Pratt didn't have a wife and kids to think about, he would've waltzed out the door arm in arm with Klein. She was grateful that he didn't— the unit losing two of their best agents in one fell swoop would've been a hard pill to swallow. Ever since, she could never suppress the twinge of anxiety whenever he sought her out in private.

"Napping on the job, are we?" Pratt teased, easing into the room. Kelley rolled her eyes at him, relaxing into the couch cushion again in the wake of his casual demeanor.

"What do you want?" She released all the breath in her lungs at once, making it clear that she was eager to return to her nap.

"I just got this back from the ME's office," he told her, holding a manilla folder aloft. Kelley scrutinized his expression, dread filling her stomach at the crinkles forming around his mouth and nose.

"It's not good, is it?"

"See for yourself," Pratt said, thrusting the folder towards her. Kelley took it, the sinking feeling in her gut growing heavier with every passing second. She knew before she opened it that whatever was in this report was going to make her job a hell of a lot harder.

Pratt waited silently, watching her expression shift as she read.

"You've gotta be kidding me..." Kelley muttered, aghast. "Cause of death: undetermined? Seriously? The man was ripped to shreds!"

"That's the other thing," Pratt began, sounding like he didn't want to say whatever was about to leave his mouth. "They got a positive ID on his dental records. Nyla's not going to like it."

Kelley knew without looking what she was about to find under the identification section of the report. The mangled, grotesque corpse belonged to none other than Leopold Thompson.

"And we can't even tell her what killed him, because we don't know," Kelley concluded, her voice clouded with disbelief.

"She clarifies in the notes section," Pratt pointed out, though he didn't sound hopeful. He crossed his arms over his chest, leaning back against the wall. Kelley kept reading, disbelief turning to confusion.

'Victim died of antemortem wounds to the torso (determination made with 85% certainty). Continued mutilation post-mortem, with no clear pattern or aim. Injuries inflicted with an unidentified sharp object (excl. blade). Exposed skin shows evidence of antemortem frostbite and post-mortem freezing. The perpetrator is inconclusive (human or animal?)'

"They can't tell?" Kelley growled, blinking up at Pratt. "They don't know if an animal did this? They've had the body for two days!"

"Apparently." Pratt grimaced, shaking his head slowly. "When I picked up the file, the assistant told me it was like nothing they'd ever seen before. No known animal attacks match this pattern of injuries, but nothing definitively suggests humans either. So, no, they can't tell."

"Jesus," Kelley exhaled harshly, falling back into the couch. "The sheriff's department has already started spreading the rumor that this was a rogue animal attack. Wildlife has been contacted. We can't just spring on the public that this could've been done by a person."

"There'd be mass panic," Pratt agreed, shaking his head again. "Until we know what we're dealing with, we can't pick a course of action. What do you want to do?"

Go home, Kelley thought bitterly.

"Get Klein and German when they're back," Kelley instructed, gingerly rubbing her temples. She'd have a migraine tonight, no question. "We can't narrow this down with the information we have, so we'll need to consider both options until we have something more concrete. And get me a weather report from the last two weeks."

"Weather?" Pratt questioned. Kelley nodded.

"I want to see how cold it was when Thompson disappeared," she explained. "Oh, and ask Nyla if she remembers anything about frost."

"Klein and German just got here," Pratt announced, gesturing to the window. "Klein is going over the logbook with Nyla. I can ask them now if you want."

Kelley stood, making her way to the sitting room window. Sure enough, Aaron and Nyla were on the front porch of the lodge while crime scene cleanup busied themselves in the lobby. Nyla looked better; she was moving around more freely now that she'd been given some proper painkillers. Even Aaron seemed more relaxed, a stark contrast to the rigid way he typically held himself during investigations. Kelley smiled, despite the complicated situation. It was nice to see Klein enjoying himself, even with something as simple as this.

As much as the team missed him, perhaps retiring to the private sector was the best thing for him after all.

"Do you see what I see?" Kelley smirked, nodding to where Aaron and Nyla were going over the Willow's logbook, huddled just a little closer together than was strictly necessary. Pratt approached the window to stand next to her, following her gaze, frowning.

"What, someone flirting with Klein?" He shrugged. "It's not unheard of. He's got the whole strong-silent-type schtick going for him."

"Sure." Kelley rolled her eyes, nodding again. "But when was the last time you saw Klein *flirt back*?"

Pratt's attention whipped to Nyla and Aaron again, watching with renewed interest. Nyla made some sort of joke that they couldn't hear, making Aaron laugh. As Pratt watched, Nyla laid her hand gently on Aaron's forearm and, to his shock, Aaron didn't pull away.

"Well, I'll be damned," Pratt whistled, long and low. "This case just got a hell of a lot more interesting."

"More interesting than a human-animal hybrid murdering hunters in the dead of night?" Kelley scoffed disbelievingly. Pratt chuckled, grinning.

"If Bigfoot himself made an appearance, I'd still say Klein getting a girlfriend was the most unbelievable thing that happened on this case."

Chapter Eighteen

NYLA

Shortly after Aaron returned from questioning Bill, he was spirited away for a meeting with Kelley and her team. Nyla didn't mind. She was tired and in desperate need of a shower.

The cabin that she now shared, temporarily, with Aaron was admittedly one of her favourites. It wasn't the nicest or the largest. It wasn't even the most modern, but there was something about the quaint décor and calming colour scheme that made Nyla love it. She'd almost picked it as her home, but the distance from the main building made things a little difficult. Besides, she really didn't have a use for two bedrooms.

When she was settled in her new lodgings, the first thing Nyla did was get herself clean. She showered, changed into pajamas, and took a little extra care in her post-shower skin routine. The cut on her cheek stung as she scrubbed away the dirt and blood from her face, but it looked healthy. She rebandaged it carefully, examining the bruises peppering her body as the steam evaporated from the bathroom mirror. It wasn't the worst she'd ever looked, but it wasn't pretty. Nyla would have to wear long sleeves for a while.

After she was feeling better, the double bed in her room looked more than a little inviting.

She stretched out on the comforter, staring up at the ceiling. Nyla was waiting for something, but she didn't realize what until the light began to fade from her window.

Bill Hannaford attacked her today. Tried to kill her. Should that... bother her?

The paramedic told her she was probably in shock. Nyla didn't think so. At least, now she didn't. She was obviously upset about the whole ordeal, but that was the extent of the mental toll. In the back of her mind, Nyla thought that she'd crack eventually, maybe when she was alone with her thoughts. But here she was, alone, exhausted, and vulnerable, and her emotions were relatively stable. Sure, she was a bit jumpier than normal, but that was hardly the worst thing. On some level, perhaps she wasn't entirely surprised that Bill had stooped to something so heinous. She, like just about every woman she knew, paid close attention to any man she met, feeling for anything that could pose a threat to her safety. She'd never felt safe around Bill, or most of the men in Somerton.

She felt safe around Aaron.

Nyla rolled her eyes at herself. Yes, she had a crush on Aaron. No, she wasn't surprised. He was exactly her type, and he was more than a little physically attractive. Whether he was interested in her, she didn't know, but it also wasn't important. They were facing upwards of seven dead hunters, with no feasible explanation of what was going on. Hooking up with the hot PI should be the last thing on her mind.

She supposed it wouldn't hurt to fantasize about it, though.

Nyla wasn't sure when she fell asleep, but when she woke up it was dark. Her phone was next to her on the nightstand, and she found a text there from Aaron, telling her he was in the sitting room if she needed anything. With a stretch, she hoisted herself out of bed.

As promised, Aaron was on the couch in the tiny space that served as a living room. Nyla paused, taking in the sight before her appreciatively. He was leaning back, one ankle hooked over his knee, reading through a series of documents that looked well beyond her scope of understanding. His face was scrunched into a serious frown, completely engrossed in whatever he was reading. Nyla let her gaze travel over him while he was distracted, taking note of his outfit. It looked like Aaron had showered too and was currently lounging in a state of undress that she hadn't expected.

Finally, he caught her staring at him, quirking an eyebrow at her.

"What?" He stiffened, confused.

"Nothing, nothing..." Nyla grinned, clasping her hands casually behind her back. "I was just wondering if you should be charging admission?"

Aaron scrunched his eyebrows at her, only cluing in when he glanced down at himself.

He was shirtless, wearing only a pair of loose-fitting grey lounge pants.

"Huh? Oh—" Aaron cleared his throat, and Nyla was sure she saw a hint of blush touch his cheeks. "Uh... I guess I underestimated how many shirts I'd need. They're hanging out to dry, but I could—"

"No, no, that's fine." Nyla laughed, circling the couch to sit next to him. She crossed her legs beneath her, angling herself to face him properly. "I was just teasing, Suits. Or... Lack-of-Suits?"

"Right." Aaron still looked a bit abashed, but he made no move to find something more modest to wear. Nyla bit back a smile.

Aaron's physique was just as impressive as she guessed it'd be. His impeccable style obscured only the fine details of his musculature, and Nyla felt no shame in taking the opportunity to fill the gaps in her mental image. In his relaxed state, Aaron's stomach was smooth, the untensed muscle forming gentle rolls at his sides and just beneath his chest. A thin line of dark hair trailed from his naval to the waistband of his pants, disappearing into the elastic. There was a matching brush of hair in the center of his chest, interrupting the otherwise unblemished expanse of brown skin.

Nyla pulled her attention away just a little too late, catching Aaron's bemused smile before he had a chance to wipe it away. She scrunched her nose in playful annoyance, directing her gaze at the paper he was reading.

"What are you looking at?"

He held up the file for her, showing her the official stamp on the back.

"It's the medical examiner's report," Aaron told her, all business now that the topic of conversation had shifted away from his unfairly toned torso. "They finished their evaluation of the body."

"Really?" Nyla leaned forward, trying to glimpse the content of the folder. "Can I...?"

"Nyla, I'm not sure you should be—"

It was too late. Nyla hadn't seen the full scope of the damage done, but she'd seen enough. The photos hardly looked real, more like stills from a Guillermo del Toro film than an actual crime scene.

"Holy shit," she whispered softly. Aaron lowered the file to let her see it properly. She almost wished he hadn't. "I can't even recognize him..."

The pictures were a collage of confusing splashes of red, brown, and black. The body— Nyla refused to call it a man, she might pass out if she did— was contorted into an unnatural sprawl of limbs. She could see from the photos that maggots had nested in the exposed flesh, dotting the decaying skin with specks of white. Another photo showed what used to be an in-tact scalp, shredded and shriveling where the skin had turned black with rot. Nyla tried to look away, but she kept being drawn back to the horror in front of her.

"What kind of animal could do something like that?" She uttered, frozen by the jagged bones erupting from the central mass of the corpse. She'd seen a number of animal attacks before, with bears topping the list as the most brutal. This... was on a whole different level.

"That's part of what this report was supposed to figure out." Aaron shook his head, looking troubled again.

"Supposed to?"

She thought he would blow her off, dismissing her curiosity as prying for unnecessary details. To her surprise, Aaron continued. Maybe he was just thinking out loud, but Nyla was happy to listen to him either way.

"The findings were... inconclusive."

"So... what does that mean?" Nyla prodded, inching closer to get a better look. Now that the shock had worn off, she could see small details in the photos that she hadn't been able to process before. Pieces of clothing, foreign debris in the wounds, things that proved the mangled mess used to be a person. "They're not sure if it's like, a bear or a wolf or whatever? They can tell that just from the body?"

"Yes and no." Aaron shrugged, pointing out one of the larger slashes on what looked to be a closeup of an arm. Each cut was uneven, like something had ripped through the muscle. The edges were dark, brown in areas and blackened in others. "They could use injuries like these to determine the kind of animal if they had a bit more time and some consults with experts, but that's not what I meant. They're not sure if this was an animal or... well, a human."

Nyla blinked.

"They think a person could've done this?"

Aaron met her gaze, his expression heavy.

"There are some sick people in this world, Nyla," he said quietly. "We can't rule it out."

"Christ..." Nyla bit her lip, trying to let that thought go as quickly as it had manifested. She looked at the folder again, trying to distract herself. "Did they at least identify them?"

Aaron hesitated, and she didn't miss the way he angled the folder away from her again. "...Yes. They're trying to get in contact with his family now."

"Who is it?" Nyla felt a jolt of something akin to hope. If nothing else, one family could get closure out of all this. "I could probably help!"

"Nyla," Aaron cut in harshly. "I don't think that's a good idea."

"Why not? Aaron, I have emergency contacts for all my guests. I could help—"

The look he gave her had Nyla snapping her mouth shut. Aaron waited, silence thick in the air between them. The realization dawned on Nyla before she was ready, but once it started, there was no stopping it.

"Oh my God... it's Leo, isn't it?"

Aaron said nothing. He didn't need to.

"Leo... Oh my God." Nyla gasped in a shuddering breath, the room suddenly starting to spin. "*Oh my God!* He doesn't even— I mean, I can't— How—"

"This isn't your fault, Nyla." Aaron's voice pierced through her panic, redirecting her attention to him. Still, guilt was running rampant through her mind and Nyla was powerless to stop it.

"I ran and left him to this." Speaking the words made the whole thing more real to her, and soon she couldn't suck in enough air. "Aaron, I left him! I should've stayed. Holy shit, *I should've stayed—*"

"Hey, look at me," Aaron commanded, slapping the file firmly onto the coffee table in front of them. "Stop. Nyla, look at me."

He grasped her chin firmly, turning her head to face him.

"You did the right thing. Running was the right thing to do. The smart thing."

"But Leo—"

"Nyla, I promise you. Whatever did this to Leo would've done this to you too." Aaron's eyes bored into hers, holding her captive with the intensity of his stare. "You can't stop this kind of carnage on a whim. The fact that you ran is the reason we're here right now, the reason that Leo might get justice. *This isn't your fault.*"

Nyla watched him and saw the sincerity on his face. She hadn't meant to speak, but when she did, the truth of her emotions left her shivering.

"Aaron... I'm scared."

As soon as the words left her mouth, Nyla wished she could take them back. Was she scared? Yes, of course she was. Men were going missing in what was essentially her backyard, and Nyla had no idea why it was happening or how to stop it. She was terrified, confused, and desperate for answers. That didn't mean she wanted to admit it aloud, especially to a man she barely knew and really liked. The last thing she needed was for Aaron to think less of her because she couldn't keep herself together.

But she'd told him the truth, and she couldn't change that now. Whatever he thought of her, she'd have to accept, even if it's that she was a scared little girl in way over her head.

She'd just have to prove to him that she wasn't.

"I think that's enough investigating for tonight," Aaron announced suddenly, using his free hand to close the folder.

"What? No!" Nyla jerked upright, realizing what she'd inadvertently done. "I didn't mean to interrupt you, I'm sorry. Please, keep going. I'll just sit over here. I'm fine, I swear."

Damn it all, Nyla bit her lip hard enough to make her wince. As if her fears were manifesting in front of her, Aaron was already pushing the folder away from them. "Aaron, wait!"

He paused, raising an eyebrow at her in surprise.

"I..." Nyla swallowed the lump in her throat, fighting back the threat of panic as it crept along her spine. She hated how much his opinion meant to her, but he was her only ally in this investigation. She couldn't lose him, or his trust, over something as ridiculous as fear. "Please, don't stop working on my account. You don't need to coddle me. It might take me a while, but I *can* handle it, I promise. I've just never seen anything like this before, so I freaked out and I spoke without thinking and—"

"Nyla," Aaron interrupted her, smiling gently. He righted himself, twisting on the couch to face her. "You've got it all wrong. It's okay, breathe."

"I *am* breathing!" She defended instinctively, realizing a fraction of a second later that he wasn't speaking literally. She flushed.

"Then try holding it for a minute," Aaron taunted, relaxing her with his ease. "Look, I'm not putting this away because I don't think you *can* handle it. I'm putting it away because I don't *want* you to handle it."

"But—"

"Hang on, let me talk." He nudged her with his knee, effectively bringing her out of her spiral with his calm cadence and reassuring atmosphere. "Nyla, come on. I've been here for 3 days now, and I've seen you in action. More action than you probably bargained for, after what happened today."

In response, Nyla's ribs throbbed.

"I know that I could walk you through every gory detail in that file," Aaron continued, laying his palm gently on her shoulder. "There's not a doubt in my mind that you'd take it all in stride, but that's not the point. This is *my* job, not yours. I look at the body so you don't have to. I wallow through the investigatory mud so you don't have to. I clean up the blood so you don't have to. Seeing a pattern?"

"I own a hunting lodge," Nyla argued half-heartedly. "If either of us should clean up the blood, shouldn't it be me?"

"Blood's not too hard to clean," Aaron shrugged, a smirk playing at his lips. "I'm sure I could find some cold water and hand soap around here somewhere."

Nyla blinked, stunned into silence.

"The FBI has specialized training programs and mandated therapy to help us compartmentalize this stuff," Aaron said. "You don't have any of that, and you're faring better than most of the witnesses I've dealt with. I'm not going to ice you out because you're *afraid*, Nyla. You're supposed to be afraid. It's my job to fix this mess so you don't have to be afraid anymore."

She didn't know what to say to that. The lump in Nyla's throat hadn't abated, but now it choked her for a different reason.

"Looking at this stuff too late at night gives me nightmares anyway," Aaron proclaimed, changing the topic and rescuing her from having to find the words to express her gratitude. He did a quick scan of the room, ending by looking at the clock. "I'd suggest we watch a movie but..."

Nyla gave an uncertain laugh.

"I used to have the TV out here," she told him, trying to distract herself. "I got too many complaints about not being able to watch it in bed, so I moved it."

"Makes sense," Aaron conceded, thinking hard for a minute. After a short time, he stood abruptly. "Fuck it, why not? Come on, we can go to my room. I'll let you pick."

"You're kidding, right?"

Aaron's bewildered expression caught Nyla off guard as she settled next to him on the bed, just enough space between them that they weren't in danger of touching. She coughed out a surprised laugh.

"What?" She shrugged, pressing 'Play' on the remote. "It's a classic!"

"It's horribly inaccurate," Aaron grumbled though she could tell from the twinkle in his eye that he was playing it up for her benefit. Nyla smiled to herself.

"It's not my fault you're threatened by such an exemplary display of investigatory prowess."

As the opening credits of *Ace Ventura: Pet Detective* bloomed into existence on the admittedly old plasma screen, Aaron seemed inclined to disagree.

"Exemplary display of investigatory prowess?" He repeated back to her, snorting. "There are no less than ten points in this movie where Jim Carrey would've landed himself in prison. And that's ignoring the blatant transphobia."

"You're right about the transphobia, I'll give you that," Nyla agreed. "But as for the 'illegal' investigating, you can just tell me what you would've done instead."

"Probably declined the offer and had a much-needed nap."

"Well then, who are you to judge?" Nyla teased, throwing a pillow at him. Aaron chuckled, hooking it under his arm and settling back against the headboard.

They watched in silence for a time, Nyla making note of all the times Aaron made a face at something that happened on screen. By the time Ace Ventura made his break in the case, she was having more fun watching Aaron.

"See, this is just ridiculous," he huffed eventually, rolling his eyes in a wide circle. "First of all, any PI worth his salt would never get themselves into this situation. What's the point of solving a crime if you then have to cover up like... six more in the process? Secondly, who steals a dolphin?"

"It's a comedy," Nyla pointed out, laughing. "It's not supposed to be realistic."

"But it is supposed to be funny."

"Don't tell me you're a Jim Carrey hater."

"I'm not a Jim Carrey hater. I'm not exactly a fan either, but I'm not a hater."

"Killjoy."

A loud crash from outside the window interrupted them, startling both Aaron and Nyla. They jumped into each other, Nyla's hand clutching Aaron's forearm, Aaron's hand shielding Nyla's torso.

"What was that?" Nyla demanded, angling herself to see out the window. Aaron was taller than her and could see without shifting more than an inch or two.

"Looks like Pratt dropped something…" Aaron mused, his posture relaxing as he took in the scene. "Ooh, a box of files. That's gonna be a pain in the ass to clean up."

Nyla felt the tension drain from her body, her heartbeat settling back to normal. "Should we go help?"

Aaron laughed, a mischievous glint in his eye.

"Not a chance."

He settled back onto the bed, but he didn't remove Nyla's hand. He paused, hesitating for a second, and then, to her surprise, Aaron wrapped his arm around her, pulling her gently against his side. It was only when she was pressed snugly against his torso that she realized why he'd offered her such comfort.

She was shaking. Shaking so hard her teeth began to clatter.

"I'm sorry," Nyla said quietly, cursing herself and forcing her limbs to be still. After what happened in the living room, she thought her embarrassment was done for the evening. "I'm not usually—"

Aaron eyed her disparagingly.

"Nyla, seriously? We just went over this." He squeezed her shoulder reassuringly. "It's fine. You're allowed to be on edge. I'd be more worried if you weren't."

"It's just not me." Nyla insisted, annoyed at herself. "I'm always the one walking headfirst into the haunted house, making friends with the zombie actors. I don't startle at things that go bump in the night."

Independent. That's what her father had called her. *Stubborn* was the less-kind word most people used.

"It gets easier," Aaron promised, lowering his voice to a soothing vibrato. "After some time passes, you'll go back to normal. You've just got to keep your head up until then."

"Easier said than done."

He didn't have anything to say to that. It was true, and there was no point arguing when they both knew it.

Nyla lost track of the movie quickly after that. She hadn't really been paying attention anyway, but now it was a completely lost cause. She'd grown accustomed to Aaron's easy touches over the short time she'd known him, yet she couldn't deny this was different, and not just because he was only half-clothed.

Aaron's chest rose and fell steadily beneath her cheek, his heart thudding steadily against her ear. The rhythmic movement lulled Nyla into a state of unguarded vulnerability, loosening her tongue perhaps a bit more than it should've.

"You know, I never even asked you," Nyla hedged, shifting against him. This was inappropriate— wildly so, but Aaron clearly didn't mind, so why should she? "Do you have a girlfriend?"

"No," Aaron answered easily, a hint of amusement in his voice. "No wife either, to answer your next question."

"I was going to ask about a boyfriend, actually," Nyla bristled, biting her lip against Aaron's chuckle.

"No boyfriend or husband," he confirmed. "I had a cat once."

"Basically the same thing."

She paused, wondering if he was going to return her question. She then realized that if she did have a partner, she probably would've disclosed that by now.

"I'm not seeing anyone either," she added absently, just in case. Aaron's chuckle deepened, and Nyla lifted her head to defend herself. "What? Why's that funny?"

"It's not," he assured her, their faces suddenly very close.

"Then why are you laughing?"

"I'm waiting," he said, smirking.

"For what?"

"For you to lose your patience and ask me what you really want to know."

"That's..."

Aaron's hand reached up to grasp her chin, holding Nyla's gaze. She held still, unsure if she was supposed to speak.

His grip on her chin was firm, his thumb pressing in just the right way to part her lips. Nyla blinked at him through her lashes, watching the way his eyes caught on her mouth. Aaron's attention blazed through her, igniting every inch of her body with searing heat.

The clock ticked loudly in the empty room; the tempo far too slow to match Nyla's racing heartbeat.

Slowly, Aaron released her. His hand lingered, sliding delicately along the curve of her jaw, caressing the slope of her neck with his knuckles. Nyla suppressed a shiver, tightening the uncertain grip she had on his arm.

"Aaron..."

His name spilled from her lips unbidden, cloaked in a sigh. Nyla watched as Aaron's eyes darkened hungrily, a muscle in his cheek twitching in agitation.

"Nyla..." Aaron inhaled sharply, shaking himself free of the trance he'd been in. "I'm sorry, I can't."

Those two words sent a shot of ice through her veins. She jolted upright, every muscle in her body tensed to flee.

"Oh... oh my God, I'm such an idiot." Nyla scrambled to stand, embarrassment flooding her. Why was she like this? Why had she pushed him? "I totally read that wrong, I'm so sorry. I'll go, I just— I'll go. Right now."

"What? No, Nyla," Aaron grabbed her arm, staying her. "You didn't read anything wrong, I promise. I want to... I just can't."

She stared at him apprehensively but saw no trace of untruth.

"Why not?"

Aaron thought hard about his answer before speaking.

"If this is... a human, there's a very good chance that both of us will need to testify in a trial. If there's any evidence of a relationship between us, it could invalidate anything we bring to the investigation." He paused. "Not to mention, if it ever gets out that I had... 'relations' with a client, I may never get another one again. I'd be ruined."

Nyla nodded slowly, letting the reality of the situation sink in.

"You have no idea how much it pains me to say this." Aaron laughed breathlessly. "But... I can't risk my job. I'm sorry."

Nyla smiled sadly, understanding tainting her disappointment.

"I would never ask you to risk your job for me, Aaron," she vowed. "It's okay."

"That's probably for the best." He gave her a sardonic grin. "If you were the one asking, I don't think I could deny you anything."

His voice dropped as he said it, injecting the words with a deep sensuality that Nyla hadn't expected. Her stomach flipped, warmth spreading in her abdomen.

"Maybe I should go," Aaron whispered, refusing to look away from the heat in her eyes.

"This is your room, so technically I should be the one leaving," Nyla teased.

"Right." Aaron cleared his throat, coming back to his senses a bit. "Well, you don't have to. I'm not kicking you out."

"You're just offering to vacate your own room to escape this situation?" Nyla laughed, straightening. She laid her hand gently on Aaron's, squeezing reassuringly. "It's fine, Aaron. You're right. We should get some sleep if nothing else."

He blinked as if remembering that they had a job to do.

"Right." He sighed eventually. "You're right."

Nyla smiled, making her way quickly to the door. He watched every move, making no attempt at hiding the way his attention lingered on her bared legs and plunging neckline. Nyla swallowed hard, reminding herself why she was leaving.

"Goodnight, Aaron," she whispered, slipping into the hall and nearly gasping at the blast of cold air that met her. His voice trailed behind her, like he was clinging to her, begging her to stay despite his words.

"Sleep well, Nyla."

Chapter Nineteen

AARON

"Look, I'm sorry, alright?"

Aaron groaned in frustration, rolling onto his back and staring pointedly down at the prominent tent in his sheets.

"It's not my fault you picked the one woman this side of the border that we can't have," he grumbled, willing his erection to abate. Instead, his cock twitched in irritation.

"You're a prick, you know that?"

This had been going on for the better part of an hour. Ever since Nyla retired to her room, Aaron was accosted with thoughts of her. He'd had an inkling that she *might* return his interest, but until now he'd been able to ignore it. He wasn't ignorant— he'd come to terms with his attraction. He also wasn't an animal— he had things under control. But then she'd gone and said something and that... that had done things to him. Things that almost made him risk it all for a taste of her supple thighs.

"Jesus," Aaron cursed, jumping as his phone alarm chimed. He wanted to do routine checks around the property, and make sure doors were locked and windows were shut. Walking around the cabin with an aching hard-on didn't seem like it would be the highlight of his night, but he didn't exactly feel like taking care of it either. With a shuddering breath, Aaron willed his hormones in check and stood.

A quick scan, and then he could come back to bed and try to sleep.

The cabin was quiet, as it should be. Nyla had gone to bed over an hour ago, and the rest of the lodge was silent. Aaron's thoughts echoed loudly in his head even as he wandered, testing the locks on all the windows.

When this case was over, or if it was determined that an animal was responsible for these attacks, Aaron would technically be free to do what he pleased with Nyla. The thought was tempting, but he couldn't help hesitating. Would she still be interested in him once this was over? Or was she being driven by adrenaline and fear? Would it look bad on him, hooking up with a client, even though he was no longer working for her? His brain was far too lust-addled to think things through properly, but he found he couldn't think of much else.

The last thing to check was the window at the end of the hall next to Nyla's bedroom. He made his way there quickly, trying not to imagine her plump ass in those damn pajama shorts just on the other side of this door.

"Aaron..."

His hand was on the doorknob, tensed and ready to burst in, when the wanton cadence of her voice finally registered with him.

Aaron froze, his heartbeat suddenly overbearingly loud in the quiet hallway.

Now that he was focussed, he could hear the way Nyla's breathing stuttered, the delicate rustle of sheets, and the almost inaudible cries she worked desperately to stifle.

She was pleasuring herself.

Aaron fought back a groan with more willpower than he thought he had left, his grip on the doorknob so tight it turned his knuckles pale. He was stunned, thoroughly and wholly rooted in place, his cock springing to rapt attention.

Nyla wasn't just pleasuring herself, he noted with gritted teeth. She was pleasuring herself *thinking about him*.

A soft moan sounded from the other side of the door, and Aaron had to turn around— he couldn't trust himself to remain in the hallway if this continued. He braced his back firmly against the cool wood of the frame, the doorknob digging into his kidney.

"Oh God," Nyla whispered, her voice ragged and broken, "*Aaron please...*"

More than once, Aaron had been accused of being able to read minds. His deductive reasoning and perception skills made him an excellent investigator, and it saved his ass on more than one occasion. To many of his clients, it seemed like he had superpowers.

He'd give anything for that accusation to be true at this moment. Aaron wanted to see what Nyla was doing to herself— what she imagined *he* was doing to her.

A sharp bolt of pleasure struck him, and he nearly choked in his efforts to remain silent. Aaron hadn't realized he was stroking himself until the gentle friction made him shiver. He wrestled his hand back to his side, intent on keeping it there.

He should go back to his room and pretend he was never here. That was the smart thing to do, the respectful thing. Nyla's hushed whimpers told him that she had no intention of being overheard. She would surely be embarrassed if she found him out here. Embarrassed, and possibly angry.

Even still, Aaron couldn't bring himself to step away. He almost wanted her to find him, to pause her ministrations long enough to notice he was there, to fling the door wide, open her mouth to scold him.

That's when he would kiss her.

Aaron wasn't as successful in keeping his pleasure silent this time. A small grunt escaped him, too quiet for Nyla to have heard.

He'd do more than kiss her, Aaron knew. Once his hands were on her body, he wouldn't be able to stop himself. She'd be wet from her attentions, slick and tight and ready for him to do whatever he pleased. Whatever she was imagining, Aaron would make sure it could never compare to the real thing.

"Fuck—!" Nyla hissed, swallowing the rest of her exclamation.

If Aaron was in there with her, she'd have no hope of even that much control. Images of her naked body writhing helplessly beneath him, crying out his name over and over until she was hoarse, her nails dragging across his skin and leaving angry welts in their wake, flooded him. His cock twitched angrily, begging to be tended to.

His fingers itched to slip inside the waistband of his lounge pants.

Aaron needed to leave. *Now.*

His room had never seemed so far away. With a deep, shuddering breath, Aaron pushed himself away from the door and padded swiftly down the hall. He didn't dare slow until he was safely inside, staring at his glaringly empty bed.

With a soft thump, his lounge pants hit the floor, and his hand went around his cock.

Sweet, tantalizing relief was quickly replaced with unrelenting need. His hand moved in quick, rapid pumps, squeezing and releasing at even intervals. Aaron's head fell back, clunking against the door.

Nyla.

He replayed the sounds of her pleasure in his mind, clinging to the melodic moans and throaty whines that left him shaking. Pictures of what he would've done if he'd opened the door— what he wanted to do now— drove his arousal to new heights.

Nyla, on her knees, her lips stretched over his shaft.

Nyla, back arched, coming undone around his fingers.

Nyla, legs spread, taking everything he had to give her.

Aaron coughed out a pained grunt as he came, hard and fast. His semen coated his hand, his thighs, the floor, even the discarded lounge pants. It was the most he'd come in months.

And yet, he wasn't satisfied.

That wasn't unexpected. Aaron knew that he would never know true relief until he'd tasted the real deal— until he finally claimed Nyla as his own.

A soft beeping interrupted his staggered breaths, reminding him that he'd only snoozed the perimeter check alarm and not dismissed it. Aaron wanted to throw the phone against the window, shattering it into a million pieces, but he restrained himself. It wasn't the phone's fault that the reminder was a double-edged sword— a signifier both of his duty, and the fact that he could never act on his desires.

Nyla was within arms reach, but Aaron couldn't have her.

Chapter Twenty

NYLA

The next morning, Nyla was surprised to find Aaron hovering outside her door, fist raised to knock. She nearly walked into him, managing to skid to a stop just before she collided with his chest.

"Good morning," she greeted breathlessly, shaking her displaced bangs from her face. Aaron didn't respond right away, scrutinizing her expression with a simmering intensity that made her squirm. "Is... everything okay?"

He held his stare for a moment longer, and then he was abruptly back to normal.

"Kelley wants us to meet her in the lobby," he explained, glancing down to see that Nyla was already dressed. She followed his gaze where it lingered on her t-shirt; it was baggy and loose, but admittedly low-cut.

"Both of us?"

"That's what she said, yes."

"Well, alrighty then. Lead the way."

Aaron worked his jaw like he wanted to say something but thought better of it. After a questioning look from Nyla, he began to make his way to the front door of the cabin.

"Did you sleep okay?" Nyla asked conversationally, not missing the way he almost... flinched?

"Fine." Aaron shrugged and paused, sneaking a glance at her as they walked. "You?"

"Like a baby," she grinned, conveniently leaving out the fact that to get to sleep in the first place, she'd had to relieve some of the tension that lingered between them when she retired to her room. As if he could read her thoughts, Nyla was certain she saw a hint of a blush on Aaron's face. Or maybe she was seeing things.

Nyla was still a little embarrassed about her emotional state the night before. She wasn't used to being so vulnerable with anyone besides Clary, leaving her feeling raw and exposed as she strolled next to Aaron. She shoved the feeling down, determined to show him that he was right to have faith in her. That she had faith in herself.

They were third to arrive in the lobby, after Kelley and German. Nyla waved to them warmly before hopping up onto the welcome desk and spinning to face the room. Kelley offered her a half-smile, clearly troubled and trying to hide it. German wore a similar expression, with a wrinkle of concern between his eyebrows. Something was wrong. Nyla caught Aaron's eye questioningly, but he seemed as in the dark as she was.

No one said much of anything until Pratt and Andrews had appeared, and then it was like the room clicked into gear. Kelley shifted the attention to her with an authoritative cough.

"I want to go over the game plan for the next few days," she said, making eye contact with Aaron as she did so. "This investigation hasn't gone as well as we'd hoped, so it would help us to have everyone on the same page.

"After reviewing the coroner's report, we can't eliminate the possibility that this is an animal attack. We also can't eliminate the possibility that this is a serial or spree killer. Our resources are already thin, but after speaking with some of you last night, I don't see an alternative option; we're going to have to follow both lines of the investigation until something turns up."

Nyla could tell from the creases around Kelley's frown that she wasn't happy about the decision. No one else seemed to be either, sharing loaded glances with the person standing nearest to them.

"We have a small team, Kelley," German rebutted, though his tone was resigned. Nyla guessed that the possibility of dividing the work wasn't news to him. "Splitting up is a luxury we don't have."

"I know," Kelley acknowledged, sounding equally resigned. "But it's one we'll have to take."

She pulled her phone out of her pocket, tapping the screen a few times before speaking again.

"German, Andrews, and I will work on the human angle. It makes sense to have the most manpower working on the most complicated path, not to mention it's the one we can actually handle. Pratt, you and Klein will look into the animal theory."

"I don't know shit about animals." Pratt snorted, shaking his head. "And Klein isn't part of the team. You can't tell him what to do."

"I've already spoken to Klein." Kelley rolled her eyes, crossing her arms over her chest. "And you agreed to this over breakfast. Stop putting on a show for Nyla."

Nyla's eyebrows shot up in surprise, but Pratt only grinned at Kelley.

"Someone has to." He shrugged absently. "I don't want her to think we're all sticks in the mud like Klein."

Nyla had figured that much out on her own, but she didn't point that out.

"Huang has been working hard over the last few days to provide us with as much help as she can." Ignoring Pratt, Kelley looked at her phone again while Nyla turned questioningly to Aaron. He leaned down to whisper in her ear.

"Ji Huang, Field Coordinator for the Division of Wildlife Resources in Wisconsin."

Nyla nodded in silent understanding.

"I received an email this morning from Huang's office, giving me the name and contact information of a couple of locals who might be able to help you on the animal front." Kelley turned to face Aaron, Nyla, and Pratt, who was standing on Aaron's other side. "A tracker, and a guide. The tracker is meeting us here within the hour," Kelley explained. "Huang detailed the situation, and he's agreed to return to the site of Leopold Thompson's abduction and try to track whatever may have taken him."

"And the guide?" Aaron nudged, sinking his hands into his pants pockets. Kelley's lips twitched in a smile.

"Huang offered to set up a meeting with the guide as well, but I told her not to bother." Kelley's eyes fell on Nyla, her expression shifting into a smirk. "I figured it would be easier to talk to Miss Jameson in person."

"Nyla?"

Aaron glanced between Nyla and Kelley in surprise. Nyla rolled her eyes at him, giving him a withering stare.

"I do run a hunting lodge, Aaron," she pointed out. "Leading guided hikes is a big part of my supplemental income. I'm the most qualified nature guide you'll find around here."

"Funny," Kelley mused. "That's exactly what Huang said."

"I'd be happy to help." Nyla grinned, feeling the excitement build in her chest. This, she could do. "Give me about 30 minutes to pack."

"We're still waiting on our tracker anyway," Kelley assured her. "Take all the time you need."

⚓︎ ❦ ⚓︎

"Nyla, I didn't mean to offend you," Aaron promised, hovering near her door while Nyla prepared a bag. She stifled a laugh, not wanting to relieve him of his paranoia just yet. "It wasn't that I didn't think you could do it. I just wasn't expecting your name to come up."

"Is that because I'm a woman?" Nyla quipped, scanning her first aid kit to make sure it was well stocked. "Or because I'm young? Need I remind you that I was the one who took you to Leo's campsite the first time?"

"No, neither," Aaron said vehemently. "Honestly! I know you're more than capable of—"

Nyla turned to face him, no longer hiding her smirk. Aaron's face fell immediately, annoyance stiffening his jaw.

"Very funny," he chastised. "I really thought you were upset at me, you know."

"I know."

She caught the sound of Aaron's grumbling as she carefully went over the final checklist in her head. Kelley said they were meeting with a tracker, so she had to account for the possibility that this trip was going to span multiple days. Nyla always had rations in her pack, along with an emergency change of clothes, but she'd recently lost her ground sheet. She'd need to grab another one from the lodge's storage room before they left.

"Don't you have to pack?" Nyla asked Aaron, eyeing him suspiciously. He hadn't left her side since that morning, and she certainly couldn't remember seeing him pack anything. Aaron shook his head, shrugging.

"I brought a pre-packed bag. It's been ready to go since I got here."

Nyla quizzed him on a few things until she was satisfied that he was as prepared as he should be. Once they were ready, they returned to the Willow's lobby. Kelley was there, talking seriously with a man that Nyla didn't recognize until he caught her eye.

"Ephraim Coady?" She gasped, a smile splitting her face. "I'll be damned!"

Ephraim held up a hand in greeting, pulling the loose fabric of his windbreaker taut. Nyla was almost sure he'd shrunk a few inches since the last time they'd seen each other. He was a thick man, with broad shoulders and sagging muscles that were once firm with regular use. He was nearing 70, but he hadn't looked it until recently. Nyla often forgot his age when speaking of him. She'd also forgotten that if they were getting a local to help them track, it would most likely be Eph.

"Nyla!" He grinned, prominently displaying his missing canine. "Long time no see! What kind of trouble have you gotten yourself into now?"

"Nothing I can't handle," she promised, dropping her bag next to the front desk. Aaron raised a brow at her as if to voice his disagreement with that sentiment, but he kept his thoughts to himself. Eph shook his head, deciding not to contradict Nyla either, returning to his conversation with Kelley.

"Then why did they call us in?"

The voice appeared from over Nyla's shoulder, taunting and familiar. She was already exasperated even before she turned to confirm her suspicions.

"Emmett? For fuck's sake." She groaned, covering her excitement with exaggerated irritation. "When they said they were bringing in an expert, I thought they were serious."

The man standing in front of her looked like he'd been plucked straight from a camping catalogue. Nyla had known Emmett for years, and he was never the pinnacle of fashion. Today was no exception. Emmett was just shy of Aaron's height and he shared his father's broad frame. He was sporting a worn, army green ballcap with a matching worker's jacket. Underneath, Nyla could see an oil-stained navy pullover that had seen better days and just the edges of a simple brown t-shirt poking out over his mud-streaked cargo pants. Despite his disastrous clothing, Emmett always had a charm about him.

He gave her a lopsided smile, winking.

"Shut it, Nyla," he teased, removing his hat long enough to shake out his thick, black hair. It was long for him, touching the tops of his ears where it was usually trimmed to an inch at most. "Bring it in."

Emmett enveloped her in a hug, just as Aaron cleared his throat to grab her attention. Nyla bit her lip to hide her smile at the pointed look Aaron was giving her.

"Aaron, this is Emmett Coady." She stepped aside for Aaron to shake Emmett's hand. "His dad, Ephraim, is our tracker."

"Nice to meet you," Emmett chirped happily. Aaron returned the gesture with a nod.

"If your father is the tracker," he began, almost accusingly, "then what brings you here?"

"Dad had a stroke last year," Emmett answered easily. Nyla remembered when it happened. Even after the medical struggle, Eph was a hard man to keep down. "His leg isn't what it used to be, so I'm here as a human crutch."

"I'm sorry to hear that," Aaron told him.

"Me too," Nyla interjected, heaving an exaggerated sigh. "Here I thought we were in for a peaceful day."

Emmett stuck his middle finger up at her.

"You're insufferable."

"As always!"

Emmett bit back a laugh, ignoring her dramatic scowl as he wandered to where his father and Kelley were talking. Nyla seated herself comfortably on the edge of the front desk, keeping decidedly silent in the face of Aaron's sudden questionable mood.

"So," he prompted eventually, sticking his hands in his pockets to look casual. "They're our local trackers, then?"

"I guess the local thing was a bit of a technicality." Nyla lifted one shoulder. "Emmett and Ephraim live in the next town over, but the grounds they work are within Somerton's border."

"Grounds?"

Nyla bit her lip again to smother her smug amusement. Aaron had already abandoned his attempt at subtlety.

"Ephraim is the maintenance worker for Lichen House," she said easily. "It's... well, a mini castle, I guess. Historic building on the other side of the mountain. The thing was falling apart when some tourism company bought it and wanted it restored, maybe turned into a B&B. They hired Ephraim to be the live-in groundskeeper while they came up with a plan, but construction never got off the ground. They still pay him though, so they must have some plan for it."

Aaron nodded slowly, taking careful mental notes.

"You two seem to know each other fairly well," he hedged.

"By-product of the business." Nyla didn't glance at him to see if he was hoping she'd elaborate on that. "Everyone involved with nature or hospitality knows each other around here. Ephraim and I cross paths all the time."

"And, uh." Aaron fidgeted. "Emmett?"

This time, Nyla didn't bother to downplay how much she was enjoying his reaction.

"He comes by every month or so to drop off a load of scrap wood for me. Easier than chopping it all myself. I leave the nice lumber for my guests, and then I burn the scraps for me."

Aaron shifted in discomfort. Nyla didn't try to ease it for him.

"So, he works with his dad?"

"Oh, no. Emmett is a bricklayer."

She said that casually, with just a hint of admiration. Aaron paused, irritation twitching in his cheek.

"Of course he is," he grumbled. Nyla thought she saw him stand just a little bit straighter. "So, he just volunteers to help you out because...?"

"Why Aaron," Nyla taunted, gently kicking him with her boot. "Are you jealous?"

"Of the handsome, muscled tradesman that runs errands for you every month out of the kindness of his heart?" He scoffed. "Why would I be?"

"Please, Emmett is like... my cousin or something. Besides, *I* wasn't the one drawing lines in the sand last night."

Aaron had the decency to blush.

"And I never said he was handsome," she said in a mischievous singsong tone. "That was all you."

"At least tell me I smell better than he does." Aaron lowered his voice so as not to be overheard, only half joking. Nyla guessed he was referring to the abundance of stains on Emmett's clothes— given Aaron's meticulous style, she wasn't surprised he'd picked up on Emmett's more careless attitude regarding his appearance.

"Emmett smells like pine, sometimes clay if he's been working," Nyla informed him shamelessly, much to Aaron's chagrin. His clothes may be worse for wear, but Emmett was always impeccably clean. "I don't remember what you smell like. I'd need more exposure for a proper comparison."

Aaron considered her for a moment, glancing back to where the others were engrossed in conversation. She watched him, curious as to what he'd do in response to her baiting in the presence of his team. She wasn't expecting anything, not with so many people around.

He cleared his throat softly, his gaze landing on something next to Nyla on the desk. He casually bumped her knee with his hip, knocking a heavy-duty flashlight perched near her thigh. It tumbled, and Aaron reached out to snag it before it hit the floor. The move brought him firmly into her space, leaning over Nyla as he righted the flashlight, his neck merely a hands width from her mouth.

"Well?" He murmured, catching her eye with smoldering deliberateness. "How do I compare, Miss Jameson?"

Nyla blinked, her heart leaping into her throat and lodging there. Automatically, she inhaled, her breath feathering over Aaron's neck as the scent of his cologne struck her. It was crisp and warm, almost smoky. She lifted her attention to Aaron's intense gaze, their faces much closer than they were a moment ago.

"I work in the woods," she whispered, her stomach somersaulting wildly. "I'm kinda sick of pine."

Seemingly satisfied with her breathless answer, Aaron held her gaze for just a moment longer before righting himself.

"Guys?"

Kelley's voice rang out clearly from across the room, drawing their attention to where Pratt had joined the conversation. Nyla jolted back into the moment, shaking away the flush she could feel on her cheeks.

"Looks like it's time to head out," Aaron announced, shouldering his bag and handing Nyla hers in the process. "Are you ready, Nyla?"

He said her name with such rich, almost sultry sincerity that Nyla was sure he knew exactly what he was doing to her. She wouldn't give him the satisfaction of watching her flounder, though. With an enthusiastic shove, she dropped from the desk onto the floor, bringing herself so close to Aaron that he needed to step back, not before she made sure that he'd felt the press of her body against his, even if it was only for a fraction of a second. She saluted the others, to whom it would've looked like Aaron simply stepped out of the way to give her more room to stand.

"Alright gents," she chirped, "let's get this show on the road!"

Chapter Twenty-One

AARON

"Klein? Seriously? Are you listening to anything I'm saying?"

Aaron shook himself with a start, turning to look at Pratt, who was staring at him in bewilderment and annoyance in equal measures. Aaron fought back the urge to fidget.

"Uh, sorry, no," he muttered, breaking eye contact. "I was focussing on the hike."

Lie.

Aaron didn't bother to check if Pratt caught his fib. It wouldn't matter much regardless.

They'd been hiking for nearly two hours now, and Aaron had never been more thankful for the company. He knew immediately upon veering from the Basin trail that if he was out here by himself, he'd be lost to the vast wilderness.

"The hike?" Pratt repeated dubiously. Well, that answered Aaron's question. He didn't respond, instead risking a glance at the object of his attention, knowing that if Pratt hadn't already guessed, he would soon.

Nyla was truly a sight to behold. Aaron knew she was capable of course. Between the short hike to the Basin and her struggles with Bill Hannaford, she'd made it abundantly clear over the last few days that Nyla Jameson wasn't one to roll over and play nice. Aaron had never seen her quite like this, though. Not while she was fully in her element, acting as the only anchor between their little group and utter disaster.

They'd found Leo's campsite quickly and Ephraim had set to work. Aaron could admit that he wasn't expecting much— not that he doubted Ephraim's abilities but, given the strangeness of this case, Aaron sincerely thought they wouldn't get lucky on the rogue animal angle. To his surprise, Ephraim found something after only 30 minutes of searching. Aided by his son, he led the group on a meandering path through the thickest part of the Basin, relying on Nyla's expertise to keep them on track.

It was as though Nyla was born in the forest. Aaron couldn't take his eyes off her; she was so at ease, weaving through the underbrush like it was second nature, displaying her prowess in a way she hadn't been able to the first time she'd introduced them to the mountain forest. Every few seconds, her attention would catch on to something seemingly innocuous, but Aaron could tell from the way her eyes narrowed that she was picking up on clues from the environment, guiding her in the right direction, keeping track of where they were and where they were going. It was fascinating, and a little irritating. More than anything, Aaron wanted to engage with her, to talk to her about what she was seeing and how she was reading the world around them. That was a difficult feat when he could barely tell a pine from a maple.

Emmett didn't have that problem.

He was next to Nyla now, hovering behind Ephraim in case his assistance was needed. The two were talking animatedly about something Aaron couldn't quite hear. Nyla laughed, and the sound both soothed him and clawed at his chest. Nyla may think Emmett wasn't interested in her, but Aaron had his doubts.

"Jesus, you're down bad."

"Huh?" Aaron snapped back to Pratt again, who was grinning like a jackal. Aaron scowled.

"Don't make that face," Pratt said, clapping Aaron on the back good-naturedly. "No shame in it. She's pretty and fun. I can see why you'd be attracted to her."

"Who says I'm attracted to her?"

Pratt laughed, full and deep. In lieu of a proper response, he just stared at Aaron in open disbelief.

"Alright, fine," Aaron grumbled, pressing his lips together against his own smirk. "But it doesn't matter. She's a client."

"Oh, what, you're going to bring a bear to court?" Pratt scoffed. "I don't think you have any legal repercussions to worry about on this one, Klein."

"It might not be a bear," Aaron pointed out sharply.

"A wolf, then."

"Shut up." Aaron sighed, lowering his voice automatically. He wasn't sure why. Nyla and Emmett were too far ahead to overhear them, but Aaron got a distinct feeling that someone was listening. Almost like the forest itself was paying attention. "You know what I'm saying. Until we have concrete proof, we can't rule out that we're dealing with a person. With the messed-up shit this guy has done to these hunters, I can't risk anything keeping him out of prison. That, and even if it is an animal, getting involved with a client could destroy my professional reputation."

"I get what you're saying," Pratt acknowledged. "But I really think you're in the clear here, Klein. Besides, if it did turn out to be a person, you know we'd all cover for you. Any one of us would vouch for Nyla's innocence, and your career is pristine. They'd have a hard time making a case for a conflict of interest as far as a conviction is concerned.

"Not to mention," Pratt continued, nearly tripping over a tree root. "Kelley isn't going to make an arrest based on flimsy evidence. On the off chance that your contributions were thrown out because of your relationship with Nyla, I can promise you Kelley will have at least a thousand backup plans."

Aaron didn't say anything, mostly because Pratt was starting to make sense and he couldn't be sure if that was his own bias speaking, or if Pratt was right. Memories of the way Nyla's body felt against him— warm, soft, molded to fit him perfectly— flashed across his mind, no matter how brief the contact had been. She'd done it on purpose, Aaron was sure of that. He couldn't decide if he was exasperated or extremely turned on by her teasing. Maybe a mix of both.

"As for your reputation," Pratt said slyly, "you wouldn't have to worry about picking up clients if you came back to the Bureau."

Aaron didn't grace him with an answer to that.

They moved along in silence for a time, traversing a dense thicket of unfortunately pointy shrubs that covered an equally unfortunate span of mud. Aaron hadn't been in the woods many times and he already decided he hated it.

"Hang on!" Nyla's voice rang out with sharp clarity, bringing the group to a halt. Aaron continued forward until he was directly behind her, his hand pressing instinctively against the small of her back. Pratt chuckled.

"What is it?" He asked urgently, searching Nyla's face for any sign of trouble. She looked concerned, but not panicked.

"Eph caught sight of something," she told him, nodding to where Emmett was helping his father over a massive stump. Aaron watched the two men navigate to a small bundle of what looked like young fir trees.

"Something alive?" Aaron guessed. Nyla's mouth twitched in amusement.

"If it was alive, we'd probably never see it," she said, gesturing around them at nothing in particular. "Animals are masters at keeping to themselves. They'll know we're here long before we catch on. Honestly, we've probably come close to dozens of animals on the way here and had no idea."

"That's not creepy at all," Pratt grumbled from behind them. Nyla smiled.

"What are we following anyway?" Aaron asked, still watching Ephraim and Emmett as they inspected the young trees. Nyla shifted his attention to something a little closer, a bush of some kind.

"Predatory animals are notoriously hard to track," she said, shuffling closer to him until her hip pressed against his thigh. Aaron tried to keep his focus on her words. "Especially in this kind of environment. The underbrush acts as a carpet, masking most of the tracks, but there are other things we can look out for: tufts of fur, broken branches, trampled leaves, discarded teeth or claws, scratch marks, urine, dung, blood, any sign at all that means an animal has passed through here.

"The problem," Nyla bit her lip, "is without any idea what kind of animal we're looking for, we can't narrow down the kinds of tracks we should be focusing on."

"So, we've been wandering aimlessly for hours?"

Aaron shot Pratt an annoyed look.

"Not aimlessly," Nyla assured him, nodding to Ephraim and Emmett again. "We have one distinct advantage right now."

"Which is?"

"We're following tracks from a kill site," Nyla looked almost nauseated as she said it, pressing on quickly. Aaron smoothed his hand over the fabric of her shirt encouragingly. "And, since Leo's body was found elsewhere, we know he must've been dragged. Any animal would have trouble leaving no trace while carting around the body of a grown man. His— the... the body would've caused a lot of damage to the foliage wherever it was dragged. That's what Ephraim has been following."

"How can you tell?" Aaron furrowed his brow, tilting his head at different angles to examine the bush. "It just looks like a normal bush. What's different about it?"

"I'm no expert," Nyla said, "but if you look closely at the base, you'll see a lot of these stems are bent or snapped. That means something walked over it or pulled something through it to cause this damage. Evidence like this I can pick up on, but Ephraim is a seasoned vet out here. He's been spotting clues I'd never have seen in a million years."

"I think it went this way," Ephraim announced suddenly, standing with Emmett's help. "Bit of old blood here on this fir."

"And the trees ahead have the lower branches snapped off," Emmett added, looking troubled. "I'm starting to wonder if it's not a cougar. The broken branches go at least ten feet up the trunk. That's way too high for a wolf or coyote."

"Cougars aren't that tall?" Pratt gaped, paling. Emmett laughed.

"No, but they can climb."

"Right." Pratt looked away, embarrassed.

"I doubt it's a cougar," Nyla countered, crossing her arms over her chest. "It attacked Leo while I was standing a few feet away. A cougar would've waited until he was alone. Or it would've attacked me when I started walking back to the lodge. Either way, it doesn't make sense."

"If it's sick, it doesn't have to make sense," Ephraim pointed out. Nyla didn't argue, but she didn't look like she fully agreed either.

"We're also assuming the thing that took Leo is the same thing that killed him," Emmett said contemplatively. "It's possible that he was killed at the campsite and then dragged off by a scavenger."

"A scavenger would've only moved him a short distance," Ephraim shot down. "Far enough away to feel safe and no more. No point in exerting so much energy."

"We need to assume that whatever killed him is what took him too," Nyla agreed. "And that it wasn't sick, or at least had some sense about it. We won't get anywhere if we don't look for *some* kind of pattern."

"Well, can we try to narrow this down?" Aaron tried, glancing between Emmett, Nyla, and Ephraim. The area of the forest they were gathered in wasn't exactly a clearing, but it was wide enough that they didn't need to cluster together. The sun filtered through the trees overhead, making Aaron's forehead sweat. "We've been tracking this thing for a while now. What have we learned?"

"It's an ambush predator," Nyla supplied helpfully. "I had no idea it was there until it attacked."

"Which means it probably hunts alone," Ephraim continued. "Something that works in a pack wouldn't need to sneak around like that. Not to mention, if there were others present, they would've attacked Nyla too."

"They probably would've attacked me first," she said assertively. Nyla held her arms out, displaying her stature to illustrate her point. "I'm smaller than Leo. Visually, I would've been the easier target."

Aaron felt a surge of discomfort at that thought.

"It was likely stalking Leo for some time, then." Emmett paused to stomp down a twig that was sticking up next to his boot, the sound echoing through the air. Aaron instinctively scanned the trees, but nothing appeared to have been summoned by the noise. "Okay. A solitary, ambush predator. Cougar sure is sounding good right about now."

"That still doesn't explain why it targeted Leo over me."

"Maybe it didn't know you were there?" Aaron guessed. He wasn't shy about the fact that he wasn't versed in wilderness survival. He knew even less about animals. Nyla shook her head.

"We'd been talking for a while by that point," she said. "It definitely knew I was there. Actually, it was like it waited for Leo to come out of the tent. Like it was specifically hunting him."

"Animals don't think like that," Ephraim muttered. "They don't single out targets for any reason other than ease of hunting. Sick, injured, small, slow, young... none of those apply to Leo. If we're tabling the sick theory for now, then it must've had another reason to go after him and not you."

"What direction did it attack from, Nyla?" Emmett prodded. She thought for a moment.

"It was hard to tell, but I think from behind Leo."

"That could be it," he continued. "If you were talking to him, then you were likely facing him. If the animal was behind him ready to attack, then you would've been facing it too."

"Animals will usually attack from behind if their prey is larger or stronger than them." Nyla pursed her lips in thought. Aaron was taking mental notes as quickly as he could, but this was foreign to him. He couldn't help feeling a surge of admiration for the sheer amount of knowledge Nyla carried with her, even if she claimed she wasn't an expert.

"This thing had to have been huge. It grabbed Leo and moved him out of my sight in less than a few seconds. Maybe it's weak relative to its size?"

"Can't be that weak if it hauled Leo all this way," Ephraim grumbled. "Could it have been smaller than you thought?"

"I mean it's possible," Nyla relented. "It was dark and raining. I didn't see exactly what happened."

"I'm telling you, cougar."

"Would you drop the cougar thing?" Ephraim reprimanded, scowling at his son. "We don't know enough to say anything for certain right now. Which direction are we heading in, Nyla?"

Aaron watched Nyla as she checked her watch, which had a small compass embedded in its face.

"If we keep going this way, it'll bring us to..." She paused, thinking. "Jackrabbit Falls? That doesn't make any sense."

"Why not?" Aaron prompted. Nyla looked up at him, her concern growing.

"Leo's body was found in the complete opposite direction."

"Have we been following the wrong tracks?" Pratt wondered aloud. Nyla began to shake her head, looking to Ephraim first to confirm. He nodded.

"We're following the *only* tracks," he clarified. "If this isn't what killed Leo, or at least what moved him, then it wasn't an animal. And if it was a human, they're comfortable in the forest. Comfortable enough to kill a man and make off with his body without leaving a trace."

"That, or they stumbled across a dead man in the woods and paraded him around like some sort of sick show and tell," Emmett said with disgust. Aaron wasn't sure which option was worse.

"A human didn't kill him," Nyla insisted, her voice brittle. "I don't know what happened after he died, but I can promise you that whatever that thing was doing to him, it couldn't have been done by a person. No way."

An ominous silence descended, one that no one was eager to break.

"We should keep following the trail," Pratt said eventually, catching Aaron's eye. "If we can, we should definitively rule out an animal perpetrator."

"We can only go for another couple of hours before we'll start losing daylight," Nyla said, squinting at the sky. "If we don't find it by... 4:30, we'll have to turn around or prepare to make camp before the sun goes down."

"Alright, that gives us another two hours of searching." Ephraim adjusted his pack, declining Emmett's offer to take it. "Let's do what we can and make a decision closer to that time."

As their group began to shuffle along, Pratt sped up to speak to Ephraim and Emmett, likely about the probability of finding anything they could use. Aaron remained next to Nyla, offering his arm to help her over a jutting tree stump. He mentally chastised himself immediately— Nyla was the last person here who'd need help navigating the terrain— but she spared him the embarrassment by accepting the help anyway.

"How are you holding up, Suits?" Nyla teased, falling into step with the rhythm of the rocky ground. Aaron rolled his eyes, doing his best to hide his labored breathing.

"I'll live," he promised. "I'm more concerned about what we've found so far. Or... what we haven't, I suppose."

Nyla nodded silently, gazing off into the trees.

"What's bothering you?" Aaron prodded, slowing to put just a touch of distance between them and the rest of the group. Not far enough to lose sight of in an emergency, but enough to avoid being overheard. "You look like you're lost in thought."

"I am," she admitted, scrunching her nose. It was growing red in the chilled air, and Aaron couldn't deny that it looked adorable even if it meant she was uncomfortable. He wished he had a jacket to offer her. "I'm trying to make sense of everything and I'm failing. It's irritating."

"Talk me through it," Aaron offered quickly. He thought he heard Pratt chuckle, but he couldn't possibly have heard his eagerness. He told himself it was unrelated.

"It's about the attack," Nyla answered absently, checking the direction of her compass again. "What we talked about back there was all true. Ambush predator, strong, solitary, maybe on the small side, but a couple of pieces aren't falling into place. I know Emmett said it didn't have to make sense if it was sick, but... I don't know. I just can't shake it."

"You mean the moving of the body?" Aaron guessed. Nyla shrugged her shoulder.

"That, but not *just* that. It would be strange for a predator of any kind to make a kill and eat so little of it. Hunting takes energy, energy that is intended to be refreshed once the hunt is over. Even if we assume that an animal killed Leo and a human moved him, that doesn't explain why he wasn't at least partially consumed."

"So," Aaron mused, "if it didn't kill these hunters for food, then why?"

"That's the part I'm stuck on," Nyla agreed. "Territory would be my first assumption. Leo was killed by a territorial animal, and someone took advantage of that."

"Is that a plausible thing to have happened 7 times?" Aaron asked doubtfully. Nyla shook her head.

"Unless a new animal has moved in and declared the Basin as its home and is killing every hunter that sets up camp there, then no," Nyla clarified, sniffling. "And even that is extremely unlikely."

"You said something about the *attack* was bothering you," Aaron reminded her, glancing up as the sky darkened above them. They hadn't used much of their two-hour window, but he was starting to wonder if it was shortening. The grey cloud cover screamed approaching weather, the temperature dropping at least a few degrees, and Aaron didn't want to be caught out in a storm. "Not the kill, the attack. What happened that's sticking out to you?"

"Sometimes I hate that you're an investigator," Nyla muttered. "Fine. Ambush predators have a pretty common approach, even if their methods are different. Sneak up, take their prey off guard, and go in for a quick kill. Usually it's a bite to somewhere vital, like the neck."

"But?"

"But," Nyla sighed, "whatever attacked Leo didn't go in for the kill bite immediately."

"How do you know?"

"I heard him," Nyla admitted, voice shaking. "When I was running back to the lodge. Leo started screaming."

Aaron slowed, absorbing this. Maybe it was the ominous implications of Nyla's observation, but Aaron could swear it was getting colder as they walked.

"Maybe it couldn't kill him right away?" he suggested, hating the gaunt look on Nyla's face. He'd give anything to change the topic, even knowing this was necessary. "It attacked him with the intent to kill, but Leo survived the initial impact and, once the animal realized, it finished him off?"

"Maybe," Nyla said quietly. He was about to offer her comfort of some kind, whatever he could think of, when a sharp pinprick of water harpooned his eye.

"Ah, shit," Aaron hissed, wiping the drop away. Nyla looked up at the sky, and her face soured. Her palms ran up the outsides of her arms, soothing the goosebumps that appeared there. Aaron wasn't just imagining things, then. It *was* getting colder. Nyla had donned a loose cotton button-up before they left the lodge, but it clearly wasn't doing much to protect her against the sudden breeze. Again, he wished he had a jacket for her.

"We need to turn around," she announced, loudly enough for the entire group to hear. In seconds, the clouds had moved in aggressively, blocking the residual light of the sun. Aaron felt a clench of fear at the promise of how dark it could get. "Weather is coming in fast."

That was an understatement. In only a few moments, it felt to Aaron like an entire season had passed. He almost expected to see his breath cloud in front of his face as he exhaled. Ephraim and Emmett looked up as well, agreeing with Nyla's assessment. Nyla and Aaron stayed put, waiting for Emmett, Ephraim, and Pratt to make their way back over the short distance that separated them.

The sky roiled, like billowing smoke high above the trees. Aaron instinctively stepped closer to Nyla, his entire body on high alert. Something wasn't right.

"Do storms come in this fast all the time?" Aaron asked, never tearing his gaze away from their surroundings. He was fighting off shakes now, his muscles tensing as the air around them plummeted to freezing temperatures. Nyla wasn't even wearing proper pants, he couldn't imagine how she wasn't shivering uncontrollably in her shorts. She didn't answer his question, but she didn't need to. The troubled look on her face told him enough.

The cold spread through them, jarring and sharp. The hairs on the back of Aaron's neck shot up, and the presence of danger suddenly screamed through his veins. Before he really knew what was happening, Aaron grabbed Nyla and yanked her to the ground beneath him just as a deafening crack sounded through the trees.

"Em—!" Nyla's cry was cut short as Aaron's hand clamped over her mouth, staring in disbelief and horror at the scene unfolding in front of them. Aaron's first thought was that the crack had been thunder or lightning from the building storm. He saw now that he was wrong.

Young trees snapped and splintered from a shadowed grove to their right, following slowly after the massive oak that had toppled just a few feet from where Aaron and Nyla were standing seconds ago. The base was shredded, its thick bark sliced into wildly curled ribbons of wood shavings from the powerful impact of something very, very sharp.

Nyla gasped into his palm, and that's when Aaron finally saw it.

At first, Aaron thought it was a trick of the light; some odd combination of shadows and shapes refracting what little sun they had left into a feral, misshapen beast lurking beneath the canopy of shuddering leaves. It couldn't be real, whatever it was. He had to be seeing things. Had to be in shock, or perhaps he'd hit his head—

And then it moved.

Inexplicably, the pool of darkness rippled like waves on the surface of a lake, revealing the outline of something very much alive. Without the sun to illuminate the creature, Aaron could only see a handful of details; it had four limbs, a hunched, skeletal torso, and an angular head with some kind of adornment he couldn't make out in the low light.

It was also right on top of them.

All of the breath left Aaron's lungs at once, leaving him frozen in place. The creature was only a few feet from them, skulking through the underbrush. Aaron couldn't risk getting his gun, it would be on them before he so much as flipped the safety. They couldn't run, not with so little distance separating them from the threat. Aaron ran through every possible scenario in his mind, dismissing them all one by one. Just when he was about to give up and try for his gun, the forest rang out with another crack, this one quieter and more recognizable.

"Aaron! Nyla!" Pratt's voice echoed off the baren trunks, making it difficult to pinpoint where he was even after his shot. "RUN!"

The creature darted away from them, presumably towards Pratt and his weapon. Nyla tensed, like she was preparing to spring, and Aaron tightened his hold on her. He'd seen witnesses run headfirst into dangerous situations, desperate to save their loved ones at any cost. He couldn't let Nyla do that. Aaron knew the best chance that any of them had for survival was to retreat. Pratt knew this too, and Aaron trusted him to convey the instruction to Ephraim and Emmett. Right now, Aaron had a job to do.

He didn't wait for Nyla to make another move; Aaron pushed himself into a crouch, grabbed her upper arm, and launched himself in the opposite direction of whatever that thing was.

An inhuman roar sounded behind them, close enough to make Aaron's heart skip, rattling his already shivering bones. The air pelted his face with tiny pricks of ice, melting on contact into chilled rain.

"No you fucking don't," Pratt growled, another shot ricocheting off what sounded like a rock. His voice was quieter now, farther away. The creature moved toward him again, away from Nyla and Aaron. "Over here, you ugly bastard!"

Another shot, this one clearly from the barrel of a hunting rifle.

"Get back to the lodge!" The shout came from another male voice in a different direction, and it took Aaron a second to realize that it was Emmett. "We'll meet you there!"

"You'd better!" Nyla threatened, panic and cold making her words shake.

"Be careful!" Ephraim added, from yet another direction. Suddenly, Aaron realized what they were doing. They were distracting it, confusing it, spinning its attention in circles so they could all get away.

Another shot, and then Aaron's boot slid out from underneath him. His body lurched forward, dragging Nyla with him as they toppled over a short ledge. Nyla dug her heels into the mud as they landed, desperately trying to stay on her feet. Aaron fell to his knee, pain zinging up the right side of his body.

"This way," Nyla instructed, ripping her arm out of his grip to snatch his fingers in a vice. She tore through the trees with purpose, and Aaron was helpless to do anything but blindly follow.

They were running downhill, that's all Aaron could tell from the limited view he had of their surroundings. Impossibly, the world was getting darker, blotting out any and all light left from the day. Nyla paused for only a second, breathing hard, before deciding on a direction and taking off again. Aaron kept as close to her as he could, gripping her hand back with enough ferocity to splinter bone.

That thing was still out there. He could hear it snapping through the underbrush. He just couldn't tell which way it was going.

"The river," Nyla announced suddenly, breathless. "We need to run through the water. It won't be able to—!"

Another crash cut her off, and a hulking shadow barreled toward them. A symphony of cracks echoed through the forest, like wood snapping in a lively fire or ice fracturing beneath their weight.

The creature lunged at them, limbs akimbo, stretching its misshapen hand to the side in preparation to strike. Each uneven jerk of its legs released another chorus of snaps, but Aaron didn't have time to examine the cause. The thing was nearly on top of them, its clawed feet leaving deep gashes in the dirt. Nyla was closer to it than he was, directly in the line of its swipe. Aaron's instincts took over, moving without thought.

Aaron threw himself in front of her, tearing his gun from its holster, raising it, and firing all in one fluid motion. The bullet connected, but so did the creature's claws. Aaron heard Nyla scream as a white-hot, burning pain lanced through his ribs. He stumbled backward, his back thudding against Nyla's front. She wrapped her arms around his stomach, catching him, pulling him back and away from the creature as it reeled and screeched.

"Shoot again!" Nyla gasped, hauling desperately on his faltering body. Aaron raised the gun in one hand, doing his best to aim at the writhing shadows in front of him. He fired another two rounds before the strength in his arm gave out and he had to relent.

"Come on, hurry!" Nyla pleaded, tugging him back a few more steps. Recovering from the shock of his injury, Aaron gathered his balance enough to follow her. As soon as she saw he was with her, she launched herself over a fallen tree and down into a dip in the terrain. There, barely visible in the dark, was the beginning trickle of a stream.

Aaron bit back a wince as he tore after Nyla, splashing through the tiny brook. The creature would surely hear them, but it didn't matter. It knew where they were already. Nyla guided him along the trail of water as it widened into something more substantial, something resembling a river and, eventually, a small lake. They skirted the edge, never venturing deeper than a few inches of water.

The creature was still following them, slower. Aaron could hear the angry rustle of detritus as it loped toward them, hindered by whatever injuries he'd managed to inflict. Could it swim? If they dove into the lake, would they be safe?

"There!" Nyla announced suddenly, taking a sharp turn into the water. Aaron stumbled after her, supposing they were about to find out if the thing was aquatic. He couldn't see what she was pointing at, but he trusted her.

Just as they reached hip depth, the sky opened.

Aaron faltered under the intensity of the rain, wincing again as pain shot through his torso. Nyla reached back for him, tugging him through the water toward something that looked like a rock. As they got closer, he could see it was a small crevice, partially submerged and barely big enough to cover them.

But it was hidden. Hidden, and surrounded by water. With luck, the creature wouldn't be able to scent them here, nor see them through the rain and shelter of the rocks.

It was a long shot, and it was all they had.

Nyla slipped herself into the crevice, pulling Aaron in after her. He held his breath against the pain of pressing his wound against the rocks, willing his heart to slow and his breath to quiet. Nyla twisted her fingers in his shirt, huddling close to keep him steady on the uneven lake floor. Aaron wrapped his arms around her, his hand cradling the back of her head, holding her against him and turning so that she was further sheltered by the small cave. If the creature found them, he didn't want her to see whatever would happen to him.

Aaron's gun was still loosely clutched in his left hand, the one around Nyla's shoulders. He wasn't sure if he could kill that thing, but he knew something without a shadow of a doubt.

He had 3 bullets left, and he'd use every single one of them to protect the woman in his arms.

Chapter Twenty-Two

NYLA

They were silent for so long that Nyla's throat felt dry.

It seemed like hours that she'd been here, crammed into this poor excuse for a cave, pressed so tightly against Aaron that she could feel the steady thrum of his heartbeat in her cheek. Her ears felt like they were filled with cotton from straining to hear any sign of the... 'thing' that stalked them. The forest was working against them, filling the air with the overwhelming sounds of the storm, drowning out everything but the rain, wind, thunder, and stirring leaves. Even still, once they'd waited so long that Nyla's legs were cramping, her soaked shirt had dried and itched her skin, her loose waves hung in clumps around her face, and she'd lost feeling in her toes, they had to accept that for the moment they were safe.

Aaron came to the realization at the same time she had, lowering his head to press his lips against her ear.

"Are you okay?" His voice scratched from his throat, low and strained from exertion. Nyla nodded mutely, tilting her head back to squint at him in the dark.

Normally, she wouldn't be able to see anything at all this far into the woods with no moonlight. As it happened, her watch had a night mode. It wasn't perfect, just enough for her to make out the familiar shapes of Aaron's face inches from hers.

"What *was* that thing?" she heard herself ask. Aaron shook his head gently.

"I was hoping you could tell me."

"I've never seen anything like that before," Nyla murmured, feeling a shudder run through her at the memory. Even now, free from the distortion of adrenaline, Nyla couldn't come up with a clear picture of what the creature looked like. It was as if she'd seen it through water or shadow, obscuring its true shape. Aaron's arm tightened around her shoulders, and he winced. Nyla's attention shot to him.

"You're hurt," she remembered suddenly, trying in vain to back away from him. The space didn't allow it, and neither did Aaron's grip on her. "Aaron, I need to look at it!"

"I'll be fine until we get out of this," he promised, but the strength of his voice wasn't convincing. Nyla loosed her fingers from his shirt, feeling gently along the curve of his chest until she found torn fabric. Aaron flinched, her fingertips snagging on something warm and wet.

"You're bleeding!" Nyla accused, her heart dropping into her stomach. "Fuck, Aaron. Why didn't you say anything? I have a flashlight on my watch, let me—"

"We can't risk being spotted by it," Aaron ground out. "Nyla, I'll be fine. I've been injured in the field before."

"Like this?"

His answering silence told her enough.

"Aaron," she implored him, laying her free hand gingerly against his cheek. "We're probably going to be stuck here for a while. I need to make sure you won't bleed out on me."

He held her gaze for a breath, but Nyla could see the fight leaving him. That worried her; he must be in a lot of pain.

"Cover the light with your hand," he told her begrudgingly, releasing her so she could maneuver around him to see properly. "The glow will attract less attention."

"Yes, sir," Nyla mocked. With her watch held carefully smothered by her index finger, Nyla turned the flashlight on and had to stifle a gasp.

The left side of Aaron's torso looked like it'd been through a massive paper shredder. His shirt was slashed from the shoulder to the base of his ribs, threads of fabric sticking to his open wounds. Nyla brought the flashlight closer, trying to get a better look, but everything was red and blending. Cautiously, she used one of the torn edges of his shirt to dab away at the blood. Aaron sucked in a sharp breath.

"I need to clean this," she told him, trying to keep the severity of the situation out of her voice. She didn't know if she succeeded. "This is a lake that runs into a river, so the water should be clean. I'd use my drinking water, but..."

But she'd lost it. Both of their packs had gone missing in their escape.

"Can't be any worse than the muck I've already got all over me," Aaron said sarcastically. Nyla couldn't disagree.

"This is going to hurt," she promised, and Aaron nodded curtly. Setting her jaw, Nyla ripped the arm off her button-up, rinsed it off as best she could, and set to work.

"Fuck," Aaron cursed, his entire body going tense as Nyla coaxed the blood from his skin. As the red dissipated, she could make out five jagged gashes stretching from the top of his shoulder, down his arm, and across his ribs. The gashes were disjointed with Aaron standing like this, but Nyla was sure if he held his arm up as if to shoot his gun, she'd see the gashes line up in the shape of claw marks. More worryingly, as the blood eased away from his injury, Nyla noticed that the colour of his skin wasn't what it should be. For one stricken moment, she wondered if the thing's claws were tipped with venom. Upon closer scrutiny, she realized she'd seen this coloration before.

The skin around Aaron's wounds had gone deathly white, standing out in stark contrast against the red blood. Nyla knew what she was looking at, but she couldn't make sense of it.

The slashes were edged by frostbite.

"Okay, I have to bind it now," she announced, keeping the strange detail to herself. There was still blood caked on him, but Nyla didn't want to push her luck too far. If she dislodged some of the bigger clots that had already formed, she was afraid he'd bleed out. Aaron nodded, his expression pinched.

Nyla ripped at the seams of her button-up, making it into a roughly shaped bandage. With Aaron's help, she wrapped it around his chest and over the worst of the injury. She couldn't cover it all from this angle, but she could get enough. More importantly, the frostbite was no longer visible.

"Ready?" she murmured, pulling softly on the ends of the bandage to tell him what she was about to do. Aaron remained silent, preparing himself. "Alright, on three. One, two..."

With a firm yank, Nyla tightened the ends of her shredded shirt into a knot. The bandage constricted Aaron's wound, dispelling a guttural groan from his chest.

"You're okay," Nyla soothed, moving back into their original positions so Aaron could collapse against the rock wall. "That will hold until we get back to the lodge, at least. You'll need to go to the hospital."

"We can't move yet," he gasped, adjusting to the pain. "It's pitch black, and we don't know where that creature went."

"It's probably nocturnal," Nyla guessed, thinking back to the moments before they were attacked. "I think it was following us for a while but didn't reveal itself until the storm moved in. I don't know about the other hunters, but Leo was killed at night. If I had to guess, it's probably sensitive to light so it can't hunt in the sun."

"So, we're here until morning?" Aaron concluded, tipping his head back onto the rock. "Great. What time is it now?"

"You don't want to know," Nyla vowed, remembering the time she saw on her watch when she turned off the flashlight. "Earlier than it should be. We're going to be here for a long time."

"How cold will it get?" Aaron asked, apparently heeding her advice on the time. "Are we going to freeze?"

"It gets chilly, not enough that we'd have to worry..." she trailed off, biting her lip. Nyla realized as the words left her that she didn't know if they were true anymore. Between the unnatural cold that accompanied the storm and the inexplicable frostbite on Aaron's ribs, she couldn't definitively say that they needn't worry. Aaron lifted his head again to look at her.

"But?"

"But we're soaked," Nyla pointed out, settling on the least odd problem they faced. "We can't stay in the water all night. We're already colder than we should be."

"We can't go out there," Aaron argued. "We'd be sitting ducks."

"It wouldn't matter anyway," Nyla agreed. "It's still raining. It's not like we'd be any drier out there."

"So, what do we do?"

That was a great question.

Nyla looked around the small space. It was far too cramped, smaller than even a broom closet should be. If Aaron and Nyla pressed as tightly as they could against opposite walls, they'd still be touching. Nyla stretched her arm above her head as high as she could reach. They had some headroom, but that wouldn't do them much good—

"Wait," Nyla twisted her arm around to feel behind her. "There's a ledge here."

"How big is it?" Aaron squinted, but it was too dark for either of them to see.

"I don't know, I'll check." Pivoting, Nyla braced her boot on a submerged rock, using the ledge to pull herself out of the water enough to poke her head above the ledge. "I'm going to turn on the flashlight again for a second."

"Hurry."

She did, illuminating the crevice just long enough to blink.

"It's small," she concluded. "I don't know if we'll be able to fit comfortably, but I think we can wedge ourselves in there if you go up first. Then I can use my legs to brace myself against the opposite wall."

"Climb up," Aaron said, coughing. "I'll be fine down here."

"Like hell," Nyla scoffed incredulously. "Aaron, you almost lost your arm. If you spend the night in the water, I'm going to be dragging your body all the way into town."

"Someone has to keep watch in case the creature comes back," Aaron insisted. "If we're both crammed onto that ledge, we'll be completely vulnerable. Down here, I can still use my gun."

"Give me the gun," Nyla shot back. "If I'm on the outside and my legs are hanging over, I should have a decent shot."

"No."

"Aaron—"

"I'm not going to let anything happen to you, Nyla." Aaron snapped. Nyla dropped back into the water, forgetting for a moment that she was supposed to be quiet and letting the splash reflect her frustration.

"Either we both get out of this alive, or neither of us does." She poked him hard in the uninjured portion of his chest in lieu of planting her hands on her hips, knowing he wouldn't be able to see the latter. "I own a *hunting* lodge, Suits. My aim is better than most. If it comes back, I'll hit it. I can promise you that."

Aaron held her glare, but Nyla wouldn't relent. Eventually, he sighed.

"Fine," he huffed, doing his best to pull himself up onto the ledge. Nyla had to help him to compensate for his shoulder, then did as she promised, shimmying up the wall behind him. She turned to plant her feet on the opposite side of the crevice, when suddenly Aaron's arm snagged her waist, hauling her back against him.

"Aaron!" she hissed. "Your wound!"

"This is my compromise," he told her. "You keep the gun, I support you. Deal?"

Nyla wanted to argue, but she didn't have the energy.

"You're infuriating," she grumbled instead, still bracing one leg on the opposite wall to alleviate some of the pressure on Aaron's arm. She was sure he smirked, but in the dark, she couldn't be sure.

"Any point in telling you to get some sleep?"

"Not a chance."

"Didn't think so." Nyla sighed. "Settle in, Suits. We're in for a long night."

Nyla didn't think she slept. She just remembered blinking to the sound of rain and opening her eyes to find none falling. A glance at her watch told her that it was just before sunrise, and for a terrifying moment, she wondered if the clouds would clear enough for them to get to safety. Aaron's breathing was labored behind her, and she didn't think he'd last another night in the cold, wet mountain forest.

She couldn't think about that right now, though. Worrying about Aaron wouldn't help.

At some point in the middle of the night, Nyla discovered she still had her walkie. It was wedged in her shorts pocket, dented and soaked through, but it was possible it still worked. She hadn't been brave enough to test it yet, though. For one, the creature could be anywhere, and the sound of a walkie might attract it. Secondly, even if they were safe enough to use it, that didn't mean Emmett and the others were. Nyla would never forgive herself if she gave them away in a misguided attempt at reaching out to them.

Slowly, much slower than she would've wanted, light began to penetrate the heavy darkness.

The time on her watch was about thirty minutes past daybreak, so the clouds must've been hanging around. With any luck, they'd continue to dissipate, but Nyla didn't want to take any chances. They had to move now, while they still could.

"Aaron?" Nyla murmured, nudging his thigh gently with her elbow. He'd fallen asleep despite his best efforts, but she wasn't sure how rested he'd be. "Aaron, come on. It's morning."

He groaned, swallowing it with a sharp gasp as he struggled to sit up. Nyla laid her hand firmly on his good shoulder, pressing him back down.

"Relax, we're fine," she insisted, shifting so her legs were poised above the water. "I'm going to get down and scope it out. Join me when you can."

"Wait," Aaron protested, clearing his throat from the strain of poor sleep. "I'm coming with you."

"Suit yourself," she shrugged, knowing there was no point in arguing. Her socks were astoundingly still damp from the night before, so when Nyla's boots sunk into the brackish water, it was less of a shock than she expected. Still, the drop in temperature sent a chill through her bones, and the thought of the Willow's mediocre bathtub situation suddenly felt like the peak of luxury.

She couldn't think about the cold too long, though. It brought up questions she wasn't yet ready to answer.

The world outside the rock crevice felt almost alien to her now. The forest was waking as they were, birdsong and the whispers of wildlife surrounding them in a comforting blanket. Nyla released her anxiety with a deep breath— for now, they were safe. It was only when the woods went quiet that she knew she needed to worry.

"Never thought I'd miss the smell of air pollution," Aaron announced, joining her on the shore. Nyla laughed, relishing in the absence of tension in her soul for the first time in nearly 24 hours. "No offense, but I could go the rest of my life without ever seeing another tree."

"Unfortunately for you," Nyla pointed out, "we have about four hours of looking at trees before we're within driving distance of a hospital. How's your arm?"

Aaron tested his range of movement with tentative stretches and fidgets. Nyla watched, trying to keep the worried expression from her face. After a few successful shoulder rolls, Aaron huffed.

"It's not perfect, but it's better." He tugged on the ends of the makeshift bandage, wincing slightly as he did so. "I don't think anything's broken. Just... slashed."

"You need stitches," Nyla frowned. "By the time we get you to a doctor, I don't know how much they'll be able to help."

"Let's focus on getting back to the lodge first," Aaron said. He held his hand out, taking the gun from Nyla. "We'll worry about the rest later."

Nyla was more worried about the vast number of infections Aaron could've contracted from their flight through the muck, but she didn't voice that concern just now. It wouldn't be helpful.

The walk back to the lodge was blessedly uneventful. Aaron grew stronger with some air and exercise, and Nyla was even able to snag him something to eat when they came across a patch of wild strawberries. Despite the panic that lanced through her when he was hurt, it did seem like it was nothing more than a surface injury at its core. By the time the lodge was in sight, Aaron was mostly back to himself.

"Go straight to the car," Nyla instructed, racing to the front door of the lobby to grab her keys. "I'm just going to—"

A blaring alarm sounded, startling her so badly that she dropped the spare key she was reaching for in the mailbox.

"What the hell is that?" Aaron was beside her in an instant, but Nyla had regained her wits. The walkie rang out harshly in the clear air, proving that it very much still worked.

"Nyla? Are you there?"

"Emmett!" Nyla pressed the call button in relief, clutching the walkie until her knuckles turned white. "Are you okay? Where's Eph? Pratt?"

"We're fine," Emmett promised, sending shockwaves of relief through her. *"Dad's a bit worse for wear but he'll live. Is Klein with you?"*

"I'm here," Aaron announced. "Are any of you injured?"

"We're mostly okay. I'm not sure about Pratt, we got separated from him last night. He was fine when we last saw him."

"Where did he go?" Aaron demanded.

"I'm not sure," Emmett paused, just long enough to make Nyla think the connection faltered. *"We tried to point out which direction would bring him back to Somerton, but I don't know if he understood."*

"Are you not in Somerton?" Nyla pressed.

"That thing chased us all the way down past King's Ledge. We managed to hole up in an abandoned bear den for the night, but we're closer to Lichen House than we are to the Willow. We're heading there now. Listen, we think the creature is nocturnal."

"So do we," Nyla agreed, entering the lodge as she spoke to Emmett. "It chased us to Dodson's Lake. We shook it by wading through the water."

"Lost your scent, or can't swim?"

"I'm not sure," Nyla admitted. "It was too far back to see us jump into the lake, and it was raining by the time it would've caught up. I wouldn't place my bets on either right now."

"*Jesus...*" Emmett's voice trailed off. "*Nyla, what was that thing? What do we do?*"

She was just wondering the same thing.

"*We* don't do anything," she corrected. "You take care of Eph and stay out of the forest after dark. This is my problem that I dragged you into, and you've more than done your part. Stay home, stay safe, and I'll figure out what to do from here."

"*Nyla—*"

"I'm serious, Em," Nyla snapped. "You've already helped more than you needed to. If anything happens to you, there won't be anyone to help your dad, so stay out of this. Are we clear?"

The line was silent.

"Emmett?" Aaron interrupted suddenly. Nyla hadn't realized he'd followed her inside. "I'll take care of her. Nothing will happen to Nyla on my watch, you have my word."

"*I'm holding you to that.*" Emmett sighed. "*For the love of God, Nyla, be careful, alright? Both of you. Don't do anything stupid and get yourselves killed.*"

"I make no promises."

"I'll make her promises for her," Aaron said, rolling his eyes.

"*That includes self-sacrifices, Klein.*" Emmett cut in. "*I want to take* both *of you out for a well-earned drink after this.*"

"He's got you there." Nyla smirked. Aaron scowled.

After another bout of well wishes, the line disconnected.

"Well, at least we have two less people to worry about," Nyla said, grabbing her car keys from her desk drawer.

"Pratt will be fine," Aaron assured her, and he sounded like he meant it. "The creature went after us and then it sounds like it doubled back to go after Emmett and Ephraim. That means it probably couldn't find Pratt."

"That doesn't mean he's safe," Nyla reminded him, not wanting to be a downer but needing to make their situation clear. "Wilderness survival isn't intuitive. There are other predators, exposure risks, dangerous terrain... we need to send out a search party for him as soon as possible."

"I'll need to update Kelley on what's happened," he agreed. "I'll tell her what's going on with Pratt. She'll handle it."

"And the creature?"

Aaron paused, considering.

"I don't know if she'll believe everything," he decided eventually. "But she'll believe enough. She has to."

Chapter Twenty-Three

NYLA

It was night by the time they left the hospital.

Aaron called Kelley from the emergency room, asking her to meet them there. As Nyla feared, they took too long to get Aaron to a doctor, so stitches wouldn't do much good for him now. The frostbite couldn't be hidden from him anymore, and both Aaron and the doctor had looked a little bewildered at that revelation. Luckily, the frostbite hadn't set in too severely and had mostly healed by the time Aaron was treated. He was going to have a nasty scar. They cleaned the wound as best they could, treated him for a few diseases and infections, and sent them on their way with a dose of preventative antibiotics. Kelley met them in the parking lot just as they were exiting the building, and they did their best to explain.

Nyla kept mostly quiet. She didn't know Kelley, and she didn't want to sound like she was influencing Aaron's retelling at all. She supplied details when Aaron's memory faltered, or when it was something to do with tracking or navigating. Otherwise, she let him fill Kelley in. Once it was all out in the open, Nyla could tell that Kelley didn't fully believe their story. To be fair to her, it *was* insane.

"So, this wasn't just a bear?" Kelley guessed. Nyla shook her head.

"No animal I've ever seen looks like that," she promised. "Not even a deformed one. It was... something else entirely."

Kelley fell silent again, thinking hard.

"Did you get anywhere on the human perp angle?"

"No," Kelley said, pushing her hand through her hair. "That's about the only reason I haven't had you both committed. That, and you just went through concussion protocol."

Nyla bit her lip.

"I know you think you saw something unexplainable," Kelley relented, hesitating. "But I can't call in specialists in monsters and ghouls. I'm treating this like a problem animal. I'm going to speak to German and Andrews, tell them what you've told me. There's a wildlife office about two hours away, so we're going to make the trip over, and I'll call you tomorrow morning to discuss the next steps, alright?"

Her tone left no room for arguing, so they didn't. Instead, they thanked Kelley for her help and Nyla brought Aaron back to the lodge.

She couldn't deny the surge of fear she felt as she parked the car as close to the lodge as possible, trying to keep their potential exposure to a minimum. The creature hadn't ventured onto the lodge's property yet as far as she knew, but Nyla didn't want to assume they were safe. Especially since they were alone.

After a long, thorough shower to remove the muck and grime they'd collected over the last 36 hours, Nyla and Aaron decided it was best to set up temporary lodging in the canteen. It was the only room on the property that was big enough to sleep in, had no windows, only one way in or out, and had reasonable access to a bathroom. She felt better locked away in the safety of the canteen, even if it left her no escape from her growing feelings for Aaron.

He'd saved her life yesterday. And he'd nearly lost his in the process. Nyla's chest felt like it would burst with the sheer volume of tumultuous emotions she'd been fighting off since their harrowing escape. Now that they were safe and alone, she couldn't hold back the flood. Aaron had fulfilled every promise he'd made to her since they met— supporting her, believing her, helping her, and now, protecting her. Her heart clenched at the thought.

"Fuck me," Aaron hissed, startling her out of her daydreaming. Nyla blinked, taking a moment to realize he was cursing the bandages wrapped tightly around his chest and arm. "That thing really did a number on me, didn't it?"

"Does it still hurt?" Nyla pressed, instinctively moving to the sink to get him a glass of water. Aaron shook his head, pushing his hand through his mess of wavy locks.

"Only when I move it too fast," he promised, taking the glass gratefully. "I almost wish I'd broken a bone. Heals more cleanly than soft tissue injuries."

"Slower though," Nyla pointed out, seating herself on the counter with her legs crossed. Aaron took care peeling off the new shirt he'd donned when he was finished showering, tossing it to the side in agitation.

"It feels like it's on fire," he explained, although she didn't ask. Nyla thought she saw a faint blush touch his cheeks again. It surprised her that Aaron was the bashful type, but maybe he was just more aware of their precarious situation than he wanted to let on. " Like I'm overheating or something, but just in that area. Like a massive cat scratch."

"It's probably full of bacteria," Nyla mused. "The antibiotics will clear up what your immune system doesn't. You'll be fine."

"Your bedside manner leaves something to be desired." Aaron chuckled, easing himself back onto the bedroll they'd laid out in the middle of the room. He stretched his good arm above his head, the waistband of his lounge pants slipping just enough for Nyla to see the deep 'V' of his hips. She allowed herself to appreciate the sight for a moment, not caring if Aaron caught her. He already knew she was attracted to him.

"Thank you, by the way," Nyla said suddenly, dragging her eyes up Aaron's prone body to find that, yes, he'd noticed her appraisal and, no, he didn't mind it.

"For what?" Aaron prompted, maintaining her stare.

"You saved my life yesterday," she explained. "Don't think I didn't notice."

"You don't need to thank me for that," Aaron dismissed. "I was doing my job. Not to mention, I would've died a hundred times over without your experience."

"Don't flatter yourself too much. I was keeping us both alive," she corrected. "You were the one who went full hero mode."

Aaron barked a laugh, flinching as the act pulled at his injury.

"I'm no hero, Nyla. I serve court summons for a living. It's not exactly glamorous." He paused, thinking. "I might've agreed with you when I worked for the Feds, but not now."

"Why *did* you leave?" Nyla pressed, curiosity gnawing at her. "You're clearly good at what you do, and your team loves you. Why did you move to the private sector?"

"No whiskey this time?" Aaron teased.

"I think we've been through enough together that we can skip it."

For a moment, she didn't think he would agree with her. The silence dragged on, broken only by the sounds of crickets outside.

"I wish I had a more interesting answer for you," Aaron said eventually, his eyes slipping closed as his breathing evened. "I'm sure you're expecting me to tell you about the last case

I worked and how I messed up and got people killed, or I saw some wild shit that broke something inside of me that'll never get fixed. But that's just not what happened.

"The truth is," Aaron shrugged, "I lost my drive. You're right, I *am* good at what I do. People have been telling me that for years, over and over. My parents were so proud of me, always telling people that I was going to make a good life for myself. Like any kid, I felt an obligation to make them happy. I liked the thought of working for the FBI, so that's what I did. And, until recently, I thought I loved my job.

"I didn't *hate* it or anything. It was a good gig. Honestly, I really enjoyed my work until about a year before I quit. It was the stupidest thing. Someone asked me why I did what I did, and I couldn't answer them. I did it because I was good at it and because I wanted to make my parents proud and because anything else felt like I wasn't living up to my potential. At some point... those reasons stopped being enough.

"I'm not jazzed about the PI thing either," he pointed out sardonically. "But it gives me a bit more control over my professional life until I figure out what I do want. I've been flipping back and forth between thinking I'm doing the right thing and telling myself I loved my old job and I'm an idiot for not going back. It's not easy reinventing your life at 35."

"How do your parents feel about it?" Nyla prodded, pushing off the countertop to drop down onto the bedroll next to Aaron. He shifted to give her more room, but he didn't open his eyes or sit up.

"That's the most annoying part," his lips twitched in a half-smile, "they didn't care at all. Dad told me I should come work for him at the office and *Madre* was just happy I'd be around more. My sister Alma told me she hung up the phone and started making *papas rellenas* before she'd even told them what I'd said."

"Papas...?"

"*Papas rellenas*," he repeated. "Bolivian dish my *madre* makes every Sunday. Mashed potato, boiled eggs, some other stuff. It's my favourite."

"Your family sounds lovely." Nyla grinned wistfully. "I've only got my dad, and he's great but I haven't seen him in about a year. He lives in Philly and works away on rotation, so it's hard to meet up regularly."

"Don't tell my mom that," Aaron smirked, "she'll all but adopt you. Alma is my only sister, but *Madre* always wanted more girls in the family."

"I guess you'll just have to hurry up and meet one," Nyla teased, pretending to examine her nails. Aaron laughed fully this time, ignoring the sting of his cuts.

"Was that an obvious attempt at steering the topic in an inappropriate direction?" Aaron taunted. "I didn't know you were a fisher, Miss Jameson."

"Not inappropriate," Nyla defended, risking a glance at Aaron's face. He was watching her with a soft smile curving his lips, his blue eyes sparkling in the lantern light. "You're single, I'm single, we just survived a near-death experience together…"

He quirked a brow, waiting for her to finish.

"I like you," she continued brazenly. "You like me, and you're already half-naked. Honestly, it's a miracle the conversation didn't get here quicker."

Aaron laughed again, carefully propping himself up on his good elbow.

"I thought you said you'd never ask me to risk my job?" His voice dropped low in his throat, warm and inviting like a lit hearth in winter. "Don't tell me you're going back on your word."

"I haven't asked you to do anything," she rebutted. "Besides, you just told me you don't want your job anymore. So, what's the harm?"

"You make a compelling argument, Miss Jameson," Aaron murmured, his attention flickering to her lips.

"I have a tendency to," she smirked. They locked eyes again, Aaron's darkening as Nyla let her desire bubble to the surface. "Where do we go from here?"

"We shouldn't 'go' anywhere," Aaron argued softly. "Nothing's changed, Nyla. Not really. Sleeping with you will wreck my professional reputation, nightmare creature or no nightmare creature."

She froze, disappointment crashing through her like water dousing a flame. She began to pull back, to stand and retreat to the bathroom for a moment to collect herself, but Aaron's hand caught the back of her neck in a firm but careful grip. Nyla sucked in a breath as he pulled her to him, his breath ghosting softly across her lips as he spoke.

"Luckily for me," he murmured, "after what we've been through today, I couldn't care less about my reputation."

He kissed her before she understood what was happening. When she did, Nyla was already swept up in him.

Aaron's kiss was slow and confident, deliberately stoking her desire into a thrumming electric spark through her veins. Nyla hummed in satisfaction, tucking her hair behind her ear and easing into the gentle movement of Aaron's lips. His hand captured her waist, tugging her closer, tightening his grip in time with the tantalizing sweeps of his tongue against hers.

They were interrupted by a pained gasp from Aaron, wincing as their movements pulled at his bandages.

"You've caught me at a disadvantage." Aaron chuckled breathlessly, easing himself back onto the cot with a soft grunt. "I think this arm is going to hinder my performance more than I'd like."

Nyla laughed, letting Aaron settle until the pinch of pain between his eyebrows smoothed again.

"Well, you'll just have to make up for it next time around," she purred, carefully stretching her leg over Aaron's hips until she straddled him, rolling her pelvis forward to rock against him. Aaron hummed in approval, his injured arm lifting just enough for him to grip the curve of her thigh tightly in his hand.

"I think I can keep that promise," Aaron murmured, waiting patiently as Nyla removed her t-shirt. "Do you have...?"

"Condoms?" Nyla finished for him, unable to resist the temptation to poke fun at him. "What? Are you telling me that 'private dicks' don't come prepared? I thought you'd be getting tail in every stop from here to Chicago."

"Ha-ha," Aaron laughed humorlessly. "I know it's hard to believe given my sunny disposition and dripping sex appeal, but this isn't something I normally do on road trips."

"I have some in the front desk if you want me to get them," she said sincerely. "But... if not, well. I'm clean. And I'm on the pill. So..."

So she trusted Aaron. And she was offering to prove it. He gently cupped the side of her face, pulling her down toward him.

"Are you sure?" He whispered, pressing a soft kiss against her lips. "I'm clean, but we don't have to if—"

"I'm sure," Nyla promised, her conviction strong. Aaron observed her expression carefully for any signs of hesitation and then, finding none, resumed their searing kiss with enthusiasm.

Kissing Aaron reminded Nyla of hot cocoa with chili pepper— warm, comforting, and rich, with just a hint of a sharp reminder that there was power and strength lurking beneath his gentle touches. Aaron was a take-charge kind of man, and it reflected in the way he took the lead between them. Even pinned beneath her, Nyla had no doubt that he was the one in control.

The night was quiet, filled only with the sounds of their breath growing ragged, of clothes gradually being discarded. When Nyla felt Aaron's skin against hers with nothing in between them, she shuddered. He was so, so *warm*. His body was firm beneath her touch, muscled and toned into a weapon in its own right. Slowly, easing into it, Nyla began to tilt her hips over his, feeling him, introducing herself to the sensation of being with him like this.

"God, Nyla," Aaron bit off a groan, digging his fingers into Nyla's hips to still her just as she picked up her pace. "Wait."

"Not close already, are you, Suits?" Nyla teased, her tongue darting from between her lips to lightly flick his nose. Aaron caught it gently between his teeth, sending a surge of lust through her. His erection was trapped between them, pressed between his stomach and her pelvis. Nyla felt him twitch.

"I can't let you have all the fun," he said, his voice dangerously low. "My arm may be out of commission, but my mouth works just fine."

"Is that so?" Nyla bit her lip, her gaze inadvertently flitting to his mouth. Aaron smirked.

"Nyla." His hand appeared at the back of her head, holding her just a hairsbreadth from her lips touching his. "Climb me. I want to taste you."

"What?" Nyla half-gasped, half-laughed. "Are you kidding? Have you seen my ass?"

"Many, many times," Aaron promised. "And yet I never get tired of looking."

"I'll suffocate you," Nyla whined, shimmying her hips for emphasis. "These curves make for a wild ride, but they're not exactly equipped with an oxygen mask. Can't we change—?"

"Breathing is overrated. Now, don't make me tell you again," Aaron growled, cutting her off as his fingers fisted in her hair. Nyla whimpered in pleasure, her heart thudding rapidly in her chest. "Do what I asked."

"But—"

"As long as you cum with my name on your lips and my tongue in your cunt, I'll greet death with pride."

Nyla blinked in stunned arousal, summoning her willpower to lift herself off Aaron's deliciously hard erection and inch her way up his body. Despite his command, she took her time, gingerly lowering her knees on either side of Aaron's head, careful not to fully sit. A hungry spark lit his eye when his mouth was finally in line with her, and a haggard moan escaped him.

"You're so wet for me already," he cursed. Suddenly, Nyla felt his arms hook underneath her knees and around her hips, his fierce grip on her pulling her down farther onto his face. She squealed, slamming her palms down on the floor to catch herself. Before she could scold him, Nyla felt the slow, deliberate stroke of Aaron's tongue.

"Oh God," she whimpered, shivers erupting down her spine. Aaron hummed his satisfaction, taking another agonizingly slow lick.

Nyla could feel the pleasure pooling in her abdomen as Aaron took his time languidly toying with her, coaxing her into a panting mess of need. His tongue lapped at her, thoroughly claiming every inch he could reach. Nyla's moans grew desperate, her hips jerking involuntarily whenever his lips ghosted higher. Aaron was in no hurry still, savoring her as if she were his last meal.

"Aaron," Nyla cried, "*Please—!*"

His lips encased her clit with a soft, teasing suckle.

"Oh!" Nyla gasped, her hips bucking. She struggled to keep her weight off him, her palms slipping on the laminate. "Aaron—!"

Another teasing suck and Nyla's hips jerked so hard that she couldn't hold herself in place anymore. She sank fully onto Aaron's face, a satisfied groan erupting from his chest as she did.

"Good girl," he grunted, tightening his grip on her thighs. "Now, scream for me."

The slow, tantalizing strokes were gone. Aaron relented, rewarding Nyla with the attention she craved. His tongue circled her clit ravenously, pausing only to prod her and swallow her gushing arousal.

"*Fuck- fuck, fuck, fuck—!*" Nyla chanted, her nails digging painfully into the floor. Pressure flooded her, building, and building until she felt like she was going to combust. "Aaron— Oh God, *Aaron!*"

Pleasure crashed over her as she came with a shuddering cry, clenching on nothing, Aaron's tongue maintaining a steady rhythm as her body pulsed. Finally, when her strength was about to give out, Nyla quickly inched her way back onto Aaron's hips, collapsing onto his chest to catch her breath.

"You're right," she gasped. "Your mouth works just fine."

Aaron laughed, pressing his lips to her forehead. Nyla closed her eyes, trying to match her breaths to the rise and fall of Aaron's torso beneath her ear.

"Not tired already, are you, *mi tesoro*?" Aaron's playful lilt tickled Nyla's ear, and she resisted the urge to roll her eyes. "I'm not quite finished with you yet."

"Easy for you to say," Nyla accused with a smile. "You get to lie down the entire time. Give a girl a break."

"When this heals, I'll make it up to you on every horizontal surface you have at this lodge," Aaron murmured, shifting his hips to encourage her into position. Nyla mewled as his erection brushed against her still-sensitive skin, her fingertips pressing sharply into his shoulders, above the bandage. "And some of the vertical ones."

Nyla's retort was cut off as Aaron eased her hips upward, gently guiding himself inside her. She gasped as she stretched to accommodate him, pulsing softly from the aftereffects of her climax.

"That's my girl," Aaron uttered hoarsely, rolling his hips until he was fully seated inside her, his palms squeezing her plump thighs and anchoring her to him. "*Fuck* Nyla, you take me so well."

Nyla moaned as he rolled his hips again, grinding his pelvic bone lazily against her clit. Nyla lifted her head, accepting Aaron's bruising kiss while his gentle thrusts and rocks grew harder, jostling her in a steady rhythm. She could feel her body coming to life again, soft waves of pleasure inching over her skin, driving her heart rate up. Her breasts rubbed hard against Aaron's chest, making her cry out against his lips.

"That's it," Aaron ground out, pumping his hips in a series of jarring thrusts followed by gentle grinding. "Cum for me again, *mi tesoro*."

Nyla felt desperation spark to life in her veins and soon her hips were moving of their own accord, chasing the pleasure Aaron was giving with each thrust. She arched her back, pushing herself into a sitting position, balancing herself with her palms pressed flat to Aaron's stomach.

"Nyla," Aaron groaned, jerking his hips erratically, his head falling back against the pillow. "*Fuck*, you feel so good."

Nyla clenched around him, and Aaron released a startled moan in response. A thrill went through her at the sound.

"Aaron, I'm gonna—" the rest of her words were drowned out by a pleasured cry as Aaron's thumb pressed against her clit, rubbing in a slow, firm circle. Nyla felt the pressure build again, driving her higher and higher until it was too much. She tried to pull away, but Aaron held fast, his thrusts stuttering as his body tensed. Nyla screamed, her orgasm fiercely shattering through her, clamping down on Aaron. He continued to thrust even as the waves subsided, until at last he found his own release, unloading himself inside her.

"Oh God," Nyla whimpered, her bones turning to jelly. She dropped onto Aaron's chest again, his spent erection slipping free of her as she did. Aaron groaned, his muscles relaxing at once, his arms winding around her naked torso and holding her close.

"You're incredible," he whispered against her hair. "Holy hell, Nyla. I think you ripped my stitches."

"They didn't give you stitches," Nyla giggled breathlessly, rolling gingerly off of Aaron to curl into his side. He rolled with her, wrapping her in his warmth. "Do you want me to check if you're bleeding?"

"And risk having to leave and go back to the hospital? Not a chance," Aaron smiled, nudging her with his nose until she tilted her head back. He kissed her, slow and sweet. "*Mi cielo*." Kiss. "*Mi ángel*." Kiss. "*Mi tesoro*."

"You'd better not be insulting me, Agent Klein," Nyla smirked against his lips, returning his lingering kisses. "I don't speak Spanish."

"My sky," Aaron translated, the endearments caressing her skin with each breath. "My angel. My treasure."

Nyla felt her heart clench happily, rewarding each nickname with a press of her lips.

"You need sleep," she whispered. "We both do."

"You sure you aren't just embarrassed that I came up with something better than 'Suits'?"

"Shut up," Nyla laughed. "You love 'Suits,' don't lie to me."

"Actually, I was always more of a *CSI: Miami* fan."

"Weirdly, I'm not surprised," Nyla bumped his nose lightly with hers. "I'm serious. I have no idea what's in store for us tomorrow, but I have a feeling it's not going to be relaxing."

"Fair point," Aaron granted, brushing her hair gently from her face. When the strength eventually returned to Nyla's legs, she helped Aaron stand and they retreated to the bathroom to clean up the lingering evidence of their relationship. When Nyla jokingly asked if she should return to her own bedroll, Aaron practically tackled her to the floor, regretting the action instantly as it pulled on his injury. Between gasping laughs, Nyla helped him right himself, curling into his good side when he was settled.

"You're a doctor's worst nightmare, you know that?" She giggled, smoothing her palm over the exposed red skin around Aaron's bandage. He relaxed under her touch, reaching above his head to turn off the lantern they were using for light. "You'd better hope that didn't reopen."

"If I bleed out in the middle of the night, at least I got laid first."

"*Good night*, Aaron," she muttered pointedly. His chest vibrated in a chuckle.

"Sleep well, Nyla."

With those murmured wishes, the canteen plunged into comfortable darkness.

Nyla wasn't sure what time it was when she finally woke. The canteen was dark, but that wasn't abnormal. Without any windows, the canteen was always dark. She stretched, reaching for the solid warmth of Aaron's body only to find herself alone in the sleeping bag.

Sitting up, Nyla fumbled for the lantern and flipped the power. The canteen came into focus, barren aside from her. Nyla glanced over her shoulder, only to see the bathroom door open and the room unoccupied.

Was it morning? Had she slept in?

Nyla grabbed her phone, dread seeping into her bones as she noted that it wasn't even 4 am.

It was the middle of the night, and Aaron was gone.

Nyla grabbed her discarded pajama shorts and Aaron's t-shirt, covering herself before venturing to the door. Aaron's lounge pants were missing, so whatever had roused him had made him feel the need to at least partially dress. Nyla tried to tell herself that was a good sign, but she was struggling with the reasoning.

The hallway outside the canteen was empty and dim. Emergency lights were always on, directing her to the nearest exit, but they weren't bright. Just enough to see without tripping.

A bang sounded from the lobby, and Nyla froze.

It was probably Aaron. Something had drawn him out of the canteen to check things out, and he was simply investigating. She didn't need to panic. Still, Nyla didn't announce herself. She closed the canteen door gently behind her, creeping forward on bare feet to see for herself what the source of the noise was.

It was silent again now, broken occasionally by the muffled sounds of shuffling. It wasn't the creature, then, was it? If it was this close, it would've attacked her by now, right?

Nyla pressed her hand against the wall for balance, her fingertips brushing the doorframe of a supply closet. She took another step, and then she was grabbed.

A scream was thrust from her throat and immediately smothered by a large, warm hand. Nyla threw her elbow back at her captor, kicking wildly when her arm didn't connect with anything. Quickly, she was yanked into the alcove of the open supply closet, pinned between the wall and a familiar body.

"Nyla, it's me," Aaron whispered in her ear, easing his grip on her as she relaxed. Nyla twisted until they were face to face, puffing out her breath in annoyance.

"Are you trying to give me a heart attack?" She demanded breathlessly. "Seriously, what is with you and grabbing people in the dark?"

"Why are you out here?" Aaron shot back, brandishing his gun in the direction of the hall. "Someone's here. I'm trying to find out who."

"Well, so am I," Nyla pouted. "I didn't know you were–"

His hand clamped on her mouth again, attention riveted to something she couldn't see.

Aaron mimed a shushing gesture and released her. Nyla sank her teeth into her tongue, watching as Aaron held his gun aloft, inching cautiously into the hallway. Nyla followed behind him, giving him room to work. Soundlessly, he stalked toward the lobby, gun prepped to fire.

Just as he reached the end of the hall, someone stepped into their line of sight.

"Jesus Christ!"

"Don't move!" Aaron barked, brandishing his gun for emphasis. The figure stumbled back, hands snapping to attention beside their face.

"Don't shoot! Klein, it's me! *It's me!*"

"Pratt?" Aaron guessed incredulously, lowering his gun a fraction. Nyla took a bold step forward, pressing the hall light switch and blinding them all momentarily.

"What the hell are you doing here?" Aaron gaped, still locked in a shooting stance. "We thought you were lost in the damn woods!"

"I was!" Pratt exclaimed, his voice evening out after his scare. "I followed Ephraim's directions and— can you put that thing down? Do I look like a ten-foot-tall bog monster to you?"

Aaron relented, dropping his gun into the waistband of his pants, flicking the safety on in the process.

"Thank you," Pratt said pointedly. "I followed Ephraim's directions, but I got off track somewhere along the way. I only found my way out because I scared the shit out of some campers. They drove me back here."

"And your first thought is to sneak around in the dark like a criminal?" Aaron criticized. Pratt raised a brow in annoyance.

"I didn't know what happened to any of you," he defended. "I went to Kelley's cabin, and it was deserted. So was mine, and yours. I had no idea if you made it back, or if you were horribly mangled somewhere in this godforsaken place. I was trying to find a phone."

"Kelley and the rest of the team went to Milwaukee to talk to Huang and to organize a proper search party for *you*," Aaron said. "Didn't any of the campers have a phone?"

"No, actually, they didn't," Pratt said haughtily. "Some sort of unplugged nature retreat thing. I was going to call the station from here."

"Bill trashed the phone when he attacked me," Nyla piped up. "I need to replace it, but I've been a little preoccupied. Bog monsters, and all."

"You knew that," Aaron said, eyeing Pratt skeptically. "You'd have had better luck searching the SUV."

"Well, excuse me," Pratt scoffed. "I'm sorry my hungry, sleep-deprived, dehydrated brain didn't come to the most logical conclusion immediately. At least I'm trying to be productive with my time, unlike some people."

Pratt's attention drifted between the red scratches adorning Aaron's shoulders, the smattering of hickeys on Nyla's neck, and the fact that neither of them was fully dressed.

"So glad my disappearance made you horny enough to bypass the pining stage of your relationship," Pratt droned teasingly. Aaron rolled his eyes, crossing his arms over his chest.

"Yes, you've done all of us a great service," Aaron deadpanned. "We could actually think without your grating commentary, for once."

"You wound me, Klein."

"Seriously though," Nyla cut in, stepping up beside Aaron who draped his arm over her shoulders. "Are you okay? Do you need a doctor?"

"I need something to drink, something to eat, and something that's not a rock to lie down on." Pratt sighed, pushing a hand through his hair. "I'll even take your fluid-soaked mattress if it means I get to sleep for half a minute."

"For you, I'll spring for the clean one," Nyla smirked, "Come on, I'll get something for you to eat while you wash up."

"Wife material, this one," Pratt said, nodding to Aaron. "Don't do something stupid and ruin it."

"Sit down before you hurt yourself," Aaron dismissed. "We'll catch you up on everything that's happened since yesterday."

✽

"So, basically, what you're saying is that Kelley thinks we're off our rockers."

The canteen was cramped with the three of them and two mattresses taking up the majority of the space. Nyla had given Aaron his shirt back after locating her own, and by the time Pratt had finished cleaning himself up in the adjacent bathroom, it was closing in on daybreak. Nyla couldn't decide if she was relieved that they wouldn't have to worry about the creature temporarily, or devastated at the little sleep she'd managed.

"I wouldn't put it quite like that." Aaron shook his head. "She believes that we saw something, but she doesn't want to accept the reality of *what* we saw."

"Can't say I blame her," Nyla chimed in, pouring the finished stovetop mac n' cheese into a bowl and setting it in front of Pratt. It wasn't fine dining, but it was better than living off nuts and twigs. "I don't want to accept the reality of what we saw either."

"Nyla, do me a favor and tell me it was a weird bear," Pratt begged, inhaling a huge spoonful of the artificially orange noodles. "A bear that got struck by lightning, maybe? Stumbled into a nuclear power plant? Bit by a radioactive spider?"

"I can neither confirm nor deny radioactive spider." Nyla smiled sadly. She'd sorted through as many possibilities as she could think of, from the mundane to the mind-numbingly stupid. None had stuck. "As for the rest, I'm afraid we're shit out of luck."

"So, then, what? An undiscovered species?"

"Whatever it is," Aaron argued, "Kelley is planning to treat it just like a loose maneater. If the wildlife office is quick, they'll have a team down here in the next three days for sure."

"They're just going to waltz into the woods and tranq it?" Pratt blinked, bewildered. Nyla handed him a glass of water to wash down his food.

"No, they'd probably try to trap it first," she supplied. She'd seen a similar situation a few years ago with a fox that had lost its fear of humans. It had bitten several kids down at the high school, so wildlife was called in to relocate it. In the end, they'd decided to send it to a sanctuary because it was too domesticated to release. Nyla doubted they'd have that problem here. "After that, they might send out a hunting party to track it and kill it."

"Three days if wildlife is quick," Aaron mused, "but I'd say two to be safe. Two days to take care of this before anyone else gets involved. The problem now is just figuring out what to do."

"Do we have to do anything?" Nyla didn't like the idea of sitting back and doing nothing, but in this case, it was an attractive option. "The wildlife people will know they're tracking a dangerous animal; they'll take precautions and they'll be much better equipped than we were. They'll see what they're up against pretty quickly, and I have no doubt they'll kill it. Or capture it. Whatever they decide to do. Can't we sit this out now that we've done our job?"

"Nyla's got a point," Aaron looked at Pratt. He grimaced.

"I'd agree, except they won't know what they're dealing with, not until it's too late."

"What do you mean?" Nyla took the chair next to Pratt, shifting to face him. "Too late for what?"

"You shot the thing, right?" Pratt asked Aaron. He nodded. "How many times?"

"Twice for sure," Aaron recalled, thinking carefully before he answered. Nyla thought back as well, confirming his count. "Three, if I hit my mark every time. But definitely two."

"So did I," Pratt agreed. "Three from me, three from you, and four from Emmett. Out of those ten, we know for a fact that eight made contact."

"It's tough," Nyla hedged, watching Pratt's expression as the words left her mouth. It was almost pitying, and that didn't bode well. "That's not necessarily unusual. Lots of large predators can survive multiple rounds if they're big and muscley enough."

"Do they typically survive multiple rounds to the head?"

Nyla blinked, stunned.

"What are you talking about, Pratt?" Aaron frowned, crossing his arms over his chest. "I don't know where I hit, I just know—"

"Both Emmett and I landed shots to its head," Pratt said, his voice dropping gravely. "Klein, I watched my bullet tear through its *skull* from right between its eyes. The thing barely stumbled. I'll grant you a tough animal can survive a few flesh wounds, but how many do you know that can bounce back from getting their brains blown out?"

Neither Aaron nor Nyla had anything to say to that.

"The wildlife group will try to kill it," Pratt agreed. "But unless they have some silver bullets or something, they won't succeed."

"Silver bullets?" Aaron gaped. "We are not seriously standing around here talking about this thing like it's a goddamn werewolf."

"Do you have any better ideas?" Pratt snapped, pushing his empty bowl away from him so violently the spoon clattered onto the table. Nyla picked it up, reaching behind her to drop it into the sink. "Last time I checked, no normal animal can regenerate, Klein."

"I can believe a lot of crap, Pratt," Aaron snapped back. "But a werewolf? No. Not a chance. That thing didn't look anything like a wolf, for one. Not to mention, it's not following the moon cycle. Besides, we found Leo's body. If he was attacked by a werewolf, wouldn't he also be a werewolf now?"

Nyla's brain caught on something that Aaron said, no matter how sarcastically. Moon cycles? Was that it? No, that wasn't quite right, but it was close. The night? They'd determined it was likely nocturnal...

"Leo was dead when we found him," Pratt pointed out. "If the others were only bitten, then maybe that's why none of their bodies have turned up. We might have a whole pack on our hands."

Only bitten. Nyla's head jerked up in realization, her memory surfacing in fragments.

"For Christ's sake, *it's not a—*"

"It's not a werewolf," Nyla said abruptly, silencing them both. Aaron looked at her in relief, until he saw the expression on her face. "But it's not an animal, either."

"What is it?" Pratt asked eagerly. Nyla shook her head.

"I think I've heard about a creature like this before." She paused to think, scrunching her brow in concentration. "I don't know why this is ringing a bell with me, but... something about it is familiar. I'm sure I've heard a story about this."

"Well, do you know how we can find out?" Pratt pressed. Aaron looked like he wanted to protest, but he didn't. Maybe curiosity was getting the better of him.

"I know who we can ask," Nyla groaned, knowing she was setting herself up for an earful. "But she's going to give me shit for it."

Chapter Twenty-Four

AARON

"Clary's Spa."

The expression that crossed Nyla's face when she heard her friend pick up was the most fascinating combination of excitement and dread that Aaron had ever seen. He would've pointed it out, but Nyla didn't give him an opportunity to speak before she launched into the purpose of their call.

"Hey Claire," Nyla began, sounding hesitant even to Aaron's ears. "What's up?"

It was 9:30 in the morning, several hours after Pratt had shown up at the lodge in the dead of night. The three of them had gotten some sleep in before the spa opened and Nyla couldn't wait any longer to get some answers, but everyone was decidedly tired. Aaron in particular felt like he was going to collapse, but he kept his discomfort to himself. He was injured, everyone knew it. No need to make a scene.

"Nyla? Hey!" Clary's voice crackled with excitement through Nyla's cell, on speaker and perched in the middle of the floor between Pratt, Aaron, and her. "I was wondering how things were going. You okay?"

"Fine," Nyla assured her, even though her grimace said otherwise. "But I have a question you're not going to like."

"I've had my coffee. Fire away."

Nyla took a deep breath, preparing herself.

"I need to know if there are any local myths about forest monsters."

The line was silent for a minute. Aaron thought that Clary might be thinking about the question, but he should've been paying closer attention to Nyla's tensed body language. Clary's voice returned, louder and full of (what he hoped was mock) outrage.

"*Seriously* Nyla?" She yelled, shorting the speaker with the sheer volume of her affront. "You're asking your *only* indigenous friend about myths and legends? Really?"

"I know, I know, I'm sorry!" Nyla rushed to defend herself, raising her voice to match Clary's. Aaron shared an alarmed look with Pratt, who had frozen awkwardly. When Aaron returned his attention to Nyla, though, her expression had taken on a lighthearted tilt that told him Clary wasn't really as offended as she was pretending to be. "To be fair, I'm not asking you."

"Alright, but you're on thin ice, Missy." Clary huffed, and Aaron knew he and Pratt had been tricked. Nyla's posture relaxed, and she grinned at the two of them. "You're lucky you're my friend. I'll get Nonna Isa."

The line went quiet again, and Aaron felt safe enough to speak. "Nonna?" He whispered. He wasn't an expert on indigenous language, but he was fairly sure 'Nonna' was a European term.

"Clary's grandmother on her mom's side," Nyla answered in a hushed tone. "They're Italian."

Pratt and Aaron looked at each other again, neither one wanting to voice their obvious questions. Eventually, Aaron's curiosity won out.

"Why are we asking an Italian—"

Clary's voice returned abruptly, cutting him off mid-thought.

"She's on her way. Give her a minute, her hip is bad today."

"No worries," Nyla chirped. She gave Aaron a sideways look, mischief sparking across her face. "Hey, Claire?"

"I swear to god if you ask me to 'smudge' anything this friendship is over."

Nyla laughed. Aaron could hear shuffling in the background of Clary's phone; Nonna Isa must be nearly there.

"Care to explain to Aaron why we're asking an 89-year-old woman from Florence about Northern Onaqwe stories?"

"What? Not what you expected, Agent?" Clary taunted. "Looking forward to hearing some ancestral tales whispered around a campfire?"

"I regret asking."

Nyla winked at him, while Pratt smothered a snort.

"My Nonna is the kindest woman you'll ever meet, but she's not the brightest bulb." Clary explained happily. "My mom and dad met here in Wisconsin, so when Mom told Nonna she was dating an indigenous man, Nonna went into panic mode trying to make him feel welcome. She invited him over for dinner and spent the whole week learning about Onaqwe culture, which was really sweet, except my dad isn't from Wisconsin. He's Maliseet from Canada. Totally different history."

"So, now Nonna Isadora has a wealth of knowledge about Oki-qwe myths," Nyla concluded slyly. "She's the perfect one to ask."

"*Ciao mia bella nipote!*" A new voice joined the conversation, warm and rough with age, bursting with enthusiasm. Aaron was immediately reminded of his family in Bolivia. "You are coming to visit?"

"Soon, Nonna, I promise," Nyla vowed, smiling fondly at the phone. "I'm sorry I can't talk long. I have something important to ask you."

"*Velocemente, velocemente,*" Nonna Isa muttered. Aaron didn't know Italian, but it was similar enough to Spanish that he could guess what was being said. "I am napping."

"I'll be quick," Nyla assured her. "I just need to know if you remember any local myths about some kind of forest monster?"

Nonna was quiet for a moment, and then a burst of rapid-fire Italian crackled through the line.

"Claire?" Nyla prompted. "Help me out on that one?"

"She's yelling at you," Clary supplied less than helpfully. "She says all the myths she knows are about some kind of forest monster. You need to be more specific."

Nyla huffed out an exasperated breath, which resulted in Nonna Isa uttering a string of words that Aaron didn't need to translate to know she was reprimanding.

"How about monsters and..." she glanced at Aaron, at his covered wound. "Cold? Ice, maybe? And darkness?"

This time, the silence dragged longer and was filled with thoughtful contemplation. Aaron watched Nyla while they waited, thinking back to the things they'd seen, things they'd felt. She was right to ask about the ice and cold. If nothing else, Aaron was sure now that the drastic temperature changes he'd been noticing were anything but normal. After some time, Nonna Isa started speaking again.

"It's a... *demone*, a demon," she suggested, and Aaron heard some rustling. "A *spirito cattivo*. What is it named, Clarissa Bella?"

"How should I know, Nonna?" Clary rebutted, sighing. "Hang on, let me get your book."

A string of Italian followed her, some of which Aaron was able to pick out, some he wasn't. Nyla was giggling all the while, understanding about as much as he was. When Clary returned, Nonna became excited.

"Chewy!" She proclaimed loudly. "It is called chewy new."

"Chewy new?" Nyla repeated dubiously. The phone shifted again, and then Clary's voice was on the line.

"Tcha, Nonna," Clary laughed. "It's pronounced cheh-win-ew. Chehwinoo. It means... man eater?"

"Appropriate," Aaron muttered under his breath.

"Aye, Clarissa Bella. Talk to your friends."

More shuffling, and then Nonna Isa was gone.

"What? Oh, hang on," Clary's voice took over, louder and more clear than she was a moment ago. "There's some kind of poem here. She wants me to translate this part. Let's see... long ago, in a galaxy far, far away..." A loud smack reverberated through the line. "Ouch! Okay, okay, I'm kidding. Jeez.

"*Quiet now, little ones, don't tell the flies to shoo/If you're loud and make a sound, you might call the Chehwinoo/Ten feet tall and made of ice, his claws turn your skin blue/The air grows cold and you hear a scream- it must be the Chehwinoo.*"

Clary paused, presumably skimming through the remainder of the poem.

"Oh, this part is interesting. *I'll whisper now as the night goes on and the moon rises new/It shuns the sun and fears the light, that sneaky Chehwinoo/Quickly now, we must make haste, we have no time to lose/Finish this tale and get inside where it's safe from the Chehwinoo.* Oh, gross. I think it eats someone."

Nyla, Aaron, and Pratt shared a troubled look.

"No, no wait, that's not right. The guy in the poem eats someone, then he *becomes* the Chehwinoo. Ew. That's way worse."

"Cannibalism," Pratt murmured. "Can't say I saw that coming."

"*Hunger is a powerful foe, but you cannot let it win/You'll lose yourself along this path, your humanity will grow thin/What would you do to survive?/Would you sin so too?/The beast inside will come alive/You are the Chehwinoo.* Well, that's not creepy at all. Why did you need to know about this, again?"

"Not important," Nyla dismissed quickly. "Could you send me that poem?"

"Sure," Clary agreed easily. Nonna Isa's voice sounded in the background again. "Uh... Nonna says a Chehwinoo is born when dark spirits punish men for heinous crimes. Their heart is swallowed by ice and their body becomes darkness. Sounds a bit... Wes Craven, but alright."

"Does the poem say how to kill one?" Nyla pressed. Aaron had just been about to ask that same question. Nonna Isa spoke again.

"The only way to kill a Chehwinoo is to kill the person who became the creature. She says you need to 'shatter the crystal,' which I think means the frozen heart?" Clary switched to Italian, verifying her guess before returning. "Yes, okay, stab it through the heart. You kill the person at the heart of the Chehwinoo, and it dies too."

"How do you stab the heart if it's encased in ice?" Aaron asked aloud, although he hadn't meant to.

"How would I know?" Clary snickered. "It's obviously a metaphor for starvation, not a literal ghoul."

Aaron, Nyla, and Pratt avoided looking at one another.

"Thanks for all your help, Claire," Nyla said, picking up her phone. "Don't forget to send me that poem, okay?"

"No problem." If Clary was suspicious of anything, she didn't show it. Aaron wasn't sure if it was a reflection of how much she trusted Nyla, or how ridiculous their queries had been. Maybe both. "I've got an appointment coming in ten minutes though, so I've gotta go. You good?"

"One more thing," Nyla added suddenly, "and this may sound stupid but... do you think you could avoid going out at night? Please?"

"Are you trying to give me a curfew? You know I'm older than you, right?"

"*Please* Claire," Nyla picked up the phone, bringing it closer to her face. "I just need you to trust me on this. If you don't, I'll start whistling."

Clary paused so long that Aaron thought she hung up. When she spoke again, her voice had changed. Cheery, but with something heavy lurking underneath.

"I hate the dark anyway," Clary said with false exuberance. "Sounds easy enough."

"Thanks, Claire." Nyla smiled. "Love you!"

"Love you too!"

The line was dead for nearly a full minute before any of them dared to speak. Aaron eased back against the cupboard door, taking some of the pressure off of his injury.

"Whistling?" He finally asked. He couldn't stand the silence anymore.

"Yeah." Nyla's shoulders dropped. "It's... an inside thing, I guess. Clary asked me to stop whistling at night because it made her uneasy, though she refused to tell me why. It seemed really important to her, so I stopped anyway. Now whenever I need to convey to her that she needs to listen to me without question, I bring up the whistling."

"Did she ever tell you why it makes her uneasy?"

"Yes."

Nyla didn't elaborate, and Aaron didn't ask her to.

Another minute went by before Nyla's phone dinged, signaling that Clary had made good on her promise. After skimming the poem, she passed it around for Aaron and Pratt to read. When they were done, the silence was somehow heavier.

"Let's think logically about this." Nyla's voice shook, like she wanted to do anything but think about this. Aaron couldn't blame her.

"You want us to think 'logically' about an ice werewolf?" Pratt stared, bewildered. Aaron felt his patience snap.

"For the love of—" he cursed, repeatedly and fiercely, in Spanish. "It's not a fucking werewolf!"

"It's an ice demon." Nyla corrected, sounding less convinced than he was. "Okay, so, how would you attack an ice demon?"

"With a keyboard and a stable internet connection."

Aaron rolled his eyes to glare at his friend.

"I know this is a big ask, Pratt," he said, already feeling his blood pressure rising to worrying levels, "but can you please try to be serious about this?"

"I am serious!" Pratt retaliated in offense. "The only ice demon I've ever met was in the latest WoW expansion, and unless you have an iron mace enchanted with flame tongue just lying around here somewhere, I can't help you."

"I didn't know you played shaman?" Aaron furrowed his brow.

"It's my secondary." Pratt shrugged. "I main priest."

"Wait a minute," Nyla sat up straight, ignoring their irrelevant bickering. Aaron diverted his attention back to her. "Pratt's onto something. Fire. It's an *ice* demon, it's gotta be weak to fire, right? We can use fire to hold it off and then we shoot it in the heart!"

"I thought we had to stab it in the heart?" Pratt looked between them in confusion, likely wondering if he'd heard wrong. "Will shooting it work? Or is the stabbing thing literal?"

"It's probably a mistranslation of 'pierce'," Aaron said thoughtfully. He didn't know if it was shock, or if he was simply at the end of his wits, but suddenly their discussion about how to tackle an ice demon felt like any other work day. He was sure he'd be talking to his therapist about that someday. "But that's just a guess. I don't know, I think it would work. Shooting a human man through the heart would kill him, so the same principle should apply here. If the human is encased in the heart, then we just need to deal a fatal blow to the human. The means shouldn't matter."

"We can't attack the Chehwinoo with fire in the middle of the forest," Pratt said, sounding dubious. "AKA the *woods*? AKA *definitely extremely flammable things?*"

"The rain might've just saved our asses." Nyla shifted again, uncrossing her legs and stretching. It was hardly the time, but Aaron couldn't help looking. Just for a second. Long enough to remember the feel of them around his hips and remind himself that he hadn't completely fallen off the deep end. "It's been damp for weeks now. Even if you completely torched a tree, it wouldn't get much farther than that."

"Great." Pratt snorted. "We attack the mythical ice creature with fire in the middle of the forest. What could go wrong?"

"It's all we've got right now."

Aaron didn't disagree. Despite the fantastic circumstances, their options were limited. They could pretend they hadn't seen what they'd seen, leave things to Kelley, leave Somerton, maybe get a psych evaluation. Even without asking, Aaron knew none of them would be comfortable doing that. Whether they were crazy or not, they couldn't walk away.

"Do we even have that much?" Pratt asked in defeat. "Aside from the fact that it hunts at night somewhere near the Basin, we don't know where this thing is. We can't just walk into this blindly. We need a plan. A concrete plan."

"I can not believe I'm about to say this but," Aaron leaned forward, taking in a sharp breath at the way his injury shifted and screamed. "Pratt? Let's plan a dungeon raid."

Chapter Twenty-Five

INTERLUDE

The Chehwinoo

Sit down, gather 'round, have a drink or two.
If you wait and fill your plate, I'll tell you 'bout the Chehwinoo.

The night is young, the wind is calm, the sky is still light blue.
If you think you're tough, then you're in luck. I'll tell you 'bout the Chehwinoo.

Long before we settled here before this town stood high,
A family man traversed this land, his pack heavy with wares.
He traveled with his wedded wife, with locks the colour of rye,
On her hip, her son did sit, sporting his father's raven hair.

The father, the mother, the son, the troop,
To Devil's Lake, their path would lead.
But misfortune fell on their little group,
On their sorrow, it would feed.

Quiet now, little ones, don't tell the flies to shoo.
If you're loud and make a sound, you might call the Chehwinoo.

Ten feet tall and made of ice, his claws turn your skin blue.

The air grows cold and you hear a scream- it must be the Chehwinoo.

Winter came before the frost, harder than ever before,
The father grew scared with every gust, as their store of food grew bare.
I must go and hunt, he said, one hand on the door,
The other reached for his young son, who screamed it isn't fair.

I'll be back before the sun,
The father unknowingly lied.
He tied his boots and took his gun,
While his wife and young son cried.

Hunger is a powerful foe, can leave you with nothing left to do.
Just be smart and play your part. Don't anger the Chehwinoo.

Where darkness lurks, where spirits hide in shadows of every hue,
Have no doubt it's lurking about. You'll find the Chehwinoo.

The father searched high and wide for signs of doe or buck,
He wandered far into the woods, where the rays of sun wouldn't touch.
He wandered as far as he dared, and when he thought he'd run out of luck,
The father came across a man, dying in a little hutch.

I have no food, he wept
I need your help, please.
From his cheeks, the tears he swept
Dripped on the father's knees.

I'll whisper now as the night goes on and the moon rises new.
It shuns the sun and fears the light, that sneaky Chehwinoo.

Quickly now, we must make haste, we have no time to lose.
Finish this tale and get inside where it's safe from the Chehwinoo.

The dying man knew not his fate as he begged for help,
The father had a terrible thought as his hunger screamed for blood.
The dying man could feed his wife, his strapping little welp.
With his gun, he shot the man and watched as he fell into the mud.

But the father had failed,
He wouldn't see his wife this night.
For if she knew, her skin would pale,
She'd stare at her husband in fright.

Hunger is a powerful foe, but you cannot let it win.
You'll lose yourself along this path, your humanity will grow thin.
What would you do to survive?
Would you sin so too?
The beast inside will come alive.

You are the Chehwinoo.

Chapter Twenty-Six

NYLA

"This might be the most ridiculous thing I've ever done," Pratt muttered, kicking wildly at a tangle of fallen branches in his path. "And I'm not even getting paid for it."

"Calm down, you're salaried," Aaron called back over his shoulder, rolling his eyes for Nyla to see. She pursed her lips to hide her smile. "Just throw a few hours of overtime on your next time report."

"I don't think an entire year of overtime would cover this."

"You could've stayed at the lodge," Nyla pointed out, prepared for the enthusiastic snort that sounded from behind her at that suggestion.

"And let you two have all the fun? No way. I want this beast— demon— thing dead."

It was early morning, the sun just barely poking over the tree line. Nyla had insisted they head out as soon as possible to get a head start on Kelley's team. Aaron and Pratt were convinced they had a few more days before the wildlife division moved in, but Nyla wouldn't risk it. Even if they found the Chehwinoo quickly, there was no guarantee they could do anything about it. Their planning had petered out after only a few loose suggestions as they all realized they had no information to build a plan *with*. Now, they needed to find the creature, form a plan, and execute it all in one fell swoop. The more time they could give themselves, the better.

Aaron was moving easier today. It had taken some convincing for him to let Pratt take the heavier bag, but he couldn't deny that he'd be more useful providing cover. His handgun rested at his side while they hiked to the Basin, two hunting rifles slung across his back. Nyla could never have imagined that moving to Somerton would eventually lead her here, trekking through the woods with an attractive PI and a sarcastic federal agent, hunting down a murderous creature of legend. It was thrilling, terrifying, and unbelievable all mixed together in a nauseating cocktail.

"I've been thinking about something," Aaron said suddenly, glancing at the sky. They had to assume that the Chehwinoo knew they were here, so Aaron was prepared to lift his gun at the slightest hint of cloud cover. "If we're to believe the story Nonna Isa told us, then that means the Chehwinoo used to be a person."

"That's my understanding," Nyla agreed, already guessing where he was going with this.

"Then who is it," he pondered, "and why were they cursed in the first place?"

Nyla paused to sort through her laundry list of questions and possible answers to that issue. She'd been wondering that very thing since last night, and she'd only made minor progress in figuring it out.

"It couldn't be someone you've met," Nyla deduced, counting backward in her mind. "The disappearances started a few months ago before you came to Somerton. But I can't think of anyone who's been missing for that long."

"No local cannibals missing out on the weekly cooking class?" Pratt interjected. Nyla snorted a laugh.

"I don't know much about Onaqwe myths, but I've learned a little from Nonna," Nyla explained, carefully stepping over a poison oak plant. She could spot them easily now, after her traumatic school trip all those years ago. "Clary was right when she said it was probably a metaphor for starvation. She just didn't realize it was also true."

"So, we're thinking about cannibalism in the context of, what, exactly?" Aaron's attention snagged on something in the trees, his body tensing. Nyla froze, but she hadn't noticed any drop in temperature suggesting the Chehwinoo was nearby. "An immoral solution to food shortages?"

"I still think that's too literal." Nyla relaxed with Aaron, continuing through the trampled underbrush. "Nonna said that dark spirits punished people who'd committed heinous crimes. I think that means we can include any kind of threat to the environment, which doesn't exactly narrow it down for us."

"I guess that's why it's targeting hunters, then." Pratt surmised. Nyla shook her head.

"Actually, no." Nyla had considered this too, but no matter which way she spun it, it didn't make sense. "Sustainable hunting is actually really good for the ecosystem around here. Helps keep populations in check. The hunters were probably just the closest available thing since they're always out in the woods at odd hours. The problem I have is that people damage the forest all the time. As much as I try to dissuade people from causing real harm, I can't stop them all. Hikers aren't being possessed every time they leave plastic water bottles in the thicket, so whoever the Chehwinoo is must've done something much, much worse."

"How could one person threaten the entire forest enough to summon ancient ice demon spirits?" Aaron squinted, looking like he was already fighting off a headache. "This isn't an episode of *Captain Planet*. Real life doesn't have the Big Bad. Things are more complicated than that."

"What about that Stein guy?"

"What?"

Nyla stopped abruptly in shock, blinking at Pratt and Aaron in equal confusion.

"Adrian Stein? No, wait, it was Stamkos. Adrian Stamkos." Pratt nodded his head once, sure of his memory. "He was building that factory out here, right? Could it be him?"

"How did you...?" Nyla shook herself free of her stunned expression, the stuttering wheels in her brain turning smoothly again. "How did you know about the Stamkos and Stein deal? I thought we nixed it?"

"Hannaford told us," Aaron explained easily. "I was going to ask you about it, but things got..."

"Supernatural?"

"Complicated."

"Well, yeah," Nyla thought back to when the pharmaceutical company made their announcement, accompanied by a grinning James Carver and a bored-looking Bill Hannaford. "The town made a deal with Stamkos and Stein a few months back. They were going to build a factory just off the interstate, but construction would've brought them across the Basin's property lines and into hunting territory. Clary and I petitioned them to stop the build. I thought it worked, that's why I didn't bring it up. Bill has a million reasons to hate me, I didn't think the Stamkos and Stein lab was high on the list."

"It must be," Aaron informed her, a troubled look taking over his features. "He told us he organized the deal himself, but I have my doubts."

"Ha," Nyla laughed humorlessly trying to imagine Bill negotiating anything, let alone a contract with a major corporation. "Bill doesn't have a political bone in his body. Carver organized the deal, not Bill. Although, he's really not much better than Bill. I'm surprised the whole thing got off the ground in the first place."

"James Carver?" Pratt piped up. "As in, Somerton Mayor, James Carver?"

"Yeah," Nyla confirmed. "Why? Were you talking to him?"

"We were trying," Pratt said. "Kelley wanted to set up an interview with him after we talked to Bill about the Stamkos and Stein deal, but we haven't been able to get a hold of him."

"That's not surprising," Nyla told them in annoyance. "Carver is as useless as tits on a bull. I've been here for 4 years, and I've maybe seen him ten times. He has a vacation home in the Keys and that's where he spends most of his time. If he knew the FBI was looking to question him, he'd be halfway to Florida before you could find his address. You'd have more luck getting the Chehwinoo in for questioning."

Pratt chuckled, picking up his pace to walk more closely behind Aaron and Nyla. The Basin felt normal as they made their way past the lake, almost too normal. Nyla found herself second-guessing the familiar terrain, worried that she was being lulled by the same ground she'd walked countless times before. She hadn't seen the Chehwinoo when it attacked Leo until it was too late. She hadn't heard it snap the tree in half when it jumped her and Aaron. Nyla wondered if it was this place that was throwing off her instincts. If she'd gotten too comfortable here.

"We're getting off track," she said, shaking off her anxiety. "It can't be Adrian Stamkos, he had a press conference last week to go over the details of his Northern Expansion Project."

"And it's not Hannaford," Aaron added. "For obvious reasons."

"The first hunter to go missing, maybe?" Pratt guessed. "He did something, turned into the Chehwinoo, and started killing the others?"

That was the best of the suggestions they'd made so far, but it still didn't sit right with Nyla. She didn't bother to voice her concerns, though, not when she didn't have a solid reason as to why.

The Basin was calm today, with an undercurrent of malaise that Nyla may or may not have imagined. Any trace of a breeze left her clutching her pocket knife, though it wouldn't do her much good. The trees breathed an unstable peace that teetered on the brink of chaos, steadily and silently building. The question now was when would the collapse begin.

Basin Lake carried into Dodson's Lake, where Nyla and Aaron had found refuge from the Chehwinoo two nights ago. It was larger than Dodson's, branching into several small rivers that snaked through the mountains. The Willow rested almost dead center between two of the more prominent streams, creating a large, misshapen V from a satellite view. Nyla had to assume the Chehwinoo was within this V, unless it could move through water, which was still undetermined. It hadn't followed them into the lake, but that could've been a coincidence. For now, they had to rely on educated guesswork. There were no pedestrian bridges crossing these two rivers, not until much closer to the town limits. If the Chehwinoo had wandered that far, someone else would've seen it by now.

"We should hit the river in another 5 miles," Nyla announced, squinting at the sky. Their progress had been a bit slower than she would normally move, so she adjusted her time estimates accordingly. "Over this ridge, we should see a flat section of forest. It's the lowest point in the Basin."

"Any tourist activity there?" Aaron asked, his voice sounding troubled. Nyla followed his gaze, but she was nearly a full head and a half shorter than him. She couldn't see what he was staring at.

"Not much," Nyla answered honestly. "Aside from the occasional hunter that makes the trip down here, it's usually quiet. It's about a three-hour hike from the main road, so even people passing through rarely make it out this way. Why?"

"I'm not sure if it's related or coincidence," Aaron said slowly, jerking his chin forward in a signal for Pratt to scout ahead. "But I rarely believe in coincidences."

Nyla was going to ask again what he was referring to, but she soon found the answer for herself.

Over the ridge and through a sparse line of trees, Nyla could see a menagerie of things that didn't belong in the woods. Bright splotches of white, mustard yellow, blue, and red peeked through the leaves, surrounded by an array of browns and greys. Nyla's stomach sank as they got closer, a hard, unyielding lump forming in her throat. They were barely out of sight of Basin Lake, and they'd just stumbled on Stamkos and Stein's build site.

After passing through the trees, the construction area unfurled in front of them, spanning wider than even the Willow's perimeter. Nyla stared in open shock, taking in the abandoned machinery, crushed trash, and haphazardly organized material. Fallen trees were once stacked neatly into piles to prep them for cutting, but now they were scattered around the grounds like toppled bowling pins. Tarps had been fitted over some of the smaller, more specialized tools, but something had ripped the waterproof fabric to shreds.

"They're not supposed to be this close," Nyla whispered, mostly to herself. "I mean, they weren't supposed to start building at all, but *this close?*"

"I have a feeling they weren't expecting any opposition," Aaron wondered, surveying the scene with a critical eye. "They started the project the same day they signed the contract. Most businesses move quickly for that very reason, avoiding public delays."

"This is protected land," Nyla complained, desperation creeping into her tone. "The Basin is a registered hunting ground, and the trails around here move through State nature parks. They can't build this close. They can't."

"If they have enough money, they can." Aaron's voice was sympathetic, gingerly pulling Nyla into a loose embrace. She let him comfort her for a moment, but they couldn't stay like that. They had a job to do.

"There's a trailer over here," Pratt announced suddenly. "It looks pretty torn up, but there might be something useful inside."

"I'll go check it out," Aaron offered, pressing a gentle kiss to Nyla's forehead. "If the Chehwinoo is nesting nearby, I doubt it'll be inside a trailer. You and Pratt keep scouting, but don't leave his side, understood?"

Nyla raised an eyebrow at him, smoothly removing one of the hunting rifles from Aaron's crisscrossed holsters.

"I'll pass along the advice." She smiled impishly. "Wouldn't want Pratt getting himself hurt."

Chapter Twenty-Seven

AARON

The trailer was falling apart. Aaron had almost felt guilty, sending Nyla off to look for the creature while he was tucked safely away in a temporary office, but now he was glad that he did. Whatever happened to this trailer, he was sure it wasn't like this when construction started. The ceiling alone was a severe hazard.

Besides, Aaron was confident that Nyla could handle herself.

He tested the strength of the floor carefully, putting one boot on the buckling aluminum and bouncing three or four times before stepping fully onto it. Some worrying creaks met his entry, but the structure held. Aaron reached for his phone, using the flashlight to search the disaster zone he was standing in. It looked like a category five hurricane had ripped through the trailer, spewing paper, garbage, equipment, and everything else into a wild array of nonsensical patterns on the floor. Aaron kicked over a few cardboard boxes, surprised when they disintegrated at his touch.

What the hell?

He squatted, poking the torn cardboard experimentally. The material sagged and gave way to nothingness, falling apart with the slightest pressure. It was like it had been soaked in water. Aaron looked around again, spotting a few other boxes suffering the same fate. There was a bag of something, crackers, he thought, perched beneath a toppled chair. Aaron could tell by looking at it that the contents had turned to mush, much like the potato chip bag he'd found at Leo's campsite. How had they ended up like that? Squished, soggy, like they'd been bogged down with water or—

Or frozen. Frozen and thawed again.

Aaron's stomach lurched in unease. He stood from his squat, casting his flashlight around the walls of the trailer. For all the dents and scratches, the frame was mostly intact. The beam from his phone bounced from uneven surface to uneven surface until it landed on something out of place.

Something red.

Aaron knew it was blood before he'd stepped closer. Nothing looked quite like old blood— somehow red, brown, and black all at once. The smell hadn't hit him yet, but Aaron knew it would. Metallic and tinged with decay, it wasn't a scent he was happy about recognizing. Luckily, blood was the only thing he found. There was no body, no evidence of something living or dying here. There was, however, a cell phone.

He'd almost missed it, buried beneath a stack of shattered hard hats. Aaron sidestepped the splashes of blood inching along the floor and walls, plucking the phone as gingerly from the pile as he could. It was new, maybe only a few years old. No passcode, but the battery was at 2%. He'd need to snoop quickly.

Texts showed nothing, just a message to the phone owner's wife that they were going to be late getting home. No social media accounts were signed in, except Twitter, but that didn't give him anything useful. Finally, Aaron opened the email app. There, he found the clue he'd been looking for.

Favor

The subject line was simple and nondescript, as was the email address it was sent from. *MailUser123456789@inbox.com.* If Aaron didn't know any better, he might've assumed it was a spam account. As it was, the email was starred and pinned to the top of the inbox, which meant that it was important. He checked the 'Sent' folder, finding a chain of messages sent to the same account. Aaron opened the initial incoming email.

Ted, it's JC. I need you to do me a favor. This petition is killing momentum, and S&S are threatening to pull out if I don't get this under control. Bill's handling things with the town, but I need someone to get me a copy of the S&S build permit. Keep this to yourself, but they've already set up in the Basin. There's a trailer just off Jedediah Path. Permit should be there. Wait until the heat cools off first, though. If it gets out that construction already started, it'll ruin me.

Thanks, JC.

Aaron read over the message again, fitting pieces together where he could. Bill was obviously Hannaford. Ted must be Ted Rourke, the last victim to go missing. Nyla had said he'd have no reason to be in the Basin, so it couldn't have been his name Aaron overheard. Well, he'd just found the reason in the email app on Ted's abandoned phone. S&S would be Stamkos and Stein, that just left JC.

JC. James Carver.

In context, it made sense. Somerton's mayor *would* be inconvenienced by the delay in construction. Aaron read on, but no other messages were sent by JC. All of them were from Ted, demanding answers.

How long am I supposed to wait?

Where is the trailer?

I'm not a woodsman, J. How am I supposed to find it?

Hello?

The emails stopped there, with no evidence as to if Ted was able to contact the sender. Aaron was about to check the call log when the phone's battery finally gave out, putting an abrupt end to his investigations. He looked up, blinking.

James Carver. Somerton's absentee mayor. Had Nyla said when she'd seen him last? Aaron couldn't remember, but if it wasn't within the last few months...

A clear picture was materializing in Aaron's mind, one of questionable political moves and environmental damage, all culminating in a dirty mayor who'd been out of touch for just long enough to give Aaron an idea of what— or who— they were dealing with. He pocketed the dead phone.

It was darker now, the sun having shifted behind a cloud overhead. Aaron emerged from the trailer, heart pounding in his ears, but he needn't have worried. Nyla and Pratt were just outside, talking seriously amongst themselves. Aaron jogged over to them, jerking his thumb back over his shoulder.

"Looks like James Carver may have been behind the illegal build site," he announced, hooking his arm casually around Nyla's waist as he reached them. Despite the fact that his stroke of fear was unwarranted, he felt better being able to see both her and Pratt. Aaron didn't think Pratt would take too kindly to having Aaron's arm around him, though. "I found a phone with some cryptic emails. Hard to say for sure, but that's what it sounded like. And there's something else."

Nyla looked up at him, her open expression so inviting that Aaron had to remind himself that now was an incredibly inappropriate time to kiss her.

"Do you remember the last time you saw James Carver?"

"The Christmas parade," Nyla answered easily, narrowing her eyes just slightly when Aaron donned a resigned expression. "You don't think he...? No, no way. Aaron, it *can't* be Carver. He's too... useless."

Even as the words left her mouth, Aaron could see that Nyla was beginning to question her own conviction. He caught Pratt's eye, and the two of them nodded in silent agreement. Nyla may be unwilling to accept it right away, but Aaron had no doubt. James Carver was their ice demon.

"And it looks like the illegal build site may be behind the sudden revival of our ancient beastie," Pratt added grimly, steering the topic away from Carver. Aaron's eyebrows shot up in surprise.

"What do you mean?"

"Over there," Pratt pointed behind him, just north of the trailer. "If you follow that path, you'll find its den. Would be pretty convenient if its home was this close to the build site and one had nothing to do with the other."

"Its den?" Aaron repeated, bewildered. "Are you sure?"

"Positive," Nyla chimed in, shaking off her confusion and doubt. "If the drop in temperature doesn't give it away, the carnage sure does."

Aaron shared a look with her, but he knew he needed to see it for himself. Disengaging, he wandered toward the rudimentary path through the trees. The foliage here was damaged enough for even Aaron to notice, stripped of life and broken in a thousand places. Even before he stepped into the forest, Aaron could feel himself start to shiver.

The path led in a wide circle, ending at the remains of a massive tree. At some point, whether by storm or rot, the tree had buckled, leaving only its colossal stump behind. Aaron approached slowly, observing his surroundings for any sign of movement. He didn't have the rifle readied. He should. He was about to sling it into his hands when he spotted something that didn't belong to the scenery, something that was decidedly out of place. Was that... snow?

It was. The shock of white against the dull browns and grey-greens of the stump snagged his attention and held on. He was so focused on the snow and ice creeping along the putrid bark that he almost missed the gaping hole in the ground, barely held together by the residual tree roots. There, he could feel gusts of icy wind swirling towards him, knocking the breath from his lungs. Aaron stilled, squinting as more of the scene came into focus. There was white, yes, and browns, and greys, and greens. There was also red. A lot of red.

He couldn't pick out any bodies, but Aaron was sure that some were around. There was too much blood for this to not be where the Chehwinoo fed. Leo's body was back at the morgue— whatever was left of it, anyway. A few of them, if not all, must be here. Aaron swallowed against the dryness in his throat, retreating to the construction site where Nyla and Pratt were still discussing.

"Do we have any rope?" Aaron asked as he got within talking distance. He didn't want to shout, not with the Chehwinoo so close. Nyla shook her head in confusion.

"No, why would we? What do you need rope for?"

"If you two can lower me in, I'll shoot it while it's sleeping," Aaron explained, checking the magazine in his handgun. "I only have one good arm, so I wouldn't be able to reliably hold the rope. I can still shoot, though."

"You're not going down there," Nyla snapped, not pausing long enough for him to argue. "We've already ruled out setting the den on fire—"

"Could have a back exit," Pratt supplied helpfully.

"—One or all of us ambushing it while it sleeps—"

"We can't see far enough into the den. Don't know what we'd be throwing ourselves into."

"—waiting until dark and ambushing it—"

"Potential back exit is a problem for that one, too."

"—and trying to sneak up on it, because we have no idea what it can and can't track," Nyla explained that reasoning before Pratt could, and he looked a little put out. "Pratt and I have an idea, we're just not sure what's the best way to execute it."

"What's the idea?" Aaron asked, only temporarily sidelining his own suggestion. Pratt tilted his head towards the construction equipment.

"Our best chance of getting a clear shot is if we lure it out into the open," he said, presumably repeating what he and Nyla had been talking about before Aaron joined them. "The thing is fast and thin. The less we have to shoot around, the better. We can set up a couple of small campfires to sort of corral it, and provide a backup weapon if things go south."

"The problem," Nyla said, "is that we're completely surrounded by trees. The site is fine, they've pretty much cleared everything already aside from a few pieces of equipment, but we can use those for cover and vantage points. We just can't figure out how to stop it from darting into the forest the first chance it gets."

"We need a way to trap it," Pratt summarized. They'd tried to form a plan before leaving the Willow, but without knowing the landscape, they hadn't gotten far. Trapping it was a suggestion that had been thrown around a few times, without any real ideas for execution. "Something to keep it here, where we actually have a chance at doing some damage."

Aaron fell silent, considering the problem. It was a hefty one, he couldn't deny that. A way to trap the Chehwinoo in the construction site, away from the trees...

"What if we build a perimeter?" Aaron said, taking stock of the site's size. "We can encase the entrance of the den and guide it straight here, then we each take a gun and whoever has the best shot takes it."

"We don't have time to build a wall, Aaron," Nyla said doubtfully. "We're three people, not a contracting firm. Not to mention, we only have a few hours until sundown. Anything we *can* build in that amount of time would never hold up to that thing."

"Unless you're suggesting we build a wall of fire," Pratt snorted. "In which case, I'm all for it. Just haul the T4 out of your ass and we'll call it a day."

A wall of fire.

Pratt was joking, but maybe...

Aaron surveyed the site again. The fallen trees were scattered, yes, but they were small and close by. If they dragged them to the edges of the site, piled on some loose branches, and made sure there were no gaps for the creature to escape, they would have a pretty solid barrier to keep the Chehwinoo where they wanted it. They'd brought flares, and matches, knowing they could likely use fire to fight. There was always the risk that the creature wouldn't leave its den if it sensed the heat, but they could avoid that if they lit the fire *after* it emerged. They'd just need a way to make sure the fire caught before the creature realized what was happening and made a run for it.

A bright orange canister caught Aaron's eye, and a full-fledged, bat-shit-insane plan formed in his mind. He turned to Pratt and Nyla, an almost manic grin on his face.

"How do you feel about blowing up a gas can?"

It took them every second of their remaining time to set up the trap.

Aaron explained his idea and, as crazy as it was, both Nyla and Pratt agreed that it just might work. Moving the trees was the hardest part, as Aaron couldn't do much to help with that. Instead, he collected as much dry matter as he could get his hands on, weaving it loosely together to form a highly flammable blanket to go on top of the wood. By the time the flames burned through the lighter debris on top, Aaron hoped that either the trees beneath would've caught, or the Chehwinoo was already dead. He wasn't betting on the latter, but he could dream.

They laid the trees out in an imperfect circle around the clearest portion of the construction site. They'd thought about extending it to include the den, increasing the chance it would get snagged in their trap, but that would've taken too much time. Instead, Nyla had pointed out that if it heard them, it would follow. They would lure it into the circle of trees, and then they'd light the gas. Whether it would catch quickly enough to properly trap it, they didn't know for sure. But it was their best idea, and right now, their only chance.

By the time sunset was nearly on them, everything was ready. Aaron couldn't move as easily as Pratt and Nyla, and he was a better shot, so they helped him onto the roof of the trailer with one rifle and his handgun. He was to shoot the gas can as soon as the Chehwinoo was inside the circle, lighting it and the gas-soaked perimeter on fire. Then he would prepare to line up a kill shot whenever he had it while Nyla and Pratt both distracted and, hopefully, weakened it with the surrounding flames and available weapons. Pratt was huddled near a small loader, the other rifle prepped to fire whenever he got an opening. Nyla was close to the trailer with an arm load of torches, ready to duck under it or slip inside if the danger got too close. As if the Basin knew what they were planning, the world around them had gone eerily silent. Not a breeze touched the trees, nor an animal rustled in the underbrush. The Basin was as silent as the grave it'd become for so many.

The air grew cold, and Aaron wondered if the soundless forest was a coincidence, or if the Chehwinoo was starting to wake.

He pulled the walkie Nyla had given him from his pocket, checking the signal. It was strong, and the battery was nearly full. They were ready, as ready as they could possibly be. The underbrush was laid out and drenched, the gas cannister was in place, Nyla and Pratt were in position. Their trap was set. Except—

Except the forest wasn't quiet anymore.

Aaron lifted his head, searching for the sound as it got closer. It was a rumble, low and familiar. Almost like...

"You've got to be fucking kidding me," Aaron pressed himself down as flat as possible, hiding from view just as the truck veered around the corner.

NYLA

"That's Bill," Nyla said instantly, panic rising in her throat. "Fuck, *that's Bill!*"

The world seemed to screech to a halt as Nyla processed what was unfolding. Their plan was barely pieced together as is, not even put into motion, and it was already falling apart.

"Hannaford?" Pratt jogged up to her, holstering his weapon just in time. Bill's old Dodge drifted into the construction zone, crunching to a stop directly on top of their gasoline-soaked underbrush perimeter. Nyla cursed. "What's he doing here? I thought he was in custody?"

"He's loaded," Nyla muttered, straightening her shoulders. According to her watch, they only had fifteen minutes until the sun disappeared behind the mountain, and Bill's stupid truck was blocking their trap. She needed to get him to leave or, at the very least, move. "He probably posted bail."

"Fuck," Pratt pushed his hand through his hair, biting hard on his bottom lip as Bill threw open the truck door with an angry kick.

"What the hell are you doing here, Jameson?"

"I could ask you the same," she fired back immediately, not bothering with any attempt at civility. "This doesn't look like a jail cell to me, Bill. Go home."

"You're trying to tell me what to do and where to go?" Bill blustered, looking outraged at the very idea. "This is a closed site! I need you two to vacate the premises. Now."

"And I need you to get in that truck, turn around, and pretend you were never here," Nyla insisted. "Tell Carver whatever mission he has you on is going to have to wait."

Bill blanked, just for a second.

"You been talking to Carver?" He demanded, stepping forcefully into Nyla's personal space. Pratt put his arm in front of her, inserting himself as a barrier. "When? What did he tell you?"

"I haven't been talking to Carver," Nyla defended, wariness creeping into her stomach and making her cautious. She didn't want to believe that Somerton's mayor, as infuriatingly incompetent as he was, could be responsible for so much death. Bill's reaction did nothing to comfort her. "As far as he's concerned, I don't even know about this place. That's really not important right now, Bill. You need to *leave.*"

"If I find out Carver's been jerking me around, I swear I'm gonna put a bullet between his beady little eyes," Bill growled. "He got me into this political shit show, and then he has the balls to vanish before all hell breaks loose."

"Sheriff Hannaford, that's not—"

"When did he vanish?" Nyla interjected, cutting off Pratt's attempt at getting Bill to leave. She had to know. She had to. "When did you stop hearing from Mayor Carver?"

"I don't know, what does it matter?" Bill huffed. "Few months ago, maybe. Why?"

Nyla looked at Pratt, at the resignation and sympathy on his face. Nyla couldn't deny it to herself anymore. Aaron was right.

James Carver was the Chehwinoo.

"Bill, listen to me very carefully," Nyla said, slowly and with as much deliberate gravity as she could muster. "I need you to leave. Something is going on here that is way above either of our pay grades, and I swear I will tell you everything tomorrow if you just get in your truck and go home. Alright?"

For just a split second, Nyla thought he was going to listen. Then the Bill she knew came out in full force, reaching into his pocket and defiantly locking his truck with the key fob.

"Bill, we don't have time for this!" Nyla cried, her patience shattering. "Move the damn truck!"

"I'm not stepping one foot off this site until you tell me what the fuck—"

The sunlight stuttered as a cloud blew past, stilling Nyla's heart in her chest.

"Bill, listen to me. We can hash this out tomorrow, alright? Right now, I need you to leave. Do you understand?"

"*Nyla, we can't wait much longer.*" Aaron's crackling voice sounded from the walkie in her hand. "*We're losing daylight. Literally.*"

"Is that Klein? Where the fuck is he hiding?" Bill made to snatch the walkie, but Nyla jerked her hand away. Pratt stepped forward, gesturing angrily to Bill's truck.

"This is an order," Pratt said. "Move the damn truck, Hannaford. This is an FBI matter, you don't have jurisdiction."

"I'm not in uniform," Bill spat. "Your 'jurisdiction' means diddly out here, city prick."

"*Nyla?*"

"Listen here you piece of shit," Pratt's patience snapped, lowering the pitch of his normally cheerful voice, "either you move the truck, or I'll hotwire the bastard and drive it into the lake!"

"Go ahead, see how good of a swimmer you are!" Bill blustered. "I sure as shit won't be hauling your ass out!"

"*Nyla!*"

"Bill, for fuck's sake!" Nyla whipped her attention to the horizon, where the last rays of the sun were quickly vanishing. "Get your head out of your ass for one goddamn second—!"

"*We're out of time!*"

Aaron's panicked bark wasn't needed. Nyla knew the exact moment the Chehwinoo left its home. The temperature plummeted, a thin sheet of frost inching along the ground towards them. Icy tendrils sparkled in the last rays of sun that reached the ground, reflecting the light in a million different directions. Nyla felt her skin erupt in goosebumps, shivers electrifying her blood and rattling her spine. Fear gripped her stomach, but Nyla couldn't listen to it. She jammed the call button on the walkie.

"Do it!"

A crack sounded through the clearing, and then everything was on fire.

Bill stumbled back in shock as the flames caught their gas trail, rapidly swallowing the thin twigs and branches. Nyla prayed they'd piled enough to last until the thicker wood below ignited, but it was too late to do anything more now. They were stuck in the middle of a raging inferno with a sputtering hellspawn, and the Chehwinoo.

"What did you do to my truck?!" Bill made to bolt toward his Dodge, but Pratt grabbed the back of his shirt and held fast. Flames licked the paint, making it bubble and crack. It wouldn't be long until the engine caught, and even Nyla didn't think Bill deserved that kind of pain. "You're insane! You're all fucking insane—!"

"Yeah, yeah, and you're gonna sue the pants off us." Pratt rolled his eyes, shoving Bill until he stumbled. "We tried to tell you, but you didn't listen. So now you're stuck here with us. Try to stay alive, will ya?"

Confusion flickered across Bill's face, and then his eyes zeroed in on something behind them. His face paled, pupils dilating to the size of dimes. Nyla knew what he'd seen before she turned, but she still wasn't prepared for the creature that was slinking along the edge of the clearing.

It moved like a spider on disjointed legs, skulking low to the ground, razor claws digging into the dirt with each jerking step. Their run-in with the creature before had been frantic, too abrupt to get a good look at what they were facing. Now, in the light of the inferno, Nyla could see all too clearly what they were up against.

"What the flying fuck is that?" Bill snapped, but the venom had left him. He was as paralyzed with fear as they were, staring in horror as the misshapen mass of sharp shadows zeroed in on them.

Every movement was choppy, delayed, almost like Nyla blinked between each second, or like a strobe light was flickering in the distance. The Chehwinoo walked like its bones were broken, but Nyla knew that did nothing to slow it down.

Not broken, she realized suddenly. *Frozen*.

The Chehwinoo was nothing more than a skeleton held together by paper-thin skin. Its body, now that Nyla could see it properly, wasn't made of shadow. It was black with death, like every inch had succumbed to frostbite.

Despite the fire, Nyla felt the air chill against her skin. It was cold, almost icy, the sweat on her brow transforming into tiny flecks of ice even as she stood there, staring into the yellow, glowing eyes of their adversary.

The Chehwinoo was awake, and they weren't going anywhere.

Chapter Twenty-Nine

NYLA

Bill's sputtered cursing resumed in earnest after the initial shock of seeing the Chehwinoo faded. Nyla pulled a flare from her shorts' pocket, poised to light it at a moment's notice.

"Stick to the plan," Pratt insisted, speaking loudly enough that Aaron could hear him from his position atop the trailer. "We get one shot at this."

"What plan?" Bill demanded, but he wasn't fully paying attention. The Chehwinoo was slowly taking stock of its surroundings, surveying the fire and calculating how high it had spread. Nyla held her breath, praying that it couldn't jump the flames. Evidently, it decided that the inferno was a sufficient barrier. For now.

Nyla watched, transfixed. Aaron had waited until the Chehwinoo was several feet inside the barrier before igniting the gas can, giving the fire time to catch before the Chehwinoo realized what was happening and tried to bolt. It worked, though the flames came to life quickly enough that Nyla doubted it would've mattered. It hugged the perimeter as closely as possible, keeping a significant distance between its fracturing body and the heat.

A shot rang out, and the Chehwinoo's shoulder splintered into a cascade of frozen shards. By the time they hit the ground, they'd melted into a puddle of crystal clear water.

"*Draw it closer,*" Aaron's voice sounded through the walkie, the static crackle catching the attention of the Chehwinoo. It whipped its head toward Nyla, Pratt, and Bill with a gut-turning crack, like bones being crushed beneath a heavy weight. "*I can't get a shot from here.*"

Nyla's grip tightened on the flare, trying to ignore the strange reactions her body was having to the contrasting temperatures. She was sweating down her arms and legs, but her face and chest were icy to the touch. Beside her, she saw Pratt shake off his jacket.

"Take a good, long look, Sheriff," he said, raising the rifle until the barrel was pointed directly at the Chehwinoo. "This is what's behind your missing hunters."

An odd look passed over Bill's face, one that Nyla didn't have time to interpret. The Chehwinoo hadn't flinched from Aaron's first shot, and now it was stalking towards them with its head tilted, assessing them, determining the best way to attack. Its eyes were huge and empty, shimmering yellow, like topaz cast under a bright light. Nyla squinted at it, realizing that it wasn't focusing on them at all. It was focusing on Bill.

"What do you know about this?" Nyla demanded suddenly, taking in the way the Chehwinoo bristled and snapped its jaws at Bill. He looked outraged that she would even think to ask.

"I don't know shit about this," he denied, faltering backward. The Chehwinoo lunged toward him, but Pratt held it back with a shot that ripped through its stomach. The creature was hunched, protecting its chest. It was smart, then. "Look, I don't... I had nothing to do with it! Carver asked me to handle the PR around this build, but the douchebag threw me to the wolves! When I posted bail, I went 'round his place to confront him, but he wasn't there. It was a ghost town, like he hadn't been home in weeks. I came here looking for answers, not to get caught up in whatever the hell this is."

"I hate to break it to you," Nyla growled, "but you're already knee deep in 'whatever the hell this is.' If you came here looking for Carver, I think you found him."

Bill stared in open disbelief, his mouth working hard with no sound coming out.

"No," he muttered, shaking his head. "No, no way. That's not... that can't be James. No. You two have done something. You've... drugged me! That's it, you drugged me with whatever you used to light this place up!"

"Bill, we didn't—"

"I'm not listening to another word from you!" Bill screamed, taking an aggressive step toward Nyla. Pratt swung the rifle around to level it at him, stopping him in his tracks. The Chehwinoo lurched forward again, but a shot from Aaron forced it to hold. "I'm getting out of here. Now. I don't know what you people are involved in, but I'm not risking my life for this. No way."

"If you run now, you're dead!" Nyla barked at him, panic making her voice crack. Bill stopped, whether because of her obvious fear or his own realization, she wasn't sure. "Our only chance of getting out of here is if we kill that thing!"

"You can't kill James," Bill said, aghast. "I'll get you for murder, Jameson! I swear it—"

"Does it look like we have much of a choice?" Pratt whipped his rifle back towards the Chehwinoo, where it was appraising them. "For God's sake, just pull out your gun!"

That, at least, Bill seemed to understand. As soon as his hand reached for his belt, the creature lunged.

Nyla dove back towards the trailer, ducking behind it and circling around the other side. She didn't see where Bill went, but she heard Pratt firing two more shots. As much as she wished they'd pepper the thing with as many bullets as possible, they had limited ammo. Every shot needed to count.

The Chehwinoo came into view as Nyla skidded around the corner of the trailer, stumbling from the damage Pratt had done. Nyla leveled her flare gun at it— she only had a single shot with it, she couldn't miss. It hadn't seen her yet, still eyeing Bill as he calculated the distance between the creature, him, and his truck. Nyla aimed the gun carefully, accounting for any movement she could reliably predict. When Bill raised his gun toward the creature, she fired.

An unholy screech erupted from the Chehwinoo's crippled jaw, like a combination of nails on a chalkboard and a dying falcon. Nyla resisted the urge to cover her ears, watching as the flare gun ate away at the Chehwinoo's mottled flesh. Globs of skin fell to the ground, collecting in the dirt and melting into slush as the Chehwinoo writhed in pain. A chunk of its shoulder was missing now, but Nyla could already see the decayed bones rebuilding themselves, the papery skin stitching back together.

Bill recovered from his shock in time to fire three rounds into the healing injury, stalling its recovery. The Chehwinoo screeched again, deeper this time. Like it was angry.

Another burst of shots from Bill's gun, depleting his remaining bullets.

Nyla watched from her position behind the trailer, fumbling with a flare torch, trying to catch Bill's attention so she could throw him a weapon. He didn't see her, true, bone-gripping fear overtaking his judgment. Before Nyla could do anything, he dropped his empty gun and stumbled backwards.

"No!" Pratt's voice, shouting over the roaring flames. "Hannaford, don't—!"

Bill turned, making a break for his truck. The vehicle was already engulfed. Even if he could get the door open, Nyla had no doubt that turning the key would result in both Bill and the truck erupting in a ball of flame. She vaulted from her hiding spot behind the trailer, catching the Chehwinoo's attention. Bill was too far ahead of her to reach, even if she chased him. All she could do was keep the monster away from him and hope he came to his senses.

As the Chehwinoo turned to face her, she realized her plan had worked too well.

If James Carver was in this creature, his hatred for Nyla simmered to the surface. The Chehwinoo hoisted itself to its full height, teetering on its hind legs like a grizzly. It pierced her with its hard, gemstone eyes, huffing out puffs of crisp, white fog. Its jaw cracked, and it screamed.

Nyla's legs abruptly unlocked and she faltered back, lighting the flare and holding it in front of her in one motion. The creature reeled as if it was expecting another shot to hit it. When it realized the flare was just a torch, it feinted forward, falling into a stuttering canter toward Nyla. It pulled back its arm, claws extended, preparing to swipe, just as Bill ripped open the driver's side door of his disintegrating Dodge. The creature's head whipped around, its focus redirected to Bill once again. Nyla readied another flare, planning to throw it at the thing if she had to, but—

But the Chehwinoo was already on the hunt.

Nyla screamed at the sudden flash of shadow that passed in front of her, accompanied by the now-familiar ear-splitting crack that shook the forest. In the light of the fire, Nyla could finally see what caused it. The Chehwinoo's jaw fully unhinged, curved, jagged teeth like broken crystals jutting in every direction. It roared, reverberating through the air like thunder.

Before any of them could act, the Chehwinoo ripped through Bill's retreating torso.

Another scream lodged in Nyla's throat as blood splattered the gravel in a wide arc, shimmering in the firelight. Bill's legs buckled, collapsing sideways with no upper body to support. His head flopped at an unnatural angle, his arms hanging limply at his sides. The Chehwinoo snapped its jaws, dispelling blood and tissue matter from its teeth with a vicious shake of its head. Bill Hannaford was dead, and he hadn't even seen it coming for him.

"Duck!" Pratt commanded, and Nyla obeyed without hesitation. She feigned to her left, hiding herself behind a large concrete slab. Pratt leveled his rifle and fired, striking the Chehwinoo in the stomach again. The creature cried out, standing on its hind legs as water and blood seeped into the ground beneath it. It was larger than Nyla remembered, and right now, it had a clear path to them. The fire was affecting it, she could see that much from the abundance of moisture that trailed after it, clinging to its skin and teeth, but it wasn't enough. They needed a big hit, something to slow it down enough to give them the opening they needed. If only she had another flare gun.

Bill's truck sputtered, some of the heated metal buckling under the weight of the fire. Nyla could see it shuddering behind the Chehwinoo, its image marred by waves of heat. An idea struck her, one that she really hoped she didn't end up regretting.

"Aaron!" Nyla screamed into the walkie, waving wildly for Pratt to take cover. "Shoot the truck!"

Aaron didn't ask questions. A shot rang out, followed by a tense moment of deadly quiet. Just when Nyla thought she'd made a mistake, an explosion split the air, swallowing the Chehwinoo in a billow of smoke.

"Shit!" Pratt's curse carried to her from his refuge behind the loader, but he seemed unharmed. Nyla risked a glance at the truck as the explosion settled, spotting the Chehwinoo limping around to the other side of the trailer. Nyla frowned, wondering why it was moving away from them, when she zeroed in on its target. The door of Bill's truck had blown clean off, landing on one of the perimeter logs on the other side of the construction site. To Nyla's horror, the door smothered just enough of the flames to give the Chehwinoo an opening.

It was going to escape.

"No!" Nyla exclaimed, but Pratt was already in motion. He tore across the construction site, moving much quicker than the injured Chehwinoo. Nyla sprinted after him, igniting her flare along the way. She skidded to a stop out of arm's reach of the Chehwinoo, waving the flare wildly in front of it. The creature recoiled, glaring hatefully at her through the red glow of flames clutched in her hand.

Pratt reached the truck door and shoved it with his boot, but it didn't move. He tried again, kicking at the disintegrating aluminum with as much force as he could muster. The door shifted, but it didn't clear the wood. Pratt cursed, looking around for something he could use.

"The PVC pipe!" Nyla screamed to him, pointing urgently at the collection of building materials gathered near the far end of the trailer. "Use it as a lever!"

Pratt jumped into action, doing exactly as she said. He grabbed the PVC pipe and shoved it under the edge of the door, balancing it on a makeshift fulcrum that Nyla was pretty sure was just a plastic bucket. With a full-body shove, the truck door lifted and began to tip off the other side of the wood. As it did, Nyla backed up toward Pratt, using the flare as a shield. The door was almost clear, giving them more time to enact their plan, when her flare gave out.

The Chehwinoo had been waiting for this. It expelled its stored energy in one massive leap, sailing clean over Nyla's head and charging at Pratt in an uneven gate. Nyla yelled in warning, and Pratt turned just in time to block the creature's swipe with his rifle. The collision sent him flying, knocking him into the still-falling truck door and outside the fire barrier. Nyla couldn't see him now, didn't know if he'd been cut or burned, but she didn't have time to wonder. She was on the ground of their trap, with three remaining flares and no other weapon, facing off against a nightmarish, furious Chehwinoo.

AARON

Aaron watched the scene unfold with panic and frustration warring for dominance in his chest. Pratt was gone. He couldn't see him from this vantage, couldn't tell if he was alive or dead. Aaron just had to hope that his friend survived because right now, Nyla was facing the beast alone. Aaron saw her pull another flare from her belt, lighting it and holding it in front of her in the same motion. The Chehwinoo slowed its advance, careful, calculating, herding her. She backed as close to the flames as she could, loosing another flare with her free hand. Aaron didn't know what she was doing until she lit it, tossing it at the Chehwinoo in an impressive throw. The creature snapped at it on instinct, catching the flare in its jaws. It screeched in pain, rearing up on its back legs and stumbling away from Nyla.

"Aaron, take the shot!" Nyla screamed, her voice cutting out intermittently on the radio. Aaron scrambled into a new position, but the dismembered body of Bill Hannaford's truck was blocking most of the Chehwinoo's torso. He shot another two rounds, both embedding themselves in the melting aluminum before ever reaching the target.

"I don't have it!" Aaron barked into the walkie. He could see Nyla, backing away as quickly as she could, sweating profusely because of her proximity to the fire. Aaron cursed in English, then Spanish, then English again, trying whatever he could to angle himself in a way that would let him end this.

A branch snapped in the flames beside Nyla and the piece of smoldering twig flicked onto her arm. She cried out, jolting away from the heat so quickly that she stumbled. The

Chehwinoo lurched forward, and Aaron's heart slammed into his throat, but Nyla saw the creature move. She swung the flare back into its face, stalling it.

Aaron released his breath, but not for long. Nyla's walkie was next to the burning truck, well out of her reach after she threw it during her fall. She was cornered, hurt, and completely out of contact.

Fuck this.

Aaron stood, sizing up the jump from the trailer roof to the ground. He wouldn't break his legs, but he'd seriously sprain something if he fumbled. Maybe even a fracture. He needed to hit the ground rolling, and he needed to do it on his left side.

"This is going to hurt like a bitch," Aaron muttered, steeling himself against the oncoming pain. Dropping the hunting rifle, Aaron braced his right foot on the edge of the trailer, patted himself down determinedly, and jumped.

NYLA

Nyla's arm pulsed in pain, radiating from the initial burn up and around her shoulder. She bit back tears, keeping her attention planted firmly on the Chehwinoo as it got closer. Her flare was about to die, and the only other one she had snapped when she fell. She was out of options, and out of escape routes.

She'd just decided to try to wrestle a burning branch from the barrier when the flare gave out, and Nyla was out of the last resource she had, time.

The Chehwinoo threw itself toward her, faltering on its crackling limbs. Nyla wasn't sure how quickly it regenerated, but she didn't wait to find out. She stole herself, scrambling to all fours and then to her feet, sprinting so close to the fire that her hair began to burn. The Chehwinoo slashed at her with its claws, reaching for her with spindly fingers, beckoning her to it. Nyla fought the instinctual urge to leap away from the fire, knowing that if she did, she'd be dead.

Pratt had the rifle. The Chehwinoo was blocking her walkie, cutting her off from Aaron. What the hell was she going to do?

Nyla's heart swelled in her throat, choking her. She couldn't breathe, but she kept running. Her legs moved without guidance, carrying her around the perimeter of their trap. The Chehwinoo followed, screeching, dragging its injured body through the dirt at a frightening speed. Nyla risked a glance over her shoulder and regretted it instantly— the Chehwinoo's lower half was damaged by the flames, its legs broken and rigid, unmoving, slowing it down as it desperately hauled itself after her. Its skeletal body tore jagged gashes in the ground where its claws penetrated, launching itself toward Nyla in stuttering lunges like a marionette on broken strings. It roared, ragged and sharp.

Ice collided with her back, pitching Nyla to the dirt. Agony swept up her side from hip to shoulder, burning and frozen at once. She hit the ground hard, skidding to a stop mere feet from the loader Pratt had used as a perch. Small shards of rock and splintered twigs snatched at her exposed skin, angering her fresh burns. When her body mercifully came to a stop, she summoned her strength and turned onto her back just in time to see the Chehwinoo reach her.

Thick, viscous slush clung to its teeth, dripping like saliva. Hefty globules splattered on the dirt, creating tiny frozen puddles where they landed. Nyla wanted to scream, but no sound would come out. The Chehwinoo loomed over her, its jaw working in a symphony of sickening pops and snaps. She was staring death in its gaunt face, and she could do nothing.

A loud crack split her ears, followed by an inhuman shriek.

Nyla screamed as something struck the ground near her left hand, showering her in a spray of dirt and ice crystals. She looked down as briefly as she dared, pausing when the small object finally registered.

A bullet was embedded in the ground, encased in ice.

Nyla looked back at the Chehwinoo, frozen, its arm reaching for her. A hole no bigger than a quarter punctured its chest and from it, water was gushing like blood. Nyla blinked. No, the water wasn't coming from the bullet wound. The Chehwinoo was... melting?

Its skeletal features sank further into its skull, collapsing in on itself like crumbling snow. The grotesque shape of its body contorted even further, limbs cracking like icicles as more and more water seeped into the dirt. Nyla yelped as its horns detached, thumping onto the ground with a wet squelch. The Chehwinoo dissolved before her very eyes, leaving behind a puddle of clear, chilled water, and sprawled in the center of it, was the disfigured body of James Carver.

"Nyla!"

Aaron's hoarse exclamation shook her from her trance. Nyla glanced up in time to see Aaron circle the body, dropping to his knees next to her and wrapping her in a tight embrace. He was bleeding, but she wasn't sure from where. He was smeared in dirt, his clothes and hair disheveled, and his handgun hung limply at his side.

"Are you okay?" She asked, pressing tightly into his warmth. Despite the fire and sweat, Nyla couldn't stop shaking. "You're hurt. Where are you hurt?"

"I'm fine," Aaron promised, wiping her hair away from her face. "Are you okay? I didn't hit you?"

It took her a second to realize he was talking about the bullet.

"No, I'm fine," she assured him. She was in pain, copious amounts of it, but she'd live. "You missed me."

"Good," Aaron sighed, tugging her closer. "I couldn't see you, but I had to shoot. If I didn't..."

"If you didn't, it would've killed me." Nyla nodded, the weight of that truth striking her hard in the gut. She fought back the urge to gag, clinging tighter to Aaron to ground her. "How did you get here? Did you... did you jump off the trailer?"

"Yes," Aaron answered bluntly, checking his side for damage. Nyla saw him wince. "I couldn't get the shot from up there. I had to improvise."

"Where's the rifle?" Nyla looked around, catching Aaron's sheepish expression. "You *left the rifle*? Aaron, what the hell?"

"I'm a better shot with this," he held his handgun aloft, shrugging like he hadn't just discarded one of the only two weapons they'd had left to take out the Chehwinoo. "Besides, it all worked out, right?"

"You're unbelievable," Nyla shook her head, trying to ignore how close to death they'd come. Suddenly, she remembered that a member of their group was still unaccounted for. "Pratt! What about Pratt? Did you see where he went?"

"I know where he fell, but I don't know what happened to him after that." Aaron stood, helping Nyla to her feet. She tested the strength of her legs before letting go of him, cringing at the way her skin protested her movements. She couldn't worry about that now. "Come on, let's go make sure he didn't have the audacity to die on us."

Despite the obvious joke, Aaron's tone was solemn. Nyla took his hand and squeezed, following him to the point in the barrier where Pratt had vanished. With her help, Aaron moved some of the crumbling wood aside using the same PVC pipe Pratt employed. They made enough room so they could slip through, and then they started searching in earnest.

"Pratt!" Aaron yelled, coughing as smoke assaulted his face. Nyla coughed too, feeling the air burn her lungs as it traveled down her throat. She repeated Aaron's call, scanning the trees for any sign of life.

"Tyler Pratt!" Aaron tried again, desperation slipping into his words. Nyla jogged ahead of him, ducking under some of the lower branches. They were close to the Chehwinoo's den now, but it was hard to say for sure how close. The temperature had returned to normal upon its death, and any evidence of snow and ice had already melted away. "Pratt! Come on, answer us!"

"I'm over here!"

The call reached Nyla first, and she only hesitated long enough to catch Aaron's eye before tearing off in the direction of Pratt's voice.

"Pratt?"

"Here! In the den!"

Nyla skidded to a halt just before the tree stump, falling to her knees to peer into the darkness. Pratt's face materialized in the soft, residual glow of the fire, looking pinched and tensed.

"Are you okay?" Aaron demanded, hitting the ground next to Nyla. "Are you hurt?"

"I'm okay!" Pratt promised, waving his phone flashlight around. "I got knocked out when the bastard threw me, and when I woke up I knew I wouldn't be able to get back into the fray. I came here to check things out, see if I could find anything useful."

"The Chehwinoo is dead," Nyla told him, "Aaron killed it. It's gone."

"That's great," Pratt rubbed the back of his neck, sounding less than enthused. His somber reaction scared her more than if he hadn't answered at all. What had he seen, heard, or found, that pushed the Chehwinoo away from the forefront of his mind? "Listen, I had every intention of covering this whole thing up and passing it off as a freak accident or something, but, uh..."

"But what?" Aaron prompted, apprehension thick in his words.

"I think we're going to need to call this in."

"What?" Nyla gasped. She was too exhausted to be truly shocked, resigned confusion taking its place. "Why? How are we supposed to explain all this?"

"We'll have to come up with something," Pratt concluded, looking behind him at something they couldn't see from ground level. "The fire, Hannaford, the hunters, we can do whatever we have to with that story. But this..." Pratt looked sick, and Nyla wondered for a moment if he was going to throw up.

"Just trust me," he said eventually, clearing his throat to dispel the waver in his voice. "You're not gonna believe what's down here."

EPILOGUE: AMELIA

Royersford, Pennsylvania

Two Months Later

"Yeah, Mom, I know."

Amelia looked up from her book at the exasperation in Sam's voice, watching as he paced the living room.

"Well, yeah, but— okay, do you want me to go or not?"

He covered a few more turns around the coffee table before he gave up, collapsing onto the couch next to her. Amelia shifted her legs enough to accommodate him, no longer paying attention to her book. It wasn't very good anyway.

"Alright. Okay. Yes, I promise. Love you too."

Sam's cell phone hit the carpeted floor with an audible thud, masked by the impressive groan coming from Sam's throat.

"So, how's Sandra?" Amelia teased, closing her book without bothering to mark the page. She already knew she would never finish it. There were many more interesting things to read. "She sounds like she's doing great."

"I remember now why I moved an entire State away," Sam said on an exhale. "Is it too late to tell her I can't come home for Christmas?"

"I think that's the fastest she's ever pushed you over the edge." Amelia chuckled, sitting up to give Sam more of her attention. "What was it about?"

"She wants me to go check on the cabin," Sam said, dropping his head onto the back of the couch, staring blankly at the ceiling of their apartment. "She's worried about the construction. Something about property value. Like she's ever going to sell the place."

"What's wrong with that?" Amelia stretched her legs out again, across Sam's lap. He let his head fall to the side to glare at her, but he didn't remove her legs either. "You've been wanting to go out to the cabin forever. Seems like a great opportunity."

"Yeah, it's perfect timing," Sam said, his voice dripping with sarcasm. "A rabid bear just tore through what, like fifteen hunters? Time to break out the camping gear!"

Amelia rolled her eyes, reaching for her water bottle to take a long sip. Sam was exaggerating and he knew it— the actual number of missing men was closer to ten, but she didn't need to point that out. The attacks had been all over the news for the last two months since the bear had been tracked and killed.

"It's a *cabin*, not a tent," she countered. "It's not like you're traipsing through the woods unprotected. Besides, they got the bear that did all the murdering."

"You think there's only one bear in the Basin?"

"You think there haven't *always* been bears in the Basin?"

Sam had nothing to say to that, dropping his hands onto Amelia's shins and squeezing gently. It felt nice, so she didn't stop him.

"What are the chances that it didn't spread rabies to *any* other animals?" Sam's resolve was waning, and Amelia could tell by the way he relaxed into the couch. It was old, bought secondhand from a yard sale when they moved in together during college. It took some serious maneuvering to break free from its sunken cushions and broken springs, which meant they almost always ended up lounging longer than they meant to. "I don't know, Am. I'd rather wait until next summer."

"Alright, so tell your mom that," she said, shrugging. "Sandra's a worrier. If you tell her you're concerned about the bear thing—"

"—then she'll never let me go there again," Sam grumbled. "You're right. Bears are bears. They're gonna do what bears do. A bear's gotta bear."

"Is the word 'bear' starting to sound weird to you, or is it just me?"

"It's just you. I can still *bear* it."

"You're un*bear*able."

Sam shoved her leg, reaching for his phone again.

"Who are you calling?"

"Ty," Sam answered easily, scrolling through his contacts and putting the call on speaker.

"You're not calling Tyler about this," Amelia argued, trying to grab the phone from him. "Sam! He's so busy, do not bother him with—"

"*Pratt.*"

"Prude," Sam shot back automatically.

"*Prick. Oh— shoot.*" Tyler's answer was immediate, but his tone dropped off in horror almost as soon as the words left him. A high-pitched, muffled voice sounded in the background, happily repeating 'prick' in a taunting singsong. "*Sorry, Izzy. No, no, don't say that word. Daddy only said it because— it's a grown-up word, okay? Just go play with Mommy, Daddy's gotta take this.*"

Sam was smothering his laughter with his palm, trying to be discreet. Amelia smacked his shoulder, unlocking her own phone to order take-out for supper. Sam was working tomorrow morning, which meant he wouldn't want to cook. She scanned the available options for their apartment complex, skirting the edge of the suburbs and downtown. Chinese food was looking like her best bet.

"*Fisher, I swear to God I'm going to murder you.*" Tyler's voice was louder now, more echoed. Amelia guessed he'd moved to the garage. "*What the hell do you want?*"

"Why do I have to want something?" Sam gasped in mock offense. "Am I not allowed to check up on my oldest, dearest friend?"

"Ahem?" Amelia raised an eyebrow at him. Sam covered the speaker, leaning over to whisper to her.

"You're my oldest, dearest, hottest friend," he corrected. "Easy mistake, but not the same."

"I'll take it."

"*If you wanted to check up, you'd text me,*" Tyler said, friendly annoyance giving way to genuine warmth. "*Not that I mind. How've you been? Still pining over—?*"

"Hey, Am's here too!" Sam interrupted quickly, coughing to cover his sudden discomfort. Amelia almost laughed. Years after their breakup, Sam still hated talking about his ex. "Say hi, Am!"

"Hey Ty," she said, relieving Sam of the situation. He saluted her in gratitude. As much as she loved teasing him, Amelia didn't like talking about Dee either. "How's the FBI life treating you?"

"*I'm in desperate need of a raise,*" he said, laughing. "*Other than that, I can't complain.*"

"That would be a first."

"Fisher, seriously. I'll nail you for tax evasion, I swear I will."

Amelia let Tyler and Sam catch up, still pondering her meal choices. The three of them, along with Sam's sister, had been close growing up. While Amelia still kept in touch with Tyler, Sam definitely talked to him more than she did these days.

"Listen, Ty." Sam cleared his throat, his free hand dropping back to Amelia's shin and rubbing absently. She almost didn't notice, engrossed in a mental debate between beef and broccoli and chicken chop suey. "How would you and Chia feel about some visitors?"

"No way, really?" Tyler's voice perked up immediately, enthusiasm and excitement clear through the phone speaker. *"You guys are coming out this way?"*

"Mom wants us to go check on the cabin," Sam explained, catching Amelia's eye briefly over her phone screen. He raised a brow at her, silently asking if she was getting food. She nodded, and he mimed an exuberant sexual gesture that she chose to ignore. Sam really did nothing to quell the dating rumors about them. "We were going to make a week out of it. Have a bonfire, movie nights, you know. College kid on Spring Break stuff."

"Maybe your Spring Break," Amelia taunted. "Mine had a lot more sex."

"Who says there won't be sex?"

"I'm so glad you and Ty are finally going to consummate your relationship."

"The Somerton cabin?" Tyler interjected suddenly, his voice hesitant. *"Like, the one we went to in high school?"*

"Unless there's another cabin you know of," Sam grinned. "Why do you sound like you're not on board now?"

"It's just..." Tyler faltered, like he wasn't quite sure how to phrase his thoughts. *"You guys want to come out here now? After what's been happening? Did you not see the news?"*

"We did," Sam said, waving frantically at Amelia to make sure she ordered him wontons. She had. "That's why we called. I wanted to run it by you, to see what you thought. They caught the bear, right? So we should be in the clear."

The line was silent for so long that Amelia had enough time to process the order, change her mind, adjust it, and reorder.

"I'm not sure, Sam." Amelia looked up; it wasn't like Ty to sound so serious, even when circumstances called for it. *"I don't think it's a great idea. As much as I'd love to see you, I think it's best if you wait until this blows over."*

"What's the big risk?" Sam frowned, tapping his foot. It was a nervous habit, one that he'd never quite been able to break. "It's not like we're going deep into the Basin or anything. Cabin county is basically on the edge of town."

"*It's not that,*" Tyler started to say something, but his voice dropped away. Amelia thought they'd lost the call, but he came back a moment later. "*Shit. I have to go; Izzy must've used that no-no word in front of Chia. I'm getting yelled at in Xhosa.*"

This time, Amelia laughed. She'd always liked Chia.

"*Seriously Fisher, I think you should wait. Alright? I gotta go. Don't be stupid, for once?*"

The call ended before Sam could form a proper response, just as Amelia got a notification that their food was on the way. Sam stared at his blank screen for longer than she was comfortable with, and then he was tapping furiously at it. She watched him for a moment, her suspicion growing with every second that he didn't say something.

"What are you doing?" She asked eventually, unable to wait anymore.

"Booking flights to Milwaukee."

"What?" Amelia swung her legs off of Sam as he stood up, pacing again while he worked. "I thought the point of getting Ty's opinion was so that you could *listen* to it?"

"Well, yeah, but then he told me not to." Sam shrugged one shoulder, like that explained everything. When Amelia still stared at him, he elaborated. "So, obviously, I have to."

"You are a literal child. And an idiot."

Sam smirked, pausing in his travel planning to wink at her.

"Yeah, but I'm *your* idiot."

"You're about to be my ex-roommate."

Another notification from her phone. Their courier was ten minutes away. That was fast, even for a weekday. Amelia tried to remember to increase their tip after the food arrived.

"Come on, Am." Sam batted his eyelashes in an exaggerated fashion. "Does next week work?"

"I didn't agree to go!"

"You have to go! You're not gonna let me go to the cabin alone, are you?" He asked like it was the most outrageous idea he'd ever heard and, while his offense was comedic, Amelia was too shocked to appreciate the spectacle.

"I was planning on it," she said pointedly. Sam finally put down his phone and stopped pacing, dropping less-than-elegantly to his knees in front of her. He took her hands in his, holding them aloft like some sort of prize. She was already exasperated and he hadn't said a word.

"What if I get mauled?" He challenged. Amelia raised an eyebrow skeptically.

"Then I have dibs on your Xbox."

Sam's attention darted to the gaming console in question, wondering if his life was worth giving up his most prized possession.

"Please, Amy Baby?" He pleaded, squeezing her hands.

"Do *not* call me that."

Sam gave her a withering look but abided by her wishes. He took a deep breath, projecting as much bravado and theatrics as he could.

"Pretty please, my tyrannical Queen? My illustrious ruler? Overlord of apartment 64C?"

"Now I want you to get mauled."

"It'll be fun, I swear!" Sam tugged on her hands again, like a kid trying to get her permission. Amelia didn't want to smile. She *really* didn't want to smile. She knew the moment that Sam realized he was convincing her, because his face lit up like a Christmas bulb. "Tyler will come over from Chicago, maybe bring Chia and Izzy if they're up for it. We'll roast marshmallows, go skinny-dipping—"

"We will not."

"—and just have an all-around good time. It'll be just like high school, except better because my sister won't be there."

"I'm telling her you said that."

"Rox knows I love her," Sam insisted. "What do you say? I'll even cover the tickets!"

Amelia knew she would agree long before he asked her again. Despite their longstanding friendship, Sam still managed to wear down her legendary resolve with relatively little effort on his part. It was infuriating, but also a little endearing.

"Fine." Amelia sighed, rolling her eyes. "But only because I'm afraid you'll get yourself killed if I don't."

"See? You do care about me."

"I can still change my mind."

"Too late, tickets booked." Sam stood in response to the knock on the door, followed by an alert telling Amelia that their food was on the other side. "Amy Baby, we're going to Somerton."

SOMERTON PRESS WEEKLY – 08/23/2022

Archaeological Discovery Stalls Construction of Somerton Pharmaceutical Lab

The town of Somerton, Wisconsin sealed a deal with pharmacy titan Stamkos and Stein in March of this year. Despite pushback from the townsfolk, construction began in early summer and continued into August before hitting a major snag.

The production lab was slated to be built in an unpopulated region around Basin Lake, just outside Somerton. Ground clearing was well under way when a local ragtag group of hikers stumbled upon a startling discovery over the weekend. On the edge of the construction grounds is a cave of Native American artifacts.

Somerton Mayor James Carver was unavailable for comment, but his office has assured us through official statements that they are taking every precaution to preserve this portion of history. What that means exactly is unclear, but we are going to keep a close eye on the situation as it unfolds.

Meanwhile, Adrian Stamkos of Stamkos and Stein is not worried. When questioned about Saturday's setback at a recent press conference, Stamkos confidently proclaimed that construction would be moving ahead in just a few weeks, as soon as the investigation was finished, and their permits amended.

"Somerton is the next step in our northern expansion project," Stamkos said. "We have every intention of moving into Canada in the next fiscal year. A hole in the ground with some broken pots is not about to delay that."

SOMERTON PRESS WEEKLY – 08/30/2022

Public Vigil to be Held for Local Sheriff, Mayor MIA

It has been two weeks since Sheriff William 'Bill' Hannaford was killed in a gas can explosion that totaled his truck and damaged several pieces of construction equipment. The funeral for the sheriff was quiet, with only his closest friends and family in attendance. This Friday, the town will be holding a public vigil for the fallen officer. The ceremony will begin at 8pm. Attendees are encouraged to park at the Sheriff's Station to pay their respects.

No word yet on if Mayor James Carver will make an appearance. Nothing has been heard from the mayor since before the accident, leaving some to speculate that he was in the truck with Sheriff Hannaford when it exploded.

PREY DRIVE

Topaz Trilogy Book Two

Coming 2023

Sign up for the VJS Books newsletter for updates on pre-orders and release dates

Also by Victoria Jayne Saunders

Deus

Join Elli Porter as she ventures deep into the Aegean Sea, facing curses, monsters, and one supremely pissed-off sea god.

Read the full summary and the first three chapters at VJSBooks.ca

Acknowledgments

Well, there you have it! My second book is done, with at least TWO MORE on the way! I hope you enjoyed the first entry in the Topaz Trilogy and are looking forward to seeing where the story goes. I know a lot of people were surprised at how quickly I wrote and published *Kill Bite* after *Deus* was released, but I for one was not. Writing is so deeply ingrained in my soul that I knew it was only a matter of jumping the first-book hurdle, and then there would be no stopping me. So, if you like my writing, that's good news for you! And, if you don't... well, I'm not sure why you've read this far but maybe you like it more than you thought? Possibly? Hopefully?

As always, I need to thank my wonderful, loving, supportive husband. I'm never going to be able to put into words how much you've done for me. A 'thank you' will never be enough.

To my friends, you are the backbone of the book. Honestly. Without your support and enthusiasm (and accountability), this book would still be locked away in a far corner of my Documents folder.

To my editor, Tanya, your thoughtful suggestions helped me take this story from an organized mess to something I'm proud to have my name on.

To my beta readers, Tanya (different Tanya) and Lety, you guys have been the real MVPs. I'm so happy that my publishing journey led me to meet you, and thank you, thank you, thank you for all your feedback and editing suggestions. I couldn't have done it without you!

Finally, to you. Yeah, you. Reading this, right now. Don't think I forgot about you. The only goal I've ever had when writing is to share these stories (I hesitate to call them 'my' stories because they're not. They're Aaron's. They're Nyla's. They belong to the characters within these pages) with people who are willing to listen, who will love them as much as I do. Thank you for giving me that opportunity.

And, as always, happy reading!

About the Author

Victoria Jayne Saunders is a Canadian author of New Adult content. A graduate of Memorial University with a Bachelor of Arts in English Literature, she spends most of her time reading, writing, and taking on a worrying amount of DIY projects. She lives in Newfoundland with her husband and arguably too many pets